A Tale of Peter

Upon This Rock

John Cosgrove

Our Sunday Visitor, Inc.
Huntington, Indiana 46750

Nihil Obstat:
Rev. Lawrence A. Gollner
Censor Librorum

Imprimatur:
✠William E. McManus, D.D.
Bishop of Fort Wayne-South Bend
December 6, 1977

ISBN: 0-87973-775-1
Library of Congress Catalog Card Number: 77-94404

Cover Design by Eric Nesheim

Published, printed and bound in the U.S.A. by
Our Sunday Visitor, Inc.
Noll Plaza
Huntington, Indiana 46750

775

DEDICATION

To my beloved
wife Mary, I dedicate
this book as a memorial
to your judgment
that it should be written,
and your constant
faith in me
that I could write it.
—*John*

CONTENTS

1

Mount Olivet: Peter in Turmoil

H E YAWNED prodigiously. He then exhumed a weary "O-h-h." He shook his shaggy head to rid his eyes of sleep. Into his ears came words sadly spoken that bestirred him to anger: "The hour is come. Behold, the Son of Man is betrayed into the hands of sinners." Looking upwards he saw the glare of approaching torches, heard the scraping of sandals on the rocky slope of Mount Olivet. "The servants of the High Priest," he muttered, "they shall not lay hand upon him." Rising, he drew the sword he had carried from the house where he and his brethren and the Master had eaten the Pasch and struck out at the advancing foe. But before he could strike a second time the Master sternly bade him: "Put away your sword. Do you not know that if I asked my Father he would send me twelve legions of angels?"

Stung by the rebuke he recoiled and with an impetuous sweep of his arm hurled the sword over a towering olive tree. His militant stature shriveled to a trembling reed. His head drooped. His shoulders sagged. Clutching at his beard he mumbled in frustration, "I tried to save him, but he chided me. He gives himself into their hands. His great work — it is cut off — all is over. All is over."

With the prisoner the soldiers were ascending the Mount of

Olives toward the road leading to the upper city. He followed them. Entering through the Fountain Gate he observed a man who also appeared to be following the soldiers, and by the light of a torch he recognized John, the youthful Apostle. Embracing John, he moaned: "I tried to save him, but he chided me. I do not understand."

"Nor do I understand, Simon. But he had a purpose. He never spoke or acted without a purpose."

Upon arriving at the gate of the High Priest's courtyard John entered, but when Simon remained without he returned, spoke to the portress, and signaled for him to come. When he entered the portress inquired: "Are you not one of this man's disciples?"

"I am not," he gruffly replied.

"I shall go in," John said. "Wait for me here."

The dank air had honed a keener edge. Huddled about a charcoal brazier near the center of the courtyard a group of men were warming themselves and commenting on the events of the night. "The Nazarene is taken at last," said one, in a tone of relief. "He gave the High Priest many a troubled hour." Another said, "His followers fled like sheep." Said another, "I pitied him. Even a false Messiah deserves loyal friends." The first speaker reflected, "For a moment I thought the big fellow with the sword would cause serious trouble, but he proved to be all froth and bluster." One of the group sidled off a few steps as if mindful to withdraw, but if this were his intention he was frustrated by the curiosity of an approaching womanservant bearing a torch. Thrusting it into his face, she said, "Why this is one of Jesus' followers!"

"I am not!" he growled shrinking into the folds of his robe. Immediately a cock crowed. "Surely you are one of them," declared a man standing near. "Your speech marks you for a Galilean." Cursing and swearing, he protested with an oath. "I

do not know the fellow you are talking about!" Immediately the
cock crowed a second time.

He staggered, as from a blow, the Master's words searing
his ears: "This night, before the cock crows thrice you shall three
times deny me." He railed at his feathered accusor: "That
damned cock! You croaker out of hell!" He fell back toward a
cloistered walk in the rear of the High Priest's palace. Gruff
words: "Out of the way, you fool!" wheeled him about, to
confront a squad of guards conducting a prisoner to a cell under
the palace. His angry retort died unspoken. In the light of a torch
he beheld a bruised, bloody face. He gazed into eyes laden with
all the sorrow in the world. He realized the terrible truth. The
Master had heard his words: "I do not know the fellow!" "Oh
Lord," he groaned, falling to his knees. "Forgive. Forgive. Forgive." For a long moment the prisoner's eyes held him in a
boundless orbit of love. Their silent message penetrated the turmoil in his mind — Simon, all is forgiven you.

Tears flooded his eyes. Grief wrenched his heart. Rising, he
rushed out of the courtyard. "Open up oh ground!" he cried.
"Bury me from the eyes and memory of men!"

But he could not avoid the eyes of men. Jerusalem was
crowded with pilgrims who had come for the feast of the Pasch.
Frequently he collided with one but he had no voice for apology
nor ear for angry remonstrations. One specially violent en-
counter threw him into a wall. Leaning wearily against the cold
damp stones he looked about like one in a dream.

Again he pursued his flight, but now with a sense of direction. A definite plan was forming in his mind. He would seek refuge in the country where the eyes of men could not search him
out. Turning about he made his way to the Northern wall and
passed through the Damascus Gate. But here, too, there were
men — faithful Jews who had come from the far corners of the
world. Their tents populated the Judean hillsides.

He turned back into the city, unaware that it was not from men he was fleeing, but from Simon. But he could not shake off this loathsome person. It dogged his every step. It cried out in condemnation: "How could I say I did not know you? What became of the Simon who spoke out: 'You are the Christ, the Son of the living God?' Now I know why you called me Satan." A gate loomed before him, the Dung Gate in the southernmost wall. He sped through it and stumbled down a bleak hillside.

At last, he found what he sought. There were no men here, no houses, and no fires, only refuse and offal and foul odors. It was Jerusalem's dumping ground — the Valley of Hinnom. Dawn was raising its gray head over Mount Olivet. Spent and weary he sat upon the ground and closed his eyes. But sleep avoided him. Sad memories stirred him — the pleading of his suffering Lord: "Could you not watch one hour with me?" His anger at the rebuke: "Put up your sword." He fingered his beard. "I flung the sword in angry protest. That must have hurt you almost as much as my denial."

A movement off to the right caught his attention. There *were* men in Hinnom! Several of them seemed to emerge from the slope of the hill. Rising, he advanced several steps but stopped abruptly when one of them, a gaunt, stooped man, with ulcerated lumps on his face, cried out mournfully the lepers' warning: "Unclean! Unclean!"

"Not as unclean as Simon bar-Jonah," he cried out.

In deference to the leper, not in fear for himself, he held his distance.

"My friends," he said, "let me send you some food."

"There is no need," the leper replied. "I am on my way to get food. My grandson is employed in the Temple. He gives us leftovers from the sacrifices."

Slowly he ascended the slope. His two companions went about gathering firewood. Simon became engrossed in moody speculation. What he had done, was done. No hand could ever erase a word of it. Could he ever again meet men face-to-face? Live among his own kindred?

Lying upon the ground he dozed fitfully. He sat up with a three-hour-old sun in his face. The lepers were sitting apart over the remnants of their meal. They offered him bread and fish, but he declined. "I cannot eat."

"But you thirst. Your lips are as dry as potsherds." He pointed to a goatskin, saying "It is clean."

Lifting the goatskin and putting the reed pipe to his lips Peter drank one fourth of it. "Greed will have its way," he apologized. "I will get you more."

"There is no need. I will meet my grandson again before the day is out." After a brief silence he said, "There is much excitement in the city. The High Priest's servants are demanding of Pilate that the Galilean prophet be crucified."

Peter groaned. Tears filled his eyes.

"Could he be a friend of yours?" asked the leper.

"The noblest, the truest of friends," replied Peter.

"I grieve with you. If you would speak to him before he suffers — even now he may be on his way to Golgotha."

Golgotha! Peter shuddered. "Friend," he said, "you have helped me. I am grateful. Peace to you and your companions."

Ascending the hill, he re-entered the city.

His way to Golgotha was blocked by a crowd of men before the Fortress Antonia shouting, "Crucify him! Crucify him!" Jesus was standing on an elevated portico beside Pontius Pilate who was washing his hands in a basin of water, saying: "I am innocent of the blood of this just man." Then soldiers seized Jesus and led him away. The crowd dispersed and many of them proceeded over a narrow street leading to the ancient gate. Peter trailed after them, down into the Tyropoeon Valley and up the steep slope on the other side. Their pace was slow. A soldier announced that the "Nazarene had fallen from exhaustion and another had been compelled to carry the tree." About a hundred paces from the second wall the ground rose to a mound twenty to thirty feet high — the place of crucifixion.

Peter did not approach the mound. Shame shackled his feet. Legs spread wide he stood motionless, his bluish robe sagging in the moist heat, arms folded across his hairy chest. He seemed unaware of the mysterious darkness settling upon the earth, until a violent shaking of the ground cast him prostrate, and heaved huge rocks out of their resting place. God is angry with his people, he thought.

Gradually the earth quieted. The sun timidly reappeared. Simon rose and leaned against the wall. Composing himself he again gazed toward the mound. One of the executioners had mounted a ladder leaning against the central cross. A woman was standing near, arms reaching upward to receive the body of its victim. "His holy mother," murmured Peter. "He is dead. They will be preparing him for burial. I should be up there with her, but I am not worthy — I am not worthy."

The spectators dispersed. The executioners returned to the Praetorium. The sun slipped behind the hills and sank into the sea. Travelers entering Jerusalem by the Ancient Gate gazed curiously at the disheveled man staring upwards toward Golgotha. But he had no eye for them. Rigidly he held his place, held it until the hilltop was deserted save for three gaunt crossed trees slowly merging in the darkening sky.

2

Jerusalem: Meeting with John Mark

JERUSALEM lay swathed in Sabbath stillness. From the roof of the Temple the mournful voice of the ram's horn had long since called the people to prayer. Men abided in the seclusion of their homes, and behind drawn shutters gave themselves to religious contemplation. Simon bar-Jonah groped through its dark silent streets. He had come to the end of three glorious years. His beloved master was dead and his hopes and ambitions had died with him. The memory of his infamy would scourge him to the day of his death. Once he paused, lifting his arms in supplication, cried out: "Oh, that I might live again that short breath of time." Finally, he came to a stone wall, and felt for a gate. When it did not yield he called out: "Open, open."

But it was not the hardy voice of the fisherman Simon bellowing above wind and wave on Lake Gennesaret. It was hoarse and weak. It brought no response. He stood waiting, harassed by shame, plagued by remorse. Finally the gate opened. "Welcome, Rabbi!" cried the porter. "My young master is much concerned over you!"

Following the porter to a room laid with fresh rushes, Simon lay upon the floor. Soon John Mark came with hot water and towels and a candle, followed by a servant with bread, wine and an earthen bowl of hot stew.

17

In sudden overpowering hunger he broke off the heel of a loaf, plunged it into the stew and lifted it to his mouth a dripping portion of bread, meat and vegetables. He crunched it noisily; he swallowed it with grunts of satisfaction. Twice he repeated this. Then, taking up the cup of wine he gulped a third of it. "On this day of sorrow I should be fasting, not feasting," he said, "but my weak nature — were you up there?"

"No, Rabbi. I was seized by the soldiers but I escaped naked, leaving my robe in their hands."

"Then it was you I saw in my flight."

"Probably, but I do not remember seeing anyone. But John, the Apostle, was there. He told me . . ."

In detail he related what John had told him of the Lord's trial, death and burial. Simon groaned, he wrenched his beard. Finally, John Mark laid him on the floor. "Try to sleep, Rabbi," he said.

Simon's grief became assuaged in the soothing alchemy of tears, and he slept. He awoke with a start, at the crowing of a cock. He shuddered. Sitting upright, he leaned against the wall, and let his mind track back through the years. One event was persistent in its recurrence — the first time he had heard of Jesus. His brother Andrew, and John, son of Zebedee, had become disciples of John the Baptist. When they prepared to journey into Judea to hear John preach they urged him to go with them. He agreed but declined to go into the desert where John was preaching. "I think he's a bit mad," he said, smiling. "I'll wait for you in the house of our friend Enos."

When they met him again in the house of Enos, Andrew said, "We have found the Messiah."

Simon smiled, skeptically. How easily his gentle brother could be taken in by tall tales. "The Messiah, eh?" he replied good humoredly. "How many soldiers does he have?"

"How quickly you judge, though you have no basis for

judgment," said Andrew, in a tone of reproof. "We spent the day with him. We believe."

"No offense, my dear brother," said Simon lightly. "For centuries our people have believed that Messiah will overcome our enemies and raise Israel above all other nations. Only a Messiah with many warriors could do that. So I prudently ask: How many soldiers has he got. And I ask, who is this Messiah and where does he come from?"

"He is Jesus, son of Joseph. He lives in Nazareth."

"A Galilean, eh? Well, if this is the time for Messiah's coming I would like him to be a Galilean."

"Let us make you known to him," urged John. "Then you too will believe."

"Don't count on that too strongly, my young friend, but I'll go with you — in the morning, perhaps."

His discussion with Andrew of that meeting with Jesus now came vividly to mind. Curbing his positive manner of speaking, he had said, reflectively, "He did not know me yet he called me by name. Then he said I would be named Rock. What did he mean? You said he was Messiah. If that be true he will disappoint many people. He will never be a warrior. He will never drive the Romans from our land."

"Tell me what you think of him," Andrew had demanded.

"He is — he is unlike any man I've ever met," he had replied. "Holiness, that's it, holiness. Holiness comes out of him, so much that you have a desire to be holy. It draws you to him. There's something more too, but I don't know how to say it."

"If he invited you would you follow him?"

"I doubt it. What would he expect of one with so little to offer? How would I make a living? If he gave up carpentry how would he make a living? I think I'd enjoy being in his company and listening to him talk, but we've got to be practical, Andrew. I wouldn't mind giving him a few shekels now and then . . ."

"Practical! Shekels!" Andrew had said, scornfully. "Beware lest your practicality blinds you to higher things!"

Another thought had engaged Simon which he did not communicate to Andrew lest he be censured for childishness. If he followed Jesus he would be obliged to abandon Lake Gennesaret. How he loved that unpredictable body of water under the Cobalt hills, at times as placid as an old woman at prayer and a few breaths later a raging demon threatening death to men and destruction to piers and sailing craft. Here was adventure, an adversary to be subdued. "How good is our life on Gennesaret," he had said to Andrew and John when they again put out in their boats. "Nothing could entice me from fickle, alluring Gennesaret."

It was a resolution that seemed as firm as the rockbound hills that surrounded the lake, but which proved to be as fragile as the waves that washed up upon it shores.

Some weeks later while he and Andrew were casting a net they observed Jesus walking upon the beach. He called to them: "Follow me and I will make you fishers of men." Immediately, acting in concert without speaking a word, they left their nets and waded ashore, Peter in his impetuosity taking the lead, and followed him.

He knew not what was expected of him, but vaguely he had sensed an opportunity for one of his dominant character to do important work and rise to high place. But the road had been strewn with many obstacles. He had experienced frustrations and disappointments. Many of his suggestions the Master had ignored. From him he had suffered humiliation and rebuke and on one occasion, a severe castigation: "Get you behind me Satan! You are a scandal to me!"

Yet the Master had honored him — permitted him to witness his transfiguration, had chosen him to execute many of his desires, and finally the highest of all honors: "Upon you I will build my Church." Pride now possessed him. "I spoke out while the others were dumb." You are the Christ, the Son of the living God. Yet, I denied him I who had boasted of my love and courage. Denied him, not to a King, but to the lowly servants of the High Priest. How could I fall so low? How could I fall so low? Now all is over. He could have overcome them with a word, with a look, but he would not. He would not.

A cock crowed unnoticed by him in his exhaustion of mind and body. Falling on his side, he slept.

3

The Road to Galilee

THE ROAD to Galilee. Peter said to his brethren, "Let us go up to Galilee, as the risen Lord bade us." At sunrise they were on their way. Westward to the blue sea, Eastward to the turbulent Jordan, the ground fell away. In one place abruptly, cut by grayish-brown gorges; in another, gradually, shouldered by gentle slopes green with fennel and wild olive. A pine or cypress tree stood vigil on a lofty crag. Clear cold water purled from roadside springs.

Many times with other pilgrims they had walked this way, their voices lifted in poignant chant from Jeremiah: "By the waters of Babylon we sat and wept, O Zion, whenever we thought of you." But there was no lamentation in their hearts today, only joy, for their beloved Lord had risen from the tomb. A joy that found expression in an ancient hymn: "I will lift up my eyes unto the hills, from whence comes blessings from the Lord who made heaven and earth. Mountains gird you about oh Jerusalem. So does the Lord encompass his people now and forever."

As the travelers mounted the hill overlooking Lake Gennesaret, Simon paused and gazed about, his heart flooding with nostalgia. Fishermen's boats rested upon the sands or swung idly at anchor; fishing nets were drying in the sun; a flock of pelicans swooped out of the north over the Cobalt hills and in gracefully descending circles came to rest upon the placid water. He was born on its shores. Since childhood it had been his playground; since the age of twelve, his living. It had lured him with the prospect of adventure, threatened him with death and shackled him to monotony and drudgery. And it had rewarded him with an indomitable spirit of self-reliance and independence. It fitted him to be an instrument for the mysterious young man from Nazareth.

During their journey from Jerusalem, Andrew said to his brother, "Henceforth you shall be a man of the world." Peter neither agreed nor disagreed. For the present he was a Galilean of the lake country. Almost every night he put out to fish; he argued with his old enemies, the salterers, for a fairer price. He visited old friends and over a supper and a pitcher of wine told them of the Lord's death and resurrection. The while he and his brethren were patiently waiting for the Lord's appearance. Finally he did appear and subjected Peter to a severe test of humility. Before the other Apostles he inquired: "Simon, son of Jonah, do you love me more than these do?" Chastened by rebukes for his boastful speech, Peter replied humbly, "Lord, you know I love you." "Feed my sheep," Jesus said and twice repeated the question. Twice Peter replied, that he loved him and Jesus said in turn, "Feed my lambs," "feed my sheep."

How compassionate he is, Peter thought. Three times I denied him and three times he gave me opportunity to declare my love for him.

On the feast of Pentecost Jerusalem again was host to many of her children. They came from remote villages in Palestine and other countries of the Diaspora to worship in the holy Temple and offer the sacrifice of leavened bread. But unlike other religious feasts which were observed with dignity and in quiet religious atmosphere, there were occurrences this day so unusual that Elezar the Prefect of the Temple felt impelled to disturb the solitude of Annas the former High Priest and make a report of them.

"We believed the Nazarene's death would end his blasphemies," he cried out, "but we were wrong! This entire day his Galilean followers have been preaching and baptizing in his name."

"It is nothing, my son," replied Annas, "a few mad fishermen whose zeal will spend itself like an arrow in aimless flight."

"Yes, they are mad, your Excellency. But with a purpose! The one called Simon Peter — his flaming eyes, his throbbing voice, his arms outstretched as if he would take the whole world to his heart — he has put a spell on the people! His garbled Hebrew and Aramaic was no impediment. I clearly understood him, and so did Jews from Parthia and Phrygia and Egypt and . . ."

"You mean he has the gift of tongues?" cried Annas.

"All of them had the gift of tongues! Men eagerly besought them: What shall we do to be saved? And they poured out those blasphemous words: 'Believe in your savior the Lord Jesus Christ. Repent and be baptized in his name!' And that is what they did! Five thousand of them!"

"Five thousand!" gasped Annas.

"An arrow's aimless flight? A spear's determined thrust!" cried the Prefect stirring in agitation about the room. "If they are not put away the whole of Judea will go over to them!"

"This is serious, but we have not the power of execution . . ."

"We have secret dungeons, Excellency!"

"If we could make a case of sedition against them," said Annas reflectively, "or of public disturbance . . ."

"I shall so instruct my servants," Elezar said, making an unceremonious departure.

One morning shortly thereafter Elezar passed a cripple lying near the Gate Beautiful, whose plea for alms he ignored. A few paces beyond he heard words spoken to the cripple which impelled him to slow his pace and listen: "Gold and silver I have none, but what I do have I give you in the name of Jesus of Nazareth. Arise and walk."

"A fake healer," he muttered, "and what a fool for trying to heal one who has not walked since infancy."

He resumed his way but after a few paces stopped in sheer amazement. The gray-bearded rack of bones running past him and rejoicing in his tremulous reed voice, was this same beggar! Turning about, he recognized Simon Peter and the youthful Apostle John, neither of whom seemed the least astonished. He waited until they had passed him and followed them — to the Temple. Simon spoke to those who had surrounded the beggar.

"Men of Israel, why do you wonder at this man? Why do you stare at us, as if it were by our strength that this man walked? Jesus of Nazareth, whom you slew gave him soundness of limb. Thus did the God of Abraham glorify his Son."

"A dangerous fellow," muttered Elezar. He summoned two Temple guards who arrested Peter and John and the beggar and confined them in a cell under the treasury. "Now I shall inform the High Priest," he said, "and put some iron into his back bone."

Perfumed beards and spotless robes bequeathed a certain luster to Annas and Caiphas and the other magistrates sitting on the upper side of the bar of justice, but the unwashed bodies and soiled garments of the two prisoners in no wise detracted from their personalities. They stood dignified and erect, with a quiet joy too mystical to be described, too challenging to be ignored. A few steps to one side, the beggar waited as though in a dream.

Annas spoke to the two Apostles. "By what power, and in what name do you act?" he demanded.

Slowly, with a gesture of authority, Simon's slab of a hand rose to full height. His deep voice rumbled through the Hall of Hewn Stone. "Princes and ancients of the people, if we are under examination regarding a benefit to an infirm man, to determine by what means he has been cured — let it be known to you and to all the people of Israel, that by Jesus Christ whom you crucified, whom God raised from the dead, by him this man stands in your presence entirely cured."

Beneath his calm exterior Annas shuddered. His troubled mind recalled a quaking of the earth, a black sky at midday, the Temple veil rent from top to bottom.

He frowned, saying, "We forbid you speaking or teaching at all in the name of Jesus."

Simon flung back defiantly: "Judge whether it is right in God's sight to listen to you, rather than to God." John supported him: "We cannot do otherwise than tell what we have seen and heard."

"Teach no more in his name," warned Annas, "else you may suffer as did he." With a gesture he ordered their dismissal.

When the court adjourned, Elezar spoke with Annas. "I have not the wisdom of the Sanhedrin, Excellency, but bear with me while in my blunt way I say what I think. This fellow will laugh at you. He will go on preaching more boldly than ever. And so, also will his followers."

Annas shrugged. "I think you are right, my son, but we cannot risk offending the people. We must wait until his popularity wanes. In the meantime, keep watch."

After a fortnight, Elezar returned.

"Excellency, every day these Galileans come to the Temple and strut about Solomon's porch like Roman centurions. They preach Jesus of Nazareth, and actually use Temple water to baptize. Many people are being subverted. They bring their sick and their lame to them, their deaf and their blind. And they cure them! I must confess to these wonders. They even lay their sick and lame on the street so the shadow of this man Simon may fall upon them."

"Surely you don't mean to say . . . ?"

"I do say! His shadow cures! Even the incurables! People are bringing their sick and their lame from surrounding towns. It is no exaggeration to say that if he is not restrained, all of Israel will go over to him."

"You should be in the Sanhedrin," said Annas, wryly. "Continue to watch. I shall importune my reluctant brothers."

Elezar continued to watch, and work. He commissioned Ruben, a young Temple guardsman, to join the new sect, and to spy upon it members, particularly upon Simon Peter. Ruben's first report confirmed the Prefect's fears. "This Simon is a power. They yield to him as to a king. Yet, he is always counseling with those called the Twelve, as if unwilling to take too much authority. They are a queer lot. All the followers give money to the Twelve, which they give to the poor. No one wants for food, clothing or shelter."

"You did well to mention this. Keep on the alert."

The young guardsman was much perturbed when next reporting to his chief. "You are right, worthy Prefect," he declared. "This man, Simon, is a menace to our peace . . ."

"You have discovered some sedition?"

"I've discovered murder! He slays with a look! A word!"

"You are mad!"

"I tell you I saw it. One of the converts, Annias, sold some property and gave money to him, representing it to be the full proceeds. Simon turned on him indignantly: "Annias, why has Satan tempted your heart to lie to the Holy Spirit and deduct some of the proceeds of your land? You have not lied to men, but to God."

"How did Simon know he had held back part of the

money?" Elezar challenged Ruben's report.

"I don't know."

"How gullible you are. I hope he took back his money."

"He didn't have time. He dropped dead at Simon's feet."

"Dead?" gasped Elezar.

"Dead as a smelt two days on the beach. Slain by Simon's flashing eyes."

"Yes, you are mad!"

"That could be," replied the guard cooly. "Even so, Annias is under ground. I helped bury him."

"He died of fright — of — of — corrupt blood!"

"Fright of Simon, perhaps. But that isn't all. Several hours later, Saphira, the wife of Annias, came to Simon. He asked her if they had sold land for a certain amount, mentioning the sum her husband had given, and she said 'Yes.' His eyes flashed again, 'How is it,' he bellowed at her, 'That you have conspired together to tempt the Holy Spirit? Behold at the door the feet of those who have been burying your husband."

"Now, don't tell me that she, too, fell dead."

"Dead as our Mother Eve! Simon said to her, 'And they shall carry you out,' and without a word she dropped at his feet. We buried her beside her husband."

Elezar sat in brooding silence. "You're right," he said, "this is double murder."

"Excellency, the Roman Procurator would laugh at such a charge. But it is proof that Simon has a strange, terrible power. If by a look or a word, he could slay this man and his wife, could he not slay the High Priest and all of the Sanhedrin?"

The Prefect paced the floor pulling nervously at his beard. "Slays with a word," he muttered. "Slays with a look. Oh, if they would only give me my way!" Within the hour he was conferring with Annas.

"This Simon possesses a strange dangerous power," the

High Priest agreed when Elezar had concluded, "but we cannot turn it against him. The Romans would laugh us to scorn were we to charge him with the murder of Annias and his wife."

Elezar gestured impatiently. "I would not charge him with murder. I would charge him with creating disorder, perverting the faithful from the holy law, plotting against the very foundation of our religious and political power. . . ."

"Ah, that is more like it," said Annas. "Arrest him and all of the so-called Twelve."

Annas and a half score of the judges filed into the Hall of Hewn Stone and solemnly took their places upon the rostrum. According to procedure the prisoners would be brought before them without delay. But on this occasion the procedure was not observed. Minutes passed, long irritating minutes. Annas frowned at the guards, and several of them hurriedly departed. How could judges mantain their austere dignity sitting like owls upon a perch with no prisoner to judge?

Finally, one of the guards returned, but not with that dignified mien and imperturbable countenance so characteristic of Sanhedrin guards. He rushed in, wild of eye and ashen of face. "The prisoners escaped!" he gasped.

Annas glowered. He flung an impatient hand. The man was mad. Prisoners did not escape from Israel's prisons. But before he could speak in reprimand another guard entered in a state of extreme agitation.

"The prisoners are gone," he said, striving to control his voice, "but we do not yet know how they escaped."

Another guard entering the court cried out: "The men you put in prison are in the Temple preaching as usual to the people. I heard one say that an angel of the Lord had delivered them."

Flushing angrily, Annas bade the guards: "Arrest them! Bring them before us! But quietly," he added in a cautious tone, "lest there be a tumult among the people."

Annas regarded the prisoners with sullen curiosity, and some fear. How did they contrive to pass through locked, guarded doors? An angel? Ridiculous! Only fools believed in angels. How insolent is this Simon Peter. He looks at me half smiling as if to say, I cured a cripple, let's see you cure one. Glaring down at him, Annas said, "We gave you strict orders not to teach in his name. Yet you have filled Jerusalem with your doctrine and intend to bring his blood upon us!"

Again that brown hairy hand shot up in solemn protest, that deep voice rumbled through the Hall of Hewn Stone. "We must obey God rather than man!"

Disdaining argument, Annas made a sign and the prisoners were removed while the court deliberated. When they were again brought in the High Priest searched their faces for signs of fear, but he saw only joy and peace. "We forbade you preaching in his name," he said to them. "You have defied us. For that you shall be scourged, thirty-nine lashes, according to our law. Again we forbid you. If you disobey, you will see an end to our mercy and forebearance.

The Apostles were led away to endure their first suffering at the hands of the disbelieving world. As the whips descended, thirteen lashes on the chest, then thirteen on each shoulder, there was no groaning, no cry of pain. Fortunately, the Jewish whips made with two straps, one of calf leather and one of ass's skin, were more merciful than the Roman scourge tipped with knobs of bone and lead, which sprayed flesh and blood over whipping post and lictor. Yet, it was a painful ordeal and an alarming portent of what was to come as a penalty for loving the Master. Through it all they encouraged one another, and when they returned to the house of John Mark, their bodies bruised and bleeding, the weaker were supported by the stronger.

Mary the mother of Jesus and several of the other women who had followed the Lord and now ministered to his disciples, oiled and bound up their wounds. Toward evening John Mark came with an explanation of their unexpected release. "Gamaliel saved you. I learned it from his servant. He warned them that if your work was of God they could not put it down, and they might find themselves in conflict with God."

"Blessed be Gamaliel!" cried one.

Simon Peter slowly rose from his pallet. "Gravely injured would be the Church," he said, "if all the Apostles were slain at one time, but it would not be destroyed. We have our Lord's promise of that: 'I am with you all days,' and 'The gates of hell shall not prevail against it. Enemies without, the Church will always have. It is the enemy within that can hurt her the most — other Judases who will betray, other Thomases who will doubt, other Simons who will deny. And there will be others — against whom the Lord warned us — false teachers — men who will teach what he did not teach, who will deny what he did teach, who will reject the meaning of his words and give a meaning of their own. Let us pray for wisdom to confute these false teachers."

4

Death and Martyrdom for Stephen

THE APPARENT reluctance of the Sanhedrin to imprison the Apostles encouraged some of their brethren to believe they would suffer no further persecution. Peter did not share their hopes. "The older members of the Sanhedrin believe that Christ's doctrine will die with the Apostles. They are reconciled to wait. But the others — they will not wait. So be prepared to suffer, even to give up your lives."

His words proved to be prophetic. The deacon, Stephen, was arrested while preaching and was brought before the Sanhedrin. Peter and Andrew were informed of this by John Mark while they were preaching in the Temple. They hurried to the Hall of Hewn Stone, which they entered as Stephen was being sentenced to death.

Across the northwest section of the city a mob pulled and dragged Stephen. A hundred paces beyond the Damascus Gate they cast him into a rock pit, Pethha-Segilah, the ancient place of stoning. Immediately a shower of stones were hurled upon him. As he staggered about more stones were cast. He fell, his body half buried, his bleeding face staring up at his executioners. The stoning ceased. The crowd began dispersing — hurriedly, furtively. Death had come into the pit. Let no man say they had lost respect for the dead.

Simon strode toward a path leading into the pit, passing a young man bearing in his arms a number of mantles and phylacteries belonging to the stone throwers. He stared angrily at him, noting with disfavor his stern thin face and hawk-like nose. The young man stared at him cooly, defiantly. Fearing Simon would denounce him, Andrew put a cautionary hand upon his brother's arm. He jerked away, obviously resenting this lack of faith in his prudence, and hurried down the path, followed by Andrew and Mark. After removing the stones, they laid Stephen's body in Simon's robe and carried it out of the pit. Andrew suggested they make a bier of the robe so they might share the burden but Simon said, "I will carry him," and lifted it to his right shoulder. Andrew did not protest. Stephen was his brother's spiritual son. This was his right. Later that day they laid it in a tomb. Simon spoke in tribute.

"Stephen, my son, when I chose you to be one of God's anointed, I had no thought, so strong were you in youth and vigor, that you would be the first of us to die. I grieve for loss of you, as for the loss of a son, but I glory in your strength and I rejoice in your reward. You are with God. You will have everlasting honor before men — first martyr for Christ, first to shed his blood as seed for Christ's Church. You have shown us how to die. When our time comes to suffer persecution and death ask our Lord to give us something of your strength, and your love. Until then, be our inspiration and our guide in the work that has been given us to do."

That night while Simon and Andrew walked in the court, John Mark joined them. "Mark," said Simon, "that man holding the cast-off clothing — he seemed to be one of the instigators of this crime. Do you know who he is?"

"I, too, was curious, Master, so I inquired of Philo, scribe to Gamaliel. The man is Saul of Tarsus, a Pharisee. He came to Judea to lead in the persecution of those who love the Lord!"

"Saul, Saul," repeated Simon, thoughtfully. "So persecution is planned. We must prepare ourselves for suffering."

These words, too, were prophetic. The next morning a boy came to him weeping. Guards broke into his house during the night and had removed his father and mother to prison. By midday reports of numerous like incidents had come to the Apostles, and by evening they had mounted to several score. Night after night the raids continued. The prisons were crowded. A few Christians were slain. Many were deprived of employment and denied the right to purchase the necessities of life.

While the faithful gave generously to aid their brethren, Simon chafed over his inability to relieve all of their suffering or to abate the persecution. Some of them became disheartened. "Saul is a demon out of hell," they wailed. "Our prayers are useless." Simon roared at them. "No prayer is useless, if said with good intent! The Lord bade us pray for those who hate us. Pray, then, that Saul may be won to the Lord."

Saul won to the Lord! They looked at him bewildered. Their father's troubles were driving him to distraction.

People began fleeing the city and soon the flight became an exodus. Peter mourned and mapped a new course. Calling together the Apostles, priests and deacons, he said:

"In my distress I failed to observe that it is not we, the teachers, who are being persecuted, but the people we have taught. Many of them are now in flight to the northern provinces. We must be shepherd to them spiritually and temporally. Half of our number shall remain here. We shall divide our money among the other half and in pairs follow them to their places of refuge. Agree among you where you shall go or cast lots for them."

"How sad that Jews should persecute Jews over religion," said Philip, one of the young deacons.

"It is the official Jews who are responsible for this persecution," Peter said, "those who have the power of office, and their minions, and that class of non-believing Jews who observed the form of our holy law but not its spirit."

"But are they not an obstacle to the conversion of many of our people?"

"A serious obstacle. We Jews were taught to venerate the judgment of the Sanhedrin and the High Priest. Therefore, when one of them declares that the friends of Jesus stole his body his words carry much weight. And there is another obstacle — the finality of death. How difficult for one to believe a dead man can be restored to life. All of you have heard how we Apostles refused to believe in the resurrection of our Lord. So we must be patient with them, and kindly, and understanding, even as the Lord was patient and kindly with us. I urge you do not speak of this as a Jewish persecution. Perhaps no more than a score or two of Jews are directly responsible."

Peter and John journeyed into upper Judea where their people lived in pastoral peace. They labored in field, vineyard and orchard, while children tended sheep. From dwellings came the rumble of stone hand mills as women crushed grain into meal. Nor was life so drab as in Jerusalem. Everywhere there was evidence of the Jews' love of colors — the greens and purples and blues of robes and mantles, the vermilions and yellows of houses, the varied shades of ornamentation on dishes and pottery; and flower beds; scarcely a dwelling without its flowerbed. Peter proudly commented on this trait of his people:

"As well as being religious and liberty loving the Jews are an artistic people. They love beauty — they create beauty. The ancient name of our country Caanan means Land of Purple, from the secretion of shell fish which was made into a famous purple dye. It is said that this developed into a liking for all colors and resulted in the cultivation of many species of flowers."

They traveled over roads they had walked with Jesus and

taught in villages where he had taught. On Mount Tabor they prayed where they had witnessed the Lord's transfiguration. "I still tremble in awe whenever I recall that day," Peter said. "How good it is to come this way again."

How this rugged fisherman has changed, John thought. He is as sensitive as a poet, as profound as a sage. Yes, and as practical as a man wise in the ways of the world. This latter characterization derived from the policy Peter adopted at the beginning of their journey. At every gathering he spoke of the need for priests. "It is not enough for you to sit in your homes and pray. You must get out and teach your neighbor. But in order to teach you yourselves must be taught. We need priests to teach and to bestow the gifts of our Church. I urge you men to search your hearts. You may find God is calling you to his service."

Worthy men responded to his call, at least one to every district into which he divided the provinces. And in every province, Samaria, Gaulonitis, Perea, upper and lower Galilee, he appointed a supervising priest, or Bishop.

All the while he was thinking of his suffering brethren in Jerusalem, and one day he said to John, "I should not abide here in comfort and security when our brethren are faced with grave danger."

"You haven't done so badly here," John said, smiling.

Then came a messenger from Andrew informing him that while the persecution had not ceased, it had abated in its severity and suggesting that he return.

"Carry on for me, my friend," he said to John. "Some of our newly ordained priests need more instruction and more fervor. Of all the Twelve you are the one best equipped to make saints of them."

He set out alone on foot. Finally he crossed the ford Betharabah where Joshua had crossed the Jordan leading the Israelites into Canaan, and strode vigorously up the rising ground toward

Jerusalem. His iron-pointed staff dug into the rocky soil, a vagrant wind whipped his blue robe about his bare calves. Many times he had walked this ground, but never with the same resolute purpose and sense of dedication that now drove him on. Simon the Galilean fisherman has become a man of the world — the new world erected by a Galilean carpenter, Jesus of Nazareth.

5

Lydda: A Priestly Ministry

PETER found his brethren more interested in a "wild tale out of Damascus" than in the prospect of further persecution. Saul, it was said, had been converted. He declared he had been chosen by Jesus Christ to preach in his name. "This could not be true. Saul was treacherous, a liar and held nothing but hatred for the followers of Jesus Christ."

"So the Lord threw Saul from his horse," said Peter with a humorous smile. "He must have wanted him very much — more than he did us, in fact, for he merely invited us to follow him. It would be well to wait until we know all the facts before we pass judgment."

Occupations crowded upon Peter, more than he had time for — administrating and preaching, instructing deacons and assisting the refugees who were returning to Jerusalem. Then came a plea from Lydda, a city twenty miles southwest of Jerusalem overlooking the plains of Sharron: "Send someone to minister unto us."

"Whom shall I send?" he warily asked himself. "I have no one." Then, after a pause, "I am wrong. I have someone, Simon. I'll send myself. I'll go in the morning."

Business details delayed his departure until after midday. He walked leisurely with a sense of relief, noting with appreciation the rugged dignity of crag, the broad sweep of valley, and the bright yellow of saffron and the reddish orange of Pomegranate against a background of green myrtle and pine. From a wild pistachio bush he picked a few yellow globules and chewed them, believing their reputed medicinal qualities would be beneficial to his gums and teeth. Knowing the location of a spring from previous journeys, he moved in its direction. At sundown, he washed his face and hands and sitting under a cypress tree, ate a supper of black bread, goat's cheese, the roasted leg of a fowl, a few figs and drank watered wine. "How comforting is this solitude," he mused. "No noise, no clamor, only the welcome chirping of crickets and the croaking of frogs."

He took off his sandals, removed from his pack a jar of ointment and carefully massaged his feet — large muscular feet, tough of sole, but free from callouses and spiney growths. Feet that had received constant care and which had borne him over many a weary mile. Replacing the ointment he pulled out a roll of heavy sail cloth, spread half of it on the ground, reserving the other half as a cover. Rising, he prayed: "Lord, I thank you for another day of life. If it please you, give me another day in your service. Protect me this night from the violence of roving animals. Give me the grace of a strong abiding faith in you, a deep love, for you and a firm hope in your Divine mercy."

When Simon reached Lydda, the brethren warmly welcomed him and lodged him in the house of Ben-Buta, a merchant in spices. Sensible of his social obligations, the merchant undertook to provide luxuriously for his distinguished guest, but to his dismay, Simon said: "I will not take your bed, my friend. A mat on the floor will do, preferably in a small alcove where my snoring will not disturb your household. Nor will I have a special servant."

"Would you have me treat you like a camel driver?" cried Ben-Buta in despair.

"I've known some worthy camel drivers," Simon said, smiling. "And while we're on the subject, let us have an understanding. The evening meal I shall be honored to eat at your table, as you graciously insist, but as for the other meals — a handful of dried peas."

"Dried peas?" cried Ben-Buta in consternation.

"Yes, and a few dried beans or lentils at midday with a cup of watered wine."

"You'll starve, Master!" moaned the merchant.

"I'll thrive," he replied, thumping his midriff, which was as flat and as hard as a shield. "I beg of you not to mention this fasting to anyone."

Simon entered immediately upon his apostolic work, teaching and baptizing, encouraging those who were wavering, lifting up those who had fallen, visiting the sick and burying the dead. The faithful admired his zeal and praised his tireless efforts in their behalf, but they were disappointed because he worked no miracles. But their awe of him prevented any mention of the subject. Finally, however, his host spoke to him.

"Master, I have a relative called Aeneas, who for eight years has been a bedridden paralytic."

"I'll go to him," said Simon, "and if he is willing, instruct him in the word of the Lord."

"He is willing, but I would have you do more. I would have you cure him."

"Cures come from God, not man," replied Simon, brusquely.

"You cured a cripple near the Gate Beautiful."

"You are wrong, my friend. God cured him, working through the lowliest of his servants."

"I am confident that if you ask him, God will work through you again and cure Aeneas."

"You are confident that God will work a miracle. Man, do

you realize what you are saying? Do you think God will jump
through a hoop? . . ."

"Oh no, Master," wailed Ben-Buta, horrified. "I . . ."

Simon waved him to silence. "Would you have your relative cured? Then pray fervently and humbly. Fast, do penance."

Ben-Buta did penance, and with him, his entire household.
Then one day Simon visited the paralytic, silently praying on the
way: "Lord, if your use of me will strengthen the faithful in their
love for you, and the non-believer will be drawn to you, then let
me not call upon you in vain." Standing by the cripple's bed he
said, "Aeneas, Jesus Christ heals you. Get up and take thy bed."
And straightway he got up and walked.

Simon rejoiced over the numerous conversions following
this cure but he was so dismayed over the people's acclaim of
him that he sternly chided them, "Think you that God did this
for my glory? No! No! He did it to show his love for you that
you might believe in him. Praise God! Not Simon!"

They obeyed him, in part. Publicly they glorified God. Privately they glorified Peter, and in time this glorification came to
the ears of people in Joppa who journeyed to Lydda and besought him to raise from the dead their "beloved Tabitha."

Patiently he said to them, "Surely you know that only God
can raise the dead to life."

With deep humility they replied, "We know that, Master.
We pray for that great favor only if he wills to grant it."

Moved by their sincere faith he accompanied them to Joppa
and they conducted him into the house where lay the body of a
woman. At his request they all withdrew. He prayed silently and
then said aloud, "Tabitha rise!" Immediately she opened her
eyes. Taking her by the hand, he raised her.

The brethren of Joppa vied with one another to give him
hospitality but he chose the house of Simon, the tanner where he
observed the same schedule of fasting. To his host's dismay he

said, "God chose to do a great work through me. I must keep close to him in spirit. Fasting helps me do that."

Rigorous fasting begets ravenous hunger. As Simon prayed on the house roof one midday he was distracted by a craving for food. The craving became so strong he had a vision of food — cattle, sheep, goats and fowls — contained in a large sheet-like vessel, suspended by its four corners in the heavens. He was delighted. But his delight turned to disgust when he saw other creatures in this vessel — swine, creeping things, and unknown beasts and birds. Then he heard a voice: "Arise, Peter, and eat." It was the Master's voice, and he boldly replied; fortified by God's law of Moses, "Far be it from me, Lord. I have never eaten anything common or unclean." The voice spoke again, with a note of chiding: "What God has cleansed, do not you call common." Three times the voice said this before the vessel disappeared.

While Simon pondered the meaning of this vision, the same voice spoke again. "Three men are looking for you. Go with them without hesitation, for I have sent them." Going down, he found three men at the door. "I am the man you are looking for," he said. "Why do you come?"

They told him that Cornelius, the Centurion at the fortress in Caesarea had been directed by an angel to send for him and he would instruct Cornelius in the word of the Lord.

Peter pondered these events. The vision of the animals and God's command to kill and eat. Understanding came to him. The command of the Old Law not to eat certain meats, was no longer binding. The vision of the Gentile Cornelius and God's command that he send for Simon Peter who would instruct him in the word of the Lord. Further understanding came to him. The interpretation of the Old Law, that God revealed himself only for the sons of Abraham was no longer valid. For the first time he understood that God should be made known to the

Gentiles. The Lord's repeated command: "Teach all nations," he had failed to comprehend. He taught Cornelius and all his household, baptized them and remained with him some days as a guest.

The Jews who had accompanied him were scandalized. "He ate and consorted with pagans! He baptized them! All this is contrary to our holy law!"

Realizing that he had been of like thought, Peter patiently explained to them why all men should be taught the Lord's word, but many were not reconciled. "The other Apostles were as close to the Lord as is Simon Peter. They will never approve a course so radical."

Well did Peter know the convictions of his brother Apostles. They had been his own convictions. His new policy was in direct conflict. Thus were drawn the lines of the first test of apostolic authority. But he would not immediately return to Jerusalem. Many engagements bound him here and it would be well for them to have more time for a consideration of this truth.

Before setting out for Jerusalem he advised his friends by messenger the hour he would meet with them in the synagogue they were using as a place of worship and urged them to have present as many of the brethren as it would conveniently hold.

When he arrived at the synagogue in Jerusalem a large, eager audience were waiting. He greeted them affectionately and opened his subject.

"For several days I visited in the house of Cornelius, a Gentile. I ate with him and his family. I instructed them and all his household in the word of the Lord and baptized them. If you have any complaint against me speak out forthrightly."

James the Elder spoke for all. "Brother Simon, you confirm all that we have heard. What was it that led you so far astray from the teachings of our holy law?"

Embracing all within his gaze Peter replied: "Knowing you

would be scandalized in me, I returned as quickly as my commitments would permit. Not to make apology, not to engage in dispute or argument, but to explain. When I have finished it will be apparent to you that I did not stray from the teachings of our Lord, but obeyed his teachings."

The Apostles exchanged amazed glances. In the old days Simon was blunt of speech, apparently too dull to engage in discussion. After the Lord named him Rock he often seemed confused, hesitant, as if reluctant to make a decision. But how he had changed in these few months! There was no uncertainty about him now. Speaking incisively with the confidence of one convinced he was uttering truth, he told them of his vision and of his argument with the Lord.

"A bad dream," twitted one of his old friends, good humoredly. "Too much strong wine, perhaps?"

"Your disbelief does not surprise me," he said amiably. "Have I not always believed as do you? But when that same voice — this you must believe if you are to carry on his work — when that same voice bade me accompany the three strangers to the house of Cornelius, and when I learned that he had been instructed by an angel to send for me so that I could teach him the message of our Lord Jesus, I understood for the first time what the Master had so often told us: 'preach the Gospel to all men . . .' " Some more of the same bad dream! "An angel would not appear to pagans!" — "Only the children of Abraham shall share in the glories of the Messiah!" — "This is a wedge that would destroy our holy law!"

"What did our Lord say when the Pharisees charged him with destroying the law?" cried Peter. "He said, 'I come not to destroy but to accomplish its fulfillment. He substituted Baptism for circumcision; instead of offering sheep and cattle in sacrifice he bade us offer his body and blood under the appearance of bread and wine. He associated with pagans. He taught and baptized them. He cured them of their ills and even raised them to life. Yet we did not understand. A habit of thought and a cherished tradition had closed our minds and sealed our hearts. The Holy Spirit came to us on Pentecost, but on this question we were deaf to his voice. A special Divine revelation was necessary for me to understand. I pray that my experience will open your minds and give you faith. If it does not — you know what the Lord said to me when I objected to him, washing my feet. If you do not believe I fear he will say the same to you: 'Then you shall have no part with me!' "

A hush settled upon the assemblage. Peter searched their faces but read no signs of doubt or opposition, only awesome wonder. The Elder James rose and began speaking.

"Simon, I yield to your judgment. It is not the judgment of Simon, the man. It is the utterance of a Divine truth by the Holy Spirit speaking through you. It is a truth often spoken by our Lord, yet it could not break through my shell of ignorance and prejudice. I salute your firm decisive way in making it known to us."

There was a general acclamation of assent from the assemblage. James continued:

"When the Lord named you Rock and made you keeper of heaven's keys and said he would build his Church upon you, I did not understand him, but I was sure he did not intend to give you final authority over His church. In fact, I did not like the idea. I was in error. All institutions must have a final authority, else there would be chaos and endless contradiction. The Church was faced with its first crisis, but we the elders were ignorant of that. I am thankful for the Church that this first test of authority you discharged in a way that convinced all of us that you were guided by the Holy Spirit."

While Peter was greeting the brethren after the meeting, Matthew said to some friends: "How our brother Simon has grown in mind and spirit and in dignity. When he gazed upon us and held up his arms to fix our attention he looked as I imagine Moses looked when he came down from Sinai bearing the tablets of the law."

6

Jerusalem: Peter Meets Saul

THE BAPTISM of Cornelius produced almost immediate results. Some Jews who fled Jerusalem during the persecution made their way to Antioch where they established a church. A few Gentiles, having heard of the conversion of Cornelius, asked to be instructed and were baptized. Their number increased until they became a substantial minority.

But differences arose between them and some of the Jews — that faction, known as Judaizers, who insisted that observation of Jewish rites and ceremonials prescribed by the Mosaic law was necessary for salvation. The Gentiles refused to observe these rites. So did some of the Christian Jews. Dissension arose, animosities developed, and became so intense and irreconcilable that Peter was informed of conditions and urged to come and "bring peace to our wounded church."

Peter could not go. He was absorbed in trying to insure peace to the church in Jerusalem, so he looked about for another and chose Barnabas, a man of distinguished appearance and of a tactful tolerant disposition.

"This dispute is turning Jew against Jew," he said sadly. "I should go but since baptizing Cornelius I have lost favor with many of our people. Bind up their wounds, my son, and pour upon them oils of tolerance and conciliation."

Barnabas kept Peter advised of conditions in Antioch. He

had reconciled a number of the brethren but his information was not encouraging. "This cleavage will continue until all of the older people have been taken to Abraham's bosom."

Peter sighed. "How excessive devotion to what is old can blind us to the virtue of what is new."

Numerous demands upon his time — apostolic administrative, private counseling and some of a social nature — for a time crowded Antioch out of his mind. Then suddenly realizing that Barnabas' letter was long overdue he hurriedly suppressed a wave of apprehension and assured himself: "All is well with him. I shall hear before long." He did hear but not by letter. Barnabas stood before him on the roof of his house, whither he had retired for prayer.

"I arrived yesterday after nightfall," he said, "with a companion, Saul of Tarsus."

"Saul!" cried Peter.

"Then it must be true."

"It is true. He has been preaching in and around Antioch. He desires to offer you his respects."

"Convey to him my respects. I would feel honored if he would sup with me, and yourself, as well."

Peter's glance swept over Saul's emaciated body. A sickly fellow, he thought. Not a very agreeable companion. A dull ponderous hulk, thought Saul, his watery eyes peering sharply. "Yes, I held their cloaks," he said, sensing Peter's thought. "His blood is upon my soul!"

"My head is bloody too," Peter said. "In anger I swore before the high priest's servants that I did not know my Lord." After a moment of tense silence he added with traditional Jewish courtesy, "Welcome brother Saul. You do honor to my house."

Having only one servant, who was preparing the meal, Peter showed his guest to a small room where there was water, towels and oils, brushes and combs. He brought him a light linen tunic and soft slippers. When they sat at table he invited Saul to ask the Lord's blessing.

Sensing Peter's curiosity Saul immediately began telling of his experience on the road to Damascus. He spoke rapidly, crisply, with suppressed emotion. When Peter asked a question he replied sharply, but not discourteously. Convinced that Saul's zeal was "eating him up," Peter offered him a cup of wine and cried out: "Marvelous! Breathtaking! How much the Lord must need you. But may I ask you to speak a bit calmer? I'm sure I missed some of what you said."

Saul took a swallow of wine. For a while he ate in silence. Then in a quieter tone he continued. When he had concluded he inquired when he could meet the other Apostles.

"Only James, a cousin of the Lord, and I are in Jerusalem at this time," Peter said. "But if you will come to the upper room in the morning for the breaking of bread you will meet many of the brethren."

As Saul and Barnabus returned to their abode, Saul spoke of Peter. "A man of strong character. Impulsive, like myself, but more self-controlled, courageous. Declared the rights of the Gentiles knowing he would forfeit the esteem of many of our people. The Lord is forming him to be a worthy foundation stone for his Church."

Others thought of Peter the Rock, "His face is a slab of granite." Or "His jawbone would anchor a sizable boat." Still others were fascinated. "What probing eyes! They demand the truth."

The following morning Peter addressed a gathering that filled the upper room. "My beloved brethren, I am privileged to make known to you our brother Apostle Saul, who has dedicated himself to serving our Lord." Speaking to Saul, he said, "In this room at this table, on the night before he died, our Lord changed bread and wine into his body and blood and gave us to eat and drink. It is fitting that you should be privileged, as we have been, to sit in his place and do the same for all of us."

In recognition of this courtesy Saul bowed graciously to Peter and with impressive dignity performed the sacred rites. At their conclusion he addressed the gathering, thanking them for their friendly reception, and with much feeling he told them of his experience on the road to Damascus, his conversion and of his sojourn in the desert preparing himself for the Lord's service. Then he said with deep emotion: "I have a strong desire to meet each one of you and embrace you in the name of our Lord Jesus Christ."

Saul began preaching in Jerusalem, but in a manner that disturbed the priests and elders of the Church. James the Apostle discussed this with Peter.

"The zeal of the man! It sweeps one off his feet. He bitterly charges the Jews with responsibility of the crucifixion of our Lord. Some of them are so angry I fear they will do him violence. You should restrain him."

"I have no right to restrain him," Peter said. "Besides, it would be useless, like trying to restrain a mountain cataract with your bare hands."

"Why, he might be slain. And that could bring about another persecution. I tell you, Simon, you should speak out!"

After some reflection Peter decided to call upon Saul at his house.

Saul received him with the courteous ceremonies characteristic of the Jewish gentleman, and poured him a cup of wine.

"I am troubled," Peter said. "Weighing the rights of one's freedom of speech against the possible death of another Stephen, I presume to ask your permission to comment on your manner of speaking."

"I know what you would say," Saul replied, striving to suppress his feelings. "That I am too vehement. I should be more conciliatory. Conciliatory!" The word crackled. "When they cried out, 'Crucify him?' When they stubbornly refuse to consider his works and his teachings?"

"Our people should not be condemned for the sins of a few," Peter said. "Most of those who cried out 'crucify him,' were instigated by those whom they trusted and respected — the High Priest and the Sanhedrin."

"What a tragedy!" cried Saul. "God honored our race by becoming a Jew man, yet how many refuse to believe in him!"

"The most sorrowful event in the history of man; agreed Peter. "But I have hopes for coming generations. They should not be so strongly bound to ancient traditions, particularly those living in other lands. And when they see Gentiles accepting that which came from the heart of the old law — should that not be an additional incentive?"

"I do not know," Saul said. "Those traditions — they are sacred, and so ancient they have become part of our blood and bone, and we are like rock in our opposition to change."

"God knew that when he revealed himself to us rather than to another race."

"Your hope rises from your love for them," Saul said. "I, too, love them. I know their adherence to the past. I pray that your hope will be realized," he added, but in a tone that signified his doubt.

Silent for a time, he said, "I dwell much on the mystery of God becoming man, and I feel glorified that he chose to become a Jew. I wish I could have known him and walked with him over the hills of Palestine. Would you tell me something about him — about his manhood?"

Peter smiled. "It will be a pleasure!" he declared. "I wish I could tell the whole world about him. There is no mystery about his manhood. He was a man like all of us, except in one respect."

He talked on and on, slowly, rapidly, sadly, joyously. With

sighs of regret and exclamations of admiration, with vibrant awe. He talked until interrupted by the mournful voice of the ram's horn on the roof of the Temple calling the people to prayer. He and Saul stood and reverently recited the ancient prayer that began with words of adoration: "Fear of the Lord is the beginning of wisdom . . ."

At the conclusion of the prayer Saul said, "Simon, you have largely dissipated my regrets for not having seen the Lord. I can see him now, the particular shade of his chestnut hair, the pigment of his skin; and his eyes — the deep brown pupils, and how they changed with his moods, the joy in them when he spoke of his Father, yes even when he spoke of the widow giving her mite to the Temple; the sadness of them when he wept over Jerusalem and foretold the destruction of our holy Temple; his sublime grace and dignity and majesty, and with it all a man who could be amused and smile at the vagaries of his disciples. I am grateful for this painting of him, Simon. I shall cherish it to the day of my death."

From the brethren Peter continued hearing complaints of Saul's vigorous preaching but he ignored their counsel to "Send him to some other place." "The Lord made special choice of him," he said. "Let us leave him to the Lord."

One day Saul came to Peter and said, "As I prayed in the Temple, the Lord bade me go from here. He would send me to the Gentiles far away."

"It is time for the rest of us to go to the Gentiles," Peter said.

With several of his disciples Saul took ship for Tarsus.

7

Apostles Announce Mission Goals

ALL OF the Apostles met in Jerusalem for the feast of the Pasch, Peter having summoned them for the discussion of a matter that could not longer be put off — their departure from Israel to teach the Gospel in other lands. A genial spirit prevailed. Difficulties were humorously exaggerated, and habits and foibles good-naturedly chaffed. Peter did not escape. "What a fine robe you're wearing," Simon the Zealot said. "And you an humble fisherman."

"What do you think of it? asked Peter swinging about so all might have a look. "One of my converts, a weaver and dyer, insisted on giving me a robe, saying the head of Christ's Church shouldn't go about looking like a camel driver. I disliked his implication, knowing some worthy camel drivers, but I accepted the robe, thinking that if the High Priest could wear purple, so should I, since my place far exceeds his in dignity. However, I shall wear it only on very special occasions.

"You wear it well," Matthew smiled. "One not knowing you would think you were born to the purple."

Finally Peter spoke of that which was foremost in the minds of all. "For a long time we have been working together in the Lord's vineyard, forging about us a strong bond of mutual affection. It is but natural that we should hope to continue until one by one we are gathered to our fathers. But we must rise above our nature. Our association must be severed. In obedience to the Lord's command, some of us must go forth into other countries. I ask you, then, to choose one for your labors. For some of you, however, I will choose, for we must ever keep in mind our brother Israelites. James, the Lord's cousin, should rule the church in Jerusalem. More than any of us he seems able to keep peace with the Sanhedrin. John has been given the care of the Lord's mother and so cannot journey far from Judea. Matthew is writing an account of the Lord's life and teachings, and for some time should remain close to the holy mother and other sources of information. Since I must be accessible to all I shall for the present remain in Jerusalem, though I prefer otherwise. After the Pasch let us meet again."

When they next met, Andrew was the first to announce his decision. "I will go to the countries of northern Asia Minor if you, my brothers, approve." Bartholomew said, "I will go down to Egypt," James the Elder said, "I would preach in Hispania." Jude chose Asia Minor, Philip, Syria; Matthias, successor to Judas, desired to preach first in Judea and then in Ethiopia; Simon the Zealot chose northern Africa; Thomas, Persia and the Indies.

They had spoken casually, as if saying no more than "I will cross over the Jordan into Parea," yet the significance of their decisions bore upon all. They pulled at their beards, rubbed their noses, palmed their brows. They regarded one another benignly, even tenderly. Finally Peter spoke, striving to keep his voice under control. "Once we part, we shall probably never be together again on this earth. At dawn let us gather for the breaking of bread."

Realizing that the hour of separation was drawing near, the Apostles gathered at Peter's house for a final breaking of bread. This ceremony had gradually taken on a format of prayer and together they prayed in a low, audible tone that throbbed with faith and love. They offered prayers of thanksgiving for God's blessings; prayers of supplication for all of their needs, spiritual and temporal. They sang verses from their favorite psalms.

At the appropriate time Peter took bread into his hands and spoke over it the same words that Jesus spoke over the bread in his hands at the last supper. All of them ate believing it was Christ's divine flesh. Then, drinking the wine Peter had likewise consecrated, they lapsed into silent meditative prayer.

Then Peter spoke, "Let us keep in mind that we are here because a Jewish maiden spoke the most important words ever uttered by man, "Let it be done unto me according to your words.' " Then he spoke again, "Silas!"

Immediately three servants entered bearing huge dishes of baked lamb and vegetables, fruit and a pitcher of wine.

In a moment laughter and the spirit of good fellowship reigned. "Just in time for my birthday tomorrow," shouted Simon the Zealot, gleefully.

In a moment Simon was being toasted by all of his companions.

At the conclusion of this ceremony, Peter said, "I offer this for your consideration. The day of Our Lord's birth should be celebrated by joyful song and music. The day of his death and for some weeks before that sad event should be given to penance, prayer and mourning. On the feast of His Resurrection let there be joy and song and glorification by horn and lyre and pipe. Impress upon your people the importance of those great feasts. And always keep this in mind. We are privileged to engage in this work because a Jewish maiden voiced the most important words ever spoken by man, 'Let it be done unto me according to thy word.' "

Simon the Zealot was the first to leave for his new missionary field. Peter walked with him down the road to Joppa where he would board a ship. When he did not speak, the Zealot inquired: "Could we be thinking of the same thing?"

"Most likely — of how I lured you from your solitude in the north country, with hints that you would be commander of the Messiah's armies."

The Zealot smiled. "Ambition stirred me, glory haunted me. I was easily lured. And what did I turn out to be? A preacher of religion — I of all men." He shook his head. Pausing, he turned about and gazed upward. "The Mount of Olives," he said proudly. "What glorious things we have seen from your royal head. I'll never look upon you again, but memory of you will always be green in my heart."

Peter swallowed hard. He embraced the Zealot and his companions and blessed them. "My heart goes with you," he said, "my heart and my prayers."

Mindful of the bitterness roused by the preaching of Stephen and Saul, Peter formulated a policy for his deacons and priests which he hoped would insure peace to the Church. "Do not preach in the Temple," he instructed them. "And when you preach in the synagogues, or at other public gatherings be temperate. Never compromise, but always be patient, kindly, and respectful of their beliefs. That is the way our Lord taught."

But there were enemies at work. Ben Ezra, priest of the Temple, addressed a gathering of Scribes and Pharisees in his house. "These fanatics thrive on persecution," he said. "If we slew them, followers a hundred-fold would rise out of their blood . . ."

"How else shall we be rid of them?" interrupted a Scribe.

"We must divide them. Some apostates who have gone over to them, being troubled in mind and heart, insist that the rites and ceremonials of our holy law shall be administered to the Gentile converts. The Gentiles refuse to submit, and speak profanely of our holy rites."

"Word of that dissension has come to me from Antioch," said one.

"It seems to be strongest there," said Ben Ezra. "We must strengthen it so that it will spread into Judea, and to wherever our people reside. Thus we shall rend them."

"Disunity does destroy," said one, "and so does the sword. Some of our Council believe we should call upon Herod's sword. If we attack this heresy from without as well as from within, it will surely fall."

Ben Ezra bowed to his colleague. "Until Herod's sword is drawn let us take this more subtle course. I have talked with Simon Peter, the head of this sect. He takes pride in what he calls their unity of doctrine and solidarity of practice. If we can sever that unity, if we can bring about a situation whereby the two factions charge each other with teaching something that is not true, they will split into conflicting sects and finally die."

"You speak wisely, my brother."

"To that end, I suggest that we send trusted followers to Antioch with instructions to join this sect and encourage others of like heart to join it. While pretending fervor, they will clamor for adherence to circumcision and all of our holy rites, and denounce those who object as idolaters and perverters of the Divine law."

"Why send them to Antioch? Why not begin here?"

"Jerusalem is the heart of the Nazarenes," Ben Ezra said. "Some of their influential leaders are always here, and they could more effectively counteract our efforts. Antioch, on the other hand, is an outpost where there is already a strong nucleus of dissenters."

"Yes, Antioch is the place," said one. "I will send a half score." Each in turn pledged assistance, until fully a hundred men could be relied upon.

After several months encouraging reports began coming to

Ben Ezra from Antioch. The dissenters were steadily increasing. Christian Jews were refusing to worship with Christian Gentiles and the breach was spreading to churches beyond Antioch. The Nazarenes were in turmoil.

Similar information came to Peter. "The needle point of heresy is becoming a wedge," he sighed.

There was substantial basis for his alarm. From sympathizers employed in the households of several Pharisees he learned that the Nazarenes were being charged with unfair distribution of food during the recent famine, and had discriminated against suffering non-believers. While the charge was false, Peter recognized its potential danger. James, the Elder, recently returned from his missionary journey in Hispania, was being bitterly denounced for his condemnation of the Pharisees. They called him another Stephen, and charged him with blasphemy and perversion of the people. Even more significant to Peter was King Herod's friendliness toward the Jewish priests and elders. He had lately been seen offering sacrifice in the Temple.

Peter and James counseled together. "The Pharisees are courting Herod," said Peter, "a man whom they secretly despise. Apparently he is lending himself to some scheme, else they would not permit him to profane the Temple by offering sacrifice."

"What mockery," frowned James. "He is not a Jew. He does not believe in God, yet he offers sacrifice. You are right, Simon. It bodes us no good."

Thereafter Peter and James supped together every night in Peter's house. But one night James did not appear. Naaman, one of his disciples, came and said, "They arrested him, Master, as we were leaving the Temple."

At dawn James was beheaded.

In the house of John Mark, Peter stood beside James' bier, his head bowed in grief. How gaunt he looks thought John.

Years have piled up on him in a single day. His first words were more like a sigh: "The first of us to die in the Lord." Suddenly a note of triumph sounded in his voice: "The first to see the Lord in all his majesty!" Then he became resigned: "The Lord could have stayed the sword as he opened locked doors, but he chose to let it fall. We lost a valiant friend. The Lord took to himself a valiant servant."

He lowered his head and went on: "James, son of Zebedee, friend since boyhood, we were not always in accord. We disputed vehemently, but never with ill will. When you caught a fish, a portion of it was mine; when you bought a new mantle, I wore it when I could. Never did I have cause to question your motive or doubt your purpose. You said not 'yes' when you meant 'no' or 'no' when you meant 'yes.' At times you were abrupt, but never unkind; often impatient, but never intolerant; ambitious for high place with the Master, but no more so than the rest of us. You gave to him in full measure your eloquence, your devotion and your love."

Again addressing the mourners he said: "My brethren, let us strive to be like James. Let us love the Lord as he loved him; labor as he labored for him; and if need be, die as he died for him."

Some of the faithful became disheartened by James' death and feared that Simon Peter would be the next to go. After the burial they urged him to go in hiding. "If they slay you, will the Church not fall?"

"Christ's Church will never fall!" Peter's booming voice reassured them. "Think you the Lord did not know I would soon be gathered to my fathers? Think you he intended his Church to drift without a rock at my death? When I die you will choose another who will serve the Lord as he commissioned me to serve him. Go ye therefore in peace and faith."

Encouraged by James' death, the Pharisees called upon

Herod and flattered him for his "just and courageous action."
"The angel who is said to have passed these men through prison
doors was helpless before your sword, O mighty King! Now, if it
please you, let it fall upon the others, beginning with Simon
Peter. He, too, was a disciple of John the Baptizer."

The following day while the faithful were gathered in the
upper room for the breaking of bread, heavy feet sounded on the
stairway. Fearfully the disciples looked at one another. "Be
calm," Peter said as he arose. Opening the door, he faced a stalwart officer armed with a short sword and a round brass shield.
"Whom seek ye?" he demanded.

"He who calls himself Simon Peter."

"I am he."

As he spoke, he remembered the Lord's words when he was
arrested in the garden, and added: "Then let these others go their
way." Turning to his friends, he said: "If it be God's will that I
die, call the Apostles into meeting so they may choose another in
my place. Be not overcome by grief. Carry on the Lord's work,
and do not forget that if he has other work for me, Herod's
sword cannot harm me, nor his prison walls contain me."

Winking at his men, the officer took Peter by the arm.
"You're a rugged practical fellow," he said. "Surely you're not
deluded by such nonsense."

"Have you never heard of the Lord, Jesus Christ?" asked
Peter. "Oh, yes," the officer answered lightheartedly. "Everybody has heard of him."

"But, alas, you know nothing of him. Let me tell you."

"Don't you think it's late for that?" replied the officer. "He
has been dead a long time."

Undismayed, Peter spoke fervently as he was led along the
street. The officer shook his head. "I cannot be vexed, so earnest
you are. You seem to think only of your dead leader. Have you
no fear of death?"

"For those who die in the Lord, death is but the gateway to eternal life, I should like to tell you about that too, my friend."

"I'd be more interested in knowing how you expect your Lord to save you."

"No matter how many walls you put around me, or how many guards stand over me, if the Lord has further work for me, I will walk out of your prison."

The officer stared at him. "I'm beginning to think you actually believe all this! And you're bold enough to warn me!"

Peter smiled, "I have a concern for you, my friend. Should I be delivered from captivity, you might be severely punished, even though it would not be your fault. I would be much comforted if you were baptized in the name of the Lord."

"Enough of this," the officer strode on with determination. Peter followed sorrowfully, believing the young captain was steeling his heart against its first faint impulse toward faith.

The prison officer bound Peter with chains and posted guards, two on the inside and two on the outside of his cell. "Now," he said, "let us see your God turn these guards into mummies and these chains into ribbons."

Several days later, near the end of the time of unleavened bread, a group of the faithful were praying in the upper room for Peter's deliverance. The stillness of the hour before daybreak was interrupted by a loud knocking at the outer gate. Soon the portress rushed back to say that it must be Peter for she had recognized his voice. They would not believe her, but when the knocking continued, they opened the gate themselves.

"An angel delivered me," said Peter simply. "He led me past the guards and through the prison gates, and then he was gone. I found myself in the street. Alone. This is a sign to me. I shall go to another place."

8

A Voyage to Antioch

ANTICIPATING that Herod's soldiers would be searching for him, Peter did not return to his house but with Aaron, a servant, secreted himself in a two-room apartment in the house of Rufus, a Galilean. He did not appear in public. Only James the Apostle knew his whereabouts and assisted him in preparing for his departure.

At Peter's invitation James came to supper one night, and found him in a small court roasting a fowl upon a spit. "Are you seeking escape from your many burdens?" he inquired smiling.

"I never escape from them," grumbled Peter. "They are with me always, like ticks on a sheep's back."

"Where is Aaron?"

"Playing at dice. I gave him a few coins and told him not to come back until he had doubled them."

"I can't imagine you encouraging one to gamble for money."

"There's no fun gambling for buttons. Hand me that bowl, please, lest I lose these drippings."

"True, but even so. . . ."

"Gambling was one of our relaxations in the Lake Country, tossing coins at a mark, wagering on boat races, and swimming races. The first boat I ever owned I won at dice."

"You amaze me! Tell me about it."

Peter smiled and wiped his brow with a towel.

"Several of us were casting dice. Chance favored me and I won steadily. Jonas lost all his money and offered his mantle as a stake. When I refused he challenged me to wager all my winnings against his boat. I liked the boat and agreed. I won. But it was only a partial victory. My father said the stakes were too high for both of us and gave Jonas one of his boats, an old one, but sturdy and bade me pay him half my winnings for the boat he had given Jonas."

He chuckled at the remembrance.

"A wise man, your father," James said.

"Only in recent years have I realized how wise he was," Peter said, reverently.

He served his guest roasted fowl with a dressing of bread and chestnuts and pomegranates, beans, lentils, a lettuce salad, honey, wheaten bread, figs and dark red Hebrew wine.

"What a sumptuous feast!" James said.

"I weary of stale cheese and dry crusts and half-cooked fish," Peter said. "Aaron is a faithful servant, but as a cook — he's a good stonemason. And besides, this will be our last meal together for a long time, perhaps for all time."

"That might be true, so I shall enjoy it. You are an excellent cook, Simon."

"I've always like cookery."

"I remember well the meals you cooked when we were traveling with the Lord. How our lives have changed since then. And for you the most portentous change of all. You are the earthly head of Christ's Church. Until the end of time men will speak of you in wonder."

"Yes, my life has changed, from Simon to Peter. I enjoyed being Simon — independent, carefree, self-sufficient, boasting and strutting as the mood came upon me, singing joyously at night upon the lake. But now as Peter, scarcely a moment am I free from care. Even when I try to lose myself in prayer cares press upon me, like ants feeding upon a carcass — cares related to the salvation and damnation of souls. I shudder when I dwell upon my responsibilities!"

Putting down his wine cup with a thump, he added: "But I wouldn't rid myself of one of them. Not for all the freedom life could give me."

"We all know that," James said, "and our Lord knew it when he chose you to bear them."

"You said men will speak of me to the end of time. That is pure fancy, my friend. Time buries all things, as sand buries entire civilizations. No man can escape oblivion, unless he be an Abraham or a Moses or a David, or a — a Jesus of Nazareth. But even if it were true I am not interested. I am concerned only in what the God man shall say to me when I stand before him in judgment. He will want to know what I did to bring peace to the Church in Antioch. I'll go there without delay. I have no passage money, but I shall work my way. I'm quite handy with sails."

"Work your way?" cried James in protest. "We are poor, Simon, but not that poor. I'll get your passage money."

"How good to have influential friends," said Peter, smiling.

After two days at sea Peter's ship entered the Orontes River and proceeded thirty miles inland to Antioch, a city lying on the plains between the green mountains of Lebanon and the rocky spurs of the Taurus range. Antioch, the pearl of the East, the city of the moon, second only to Rome in power and grandeur, and in many respects surpassing Rome as a dwelling place. Its streets were wide and clean, and bounded by expansive parks with grass and flowers and trees and fountains. Four boulevards crossed the city from east to west, and the Corso Boulevard, in the southern section, provided two lanes for traffic, one for heavy commerce, the other for chariots and pleasure vehicles. On each side were covered porticos for pedestrians.

What a contrast to the narrow crooked streets of Jerusalem, thought Peter, with its rows of gloomy houses which shut out air and light from their dwellings. Here we see single houses with wide spaces between, some with glass windows! "Marvelous!" he cried.

"I lived here for a time, Rabbi," said Jonas, one of his companions. "You see only a portion of its magnificence. These lamps, for instance. They throw a bright light over the streets. There are numerous theaters, temples, baths, aqueducts, artistic specimens of statuary, and stadia for races and gladitorial games."

"The people seem well-dressed," said Peter.

"And they are well-fed and well-housed, most of them. And our own people — about a third of the population of half a million, share in this prosperity — in varying degrees, of course."

"That is to say, there is poverty here and destitution and beggary."

"Yes, Rabbi, as in all other populous cities."

"And among the Gentiles there is depravity and abominations like unto Sodom and Gomorrah. They have a place, the beautiful Grove of Daphne but its beauty is used to conceal much of their depravity."

"Be not too critical of them, my son. Men who know not the true God easily fall into worship of other gods — sensuality and pleasure."

That night the travelers slept in the house of Barnabas, located in the Epiphana, the Jewish quarter, and from Barnabas Peter received a detailed report of Church matters. It was having a slow but steady growth among the Jews and due to the eloquent preaching of Saul a large number of Gentiles had been baptized. The differences between the Judaizers and the Gentiles had not been reconciled but their animosity had been curbed "at least for the present." "But this is only a truce," added Barnabas, "not a peace. Some day, I fear, this ill feeling will erupt with a force that will sunder the followers of Christ into two bitterly contending churches."

"That thought haunts me constantly," said Peter.

"And this dissension is being fomented by some of our own people from Jerusalem who falsely declared belief in Our Lord and were baptized."

"I suspected that," Peter said. "One of them confessed to me when he became a true believer."

Peter had come to a country where Greek was the language of the people, but he knew not a word of it. He decided to learn and asked Barnabas to find him two scribes who could teach him. Joseph, a Jew, and Ignatius, a Greek, became his instructors.

He began meeting with the brethren, in their houses, since they had no temple, where a small number would be gathered, assisted by an interpreter in the houses of the Gentiles. But to his dismay he discovered they were not one body. With rare exception the Judaizers and the "liberal" Jews and the Gentiles met only with their own kind. We must have a temple where all may meet together, he decided, but for the present he kept this decision to himself.

The division among his people he used as a text for instruction. To the Judaizers he said, "You say you love God. God says you cannot love him when you have enmity for your brothers who do not agree with you in your interpretation of the Law of Moses. And I say entrust its interpretation to the Church that he founded."

The "liberal" Jews and the Gentiles were told to "Disagree with the Judaizers, not in hatred or enmity, but in kindness, patience and understanding. Have respect for their veneration of ancient sacred traditions."

To his priests Peter sadly admitted that his teachings were bearing little fruit. "The Judaizers speak with less bitterness in public for their brethren, but they have not budged from their views."

"Even that is no small achievement, Master," Barnabas said. "You were the physician with the right remedy, the gentle word, the patient manner."

"Thank you, my son, but we must have more, something that will bring them together. A temple! Where all may worship standing side by side."

Knowing his people were too poor to build a temple he prayed and pondered over what might serve as one. "A cave!" he cried out one night, suddenly rousing from a sound sleep, "our Lord's first temple was a cave!"

He urged his people to search for a cave but some of them were indifferent. It was not fitting to worship in a hole in the ground. Others could not find time for such a useless effort. Those who responded to his appeal could find no suitable place.

So he roamed the countryside himself, with several neophytes. After several days of fruitless search he stopped on the slope of Mount Stauris about two miles from Antioch. As he looked about he observed a huge face of rock that seemed to be upholding a rock spire that vaguely resembled Mount Moriah. "This is the place," he said quietly.

In the cave a half score of skilled quarrymen were hewing out rock. Peter and all of his priests were soliciting money to pay expenses. Some two months later he surveyed an excavation about forty feet long, thirty feet wide and twenty feet high with a smooth floor and a ponderous wooden door closing off the ten foot entryway. A stone table, the "table of sacrifice" stood at the far end close to the wall.

On the day of the Sun following its completion Peter dedicated the grotto and conducted the service known as the breaking of bread to a congregation of more than three hundred worshippers, with more than twice that number on the outside. He had thoughtfully prepared for this occasion and began the service by a recitation from one of the Psalms of David: "I will go to the altar of God. To God the joy of my youth. Our help is in the name of the Lord who has made heaven and earth."

After the service he thanked all who had "given generously of money and labor to this work for God," and concluded with a recitation from the 50th Psalm: "Create in us a pure heart, O God, and a resolute spirit renew within us. Cast us not from thy face. Restore to us the joy of your salvation."

9

Antioch: Teaching and Preaching

WHEN the Roman Gallio visited his friend Xanthus, a representative in Antioch of Roman financial interests, he mentioned that one of his slaves had embraced a strange new religion. "His god is a Jewish carpenter who was crucified by Pilate the Roman Procurator."

"Jesus of Nazareth, a village in Galilee," Xanthus said. "His followers gave him another name: Christ, meaning the Anointed or the Holy One. Here we know them as Christians, the first time they have been so designated, I am told."

"An appropriate name," Gallio said.

"Their leader, Simon Peter has been here for some time."

"A wild-eyed fanatic no doubt."

"He is a well-balanced blend of religious zeal and shrewd practical business, an organizer, an executive. He tells his people they must do more than love God, they must love men, all men, not just the members of their religion."

"Rather fatuous, don't you think?"

"Perhaps, if he did nothing but preach. But he teaches them how to love. He divided the city into districts and appointed men to seek out the poor. Others gather food and clothing which is stored in accessible places for distribution. Some orphan children were placed in private homes and others in a foundling home staffed by regulars and volunteers. Still others, himself included, solicit funds to carry on this work. If one grumbles over the resultant sacrifice of his ease and comfort he will say, if you do not love men your professed love of God is a mockery. Suppose we go for a drive. You might see him."

"At this late hour?"

"I am told he never sleeps," said Xanthus, smiling.

As they rode along one of the boulevards Gallio inquired, "Isn't the Grove of Daphne near here?"

"Those torchlights are near one of its entrances."

"What a strange place for lights."

Upon coming closer they could see the reason for the lights. A man was standing on a cask between two torches implanted in the ground, exhorting a small group of people.

"That's the man," Xanthus said, "They call him the Rock."

"Not inappropriately named," Gallio said.

Peter's voice could be distinctly heard. "Subdue your lusts! Cease your abominations! Pray to the true God to give you the grace of repentance!"

"His Greek is a bit thick," Gallio said, "but understandable. Does he have many listeners?"

"Not among those who come here at night. But elsewhere — a friend of mine, a man of wealth and learning, and a convert, informs me he has many converts, Gentile as well as Jew." After listening for a while Gallio said, "He seems learned in Hebrew lore and history. Was he formerly a member of the Jewish Sanhedrin?"

Smiling, Xanthus said, "he was an unschooled Galilean fisherman."

"Amazing! I would like to meet him!"

"And so would I. I shall invite him to dine with us."

Xanthus called at Peter's house and introduced himself. "I know you through my friend Photius."

"Dear Photius!" cried Peter. "His friend is most welcome

in my house, for I know he comes as a friend."

"I'm a Greek bearing gifts," Xanthus said. "Beware of me."
Taking Peter's hand he placed in it a leather bag of coins.

"Oh what a generous gift!" cried Peter.

"It is more of a bribe."

"A bribe?"

"To induce you to dine with me and a friend from Rome
who is anxious to meet you."

Peter smiled. "Must I be bribed to accept your gracious
hospitality?"

"Then give the money to your poor," laughed Xanthus. "I
shall call for you at sundown tomorrow, if that hour is agreeable
to you."

When Xanthus departed, Joseph, one of Peter's scribes,
came with writing equipment, Peter said, "We shall put off writing, Joseph. I am more interested in clothes — raiment for the
body."

Joseph stared at him, amazed.

"Purchase for me a new robe, a purple robe of silk and
wool and a white tunic of soft texture. Here is money. It was
given me for the poor."

"No one is poorer than you, Master," declared Joseph.

"That could be debated, Joseph, but I'm giving myself the
benefit of the doubt. I've been invited to dine with Xanthus and
his friend from Rome. I ask you: Should the head of Christ's
Church be dressed like a camel driver?"

Joseph cried out joyously. "How I have prayed for this day!
But don't you think you should walk the full mile?"

Peter regarded him suspiciously.

"Your hair and beard, Master! Come with me to Samuel.
He is the best barber in Antioch and one of the faithful."

Ignoring Peter's feeble protests, Samuel plied brush, comb
and scissors and crowned Peter's head with a billow of foam. But

when he said it would be a pleasure to oil and crimp such a magnificent beard Peter indignantly rebelled. "And have me look like Caiphas, the High Priest?"

"No Master, like our beloved Lord. I've heard that his good mother did the same for his hair and beard."

"So she did," muttered Peter, "but don't get the idea this will be something regular."

When these ministrations were completed Samuel took hold of Peter's right hand and shook his head ruefully. "An honest rugged hand, Master," he said. "but it lacks gracefulness. These calluses should be peeled; the fingernails should be trimmed and polished. A man's hand bespeaks his gentility."

"Not so much as his heart," countered Peter, "but have it your way."

When Peter walked from his house to the waiting carriage, escorted by Xanthus and Gallio, his household looked on with admiration. "How noble he looks," Joseph said. "He makes me proud to be a Jew."

Sensing what was expected of him, Peter acquainted his hosts with the major precepts of the Mosaic Law and in reply to numerous questions, explained how, by means of that law, God had revealed himself to the Jews and how, through the teachings of Jesus, of Nazareth, "who was both God and man," he revealed himself to all men.

"God become man?" cried Gallio, shaking his head.

Peter explained how that occurred and quoted passages from the Hebrew Prophets wherein God's incarnation was foretold.

"You say he became man to die in atonement for the sins of man," Xanthus said. "How noble! How heroic! But why? If your God is all powerful, all wise — why could he not have atoned in some other way? Why submit to the degradation of death by crucifixion?"

After a long silence Peter replied, "So that we might realize the heinousness of sin. So men might be sensible of his great love for them."

Xanthus poured more wine into Peter's cup. "What an idealistic world you portray for us, Rabbi," he said. "Occasionally, for a moment, we might rise to that high-plane, but to make it a way of life — even you must admit, it is beyond our nature."

"Not if we use the means my Lord has given us," Peter replied. "To use his own words, he is 'the way, the truth and the life.' "

"It must have some attraction," Gallio said, and he told Peter of the small group of Roman slaves who were Christians.

"Christians in Rome?" cried Peter, "and they have no one to minister to them!" In a quieter tone, he said, "Tell me something about Rome, that might be helpful to a visitor."

"If you come to Rome I would be honored if you were our guest."

"Thank you, noble Roman. It may be only a dream, but if God wills . . ."

From his numerous questions about the government, the religion and the social and economic life in Rome, Peter obtained information which he said "will be most helpful if ever I visit your great city." After a short silence he said reflectively, "Rome is the heart of the world. Some day it might be the heart of Christ's Church."

10

A Fisher of Men

WHEN Peter had not risen two hours after sunrise, Joseph his scribe went to awaken him. But he lay in such deep slumber his head cradled in the bend of his right arm, his hairy chest rising and falling rhythmically, Joseph did not arouse him. How dedicated to the Church he is, the scribe was thinking. His gaze is fixed upon the future yet bound by old customs. And he is so self-critical. "I should not be so lenient with the Judaizers," "I am neglecting the poor and those languishing in prisons. I should provide better refuge for outcast women" — "Lord, you should have chosen a more worthy head."

As Joseph turned to leave, Peter awakened and sat up upon his straw pallet. Joseph apologized for disturbing him.

"Sluggards should be disturbed," Peter said.

"I hope you had an enjoyable evening, Master."

"Most enjoyable. Gracious hosts, intelligent conversation — savory food, delicious wine, an atmosphere of beauty and refinement. I fear I took a little too much wine."

Joseph smiled.

"I was embarrassed. My Greek — it gets mixed with my Aramaic and my Hebrew, but my hosts were patient and most interested in our Lord and his teachings. So I kept talking. I could sense their increasing respect and admiration for him."

"How eloquent you are when speaking of our Lord. But you must still be weary. Try to sleep."

"No. No." Behind his large hand Peter yawned. He shook the sleep from his eyes. "I learned from Gallio that there are Christians in Rome! Jews and Gentiles! But they have no one to minister to him!"

Gazing into Joseph's eyes, he went on: "You are a worthy priest, my son. You have sacrificed much for our Lord's Church. Would you be willing to sacrifice even more?"

Thoughtful for a few moments Joseph replied, "I will go wherever you send me, Master, but I question my worthiness and my willingness to sacrifice, as a priest should. Could I give all of myself as you have given!"

"Of yourself, you could not," Peter said. "Of myself I could not. Only by prayer can that be done. Ardent prayer. Burn our Lord's ears with the heat of your prayers."

Joseph smiled.

"Pray like the Canaanite woman, vigorously, insistently. She asked our Lord to help her afflicted daughter, but he ignored her. She besought him again and he spoke harshly to her. 'It is not fair to take the children's bread and cast it to the dogs.' She was not discouraged. More determined than before, she said it was fair for dogs to eat the crumbs that fall from the Master's table. He was so pleased that he praised her faith and instantly cured her daughter."

"I admire her courage," Joseph said.

"Talk to God as if he were walking beside you, simply, confidently, short, trenchant prayers, for the grace to persevere, for guidance in your judgments, to quicken your compassion for suffering man, in honor of his infinite Majesty, for the strength to resist temptation to sin. Let not an hour of the day pass that you do not speak to God."

"You give me courage, Master," Joseph said.

"I would go to Rome, but many duties hold me here. But I shall follow you, in a year, two years. Prepare the ground for me."

"Rome," said Joseph, in a tone of uncertainty. "It is so remote from the spirit of our world . . . so . . ."

Peter gripped Joseph's arm. "Rome is the heart of the Western world!" he declared, "as Antioch is the heart of the East. If its heart can be made Christian so, in time, will its head and its hands and its feet . . ."

Moved by Peter's fervor, Joseph inquired, "How soon would you have me go, Master?"

"We shall consult with Gallio. A letter of introduction from him to his Christian servant should be helpful."

A fortnight later on the deck of a ship about to sail for Rome, Peter blessed the young man kneeling at his feet. Then raising him, he embraced him, kissed him on both cheeks and hurried down to the pier.

His contemplated journey to Rome imposed another burden upon Peter. He asked Anithas, his scribe, to find someone who could teach him Latin. "I must go to Rome."

"Latin will be difficult for a man of your age, Master," said Anithas, laying down his quill.

"I realize that. I did not know how to read or write Aramaic or Hebrew until after I became an Apostle, and I'm not proud of the progress I've made. So I'll limit myself to speaking it, as I do Greek, and leave the reading and writing to learned scholars like yourself."

"You would go to Rome, Master? At your age? Don't you think you should ease up a bit in your activities?"

Peter closely regarded the young man. "What makes water fit to drink?" he inquired. "Motion. What strengthens our bodies and sharpens our minds? Motion. If I am to obey my Lord's commission I must keep in motion physically, mentally and spiritually. I must be able to communicate with people."

Peter's efforts to establish a better understanding between the Gentile Christians and the Judaizers, brought no permanent results. Their ill feeling would suddenly flare up, usually from some insignificant incident difficult to trace. Then from a wholly unexpected source, these differences became a matter of public comment.

When Saul and Barnabas returned from Jerusalem, whither they had journeyed to help the sufferers from the famine there, a large number of the brethren assembled in the grotto church to welcome them. But Saul was not in an amiable mood. He addressed Peter in the Aramaic form of Rock, "Kephos," and said, "if you who are a Jew, live like a Jew, how is it you compel the Gentiles to live like Jews?"

A hush settled over the assemblage. The indignant retort on Peter's lips remained unspoken. His tone of voice was calm and conciliatory.

"Upon coming to Antioch I found a home in the district where most of the Jews lived. Upon learning that this was displeasing to some of our Gentile brethren, I undertook to live an equal time with Jew and Gentile, abiding in house to house so as to show no favoritism. While I lived with our Gentile brethren they showed me most respectful deference, and over my objection they would live as I lived, like Jews. I made no rule requiring this, but I could not speak out too strongly against their courtesy, lest I offend them. While my purpose was to reconcile the differences between Jew and Gentile, I now recognize that my method was unwise and justifies the criticism of our brother Saul. Henceforth I shall live apart from them, while remaining accessible to all, ever mindful that we are one in the body of our Lord Jesus Christ."

When a few of Peter's friends criticized Saul for his "quarrelsomeness" he gruffly rebuked them. "Living with the Jews, and then with the Gentiles! As if I had two families instead of one! A wedge of disunity. But I could not see. Saul spoke wisely. We should not reject words of wisdom even though they savor of gall instead of honey."

While Peter's thoughts of apostolic labor were reaching out toward Rome, thoughts of a personal nature transported him to the coast of the Black Sea, whence he had just received a letter from Andrew.

"Andrew is lonely for the old times," he murmured. "And I am lonely, too. Oh if we could have a few days together."

He began writing, his rough scrawl roving vagrantly over the papyrus.

"You are yearning for Lake Gennesaret and to cast a net again with James and John and myself. I share in your yearning for the pitch of a boat in a squall, the snap of a sail, the splash of spray in our faces. Our life was never dull. We had our share of adventure and an occasional bout with grave danger.

From an oak chest he removed a blanket, a tunic, a robe, a jar of medicated ointment and a small sack of coins. Calling a servant he bade him wrap them in one bundle "against the weather," seal the letter and send them to Andrew by the neophyte Stephen.

"Now I am going out for a while," he said, "and be not concerned if I do not return until morning."

He made his way to the river and followed it downstream to a pier where boats were moored and three men were working with fishing nets. One of them, Philo, the father of the others, cried out, "Master! How good of you to visit us! I never thought you'd have time to accept our invitation."

"I've been trying to steal a little time," Peter said, embracing Philo and his son, "but something always interfered. Then I got a letter from Andrew that made me lonely, so I shook off everything and started for the river. We will fish tonight."

"Cyrus," said Philo, "go tell your mother that the Master will sup with us."

Gazing about, Peter took note of Philo's roomy stone house far back from the river on high ground, the sturdy stone steps leading up to it, boats tied to the pier, fish nets stretched between stakes, cordage and sail cloth in compact piles. "You have a good fishery," he said, "everything is shipshape."

"Thank you, Master," said Philo, "but nothing like you had on Lake Gennesaret, from what I've heard."

"Tales grow with the telling," said Peter, smiling, "but I'd say we were good water men."

After supper Philo and his sons were joined by three other men and in two boats they put out into the river. Philo offered Peter the tiller, but he declined, "I don't know the river. I'll man the oars."

In each boat one man steered, one rowed and the other tended the net which was strung between the two boats. The extra man, in Peter's boat, would assist in raising the net to take in the fish that were caught. By the light from hooded candle lanterns, they would be gutted and packed in small kegs between layers of salt.

The fish were plentiful. The work was tiring. Finally Philo directed the boats to a small island. "Let's rest awhile and refresh ourselves," he said.

Sitting on the sand they ate bread and cheese and drank wine from a goatskin. "You brought us luck, Master," Philo said.

"Not as much as the Lord brought us on one occasion," he replied, and told of the huge draught of fishes they had taken at his direction.

In response to their eager questions, Peter told them many things about Jesus. "He was not always preaching nor instructing us. As we sat around a fire at night or in the shade by day on the bank of a brook, he would tell us of his boyhood and young manhood; how Joseph his foster father taught him the carpenter trade. And how he enjoyed talking about his mother. All of us love our mothers, but Jesus — I can't describe it, but we all knew he loved his mother in a way — I can't describe that, either. There was something supernatural about it, something holy."

"You would kind of expect that of God, wouldn't you, Master? Loving his mother something special."

"Well spoken, my friend," Peter said. "Very well spoken."

"I'd like to hear more about him, Master," Philo said, "but we have a long hard pull up stream . . ."

"I've been thinking of that," Peter said.

About an hour after sunrise they made the boats fast to the pier. After breakfast Peter yielded to Philo's persuasion to "lie down for an hour." He slept until midafternoon.

At dusk Peter arrived at his house. Philip, a young deacon who had succeeded Joseph as scribe, greeted him cheerily. "It is good to see you, Master! You look quite rested."

"Ah, my son, there's nothing like a night of fishing to rest both mind and body."

"I wouldn't know, Master. I've never fished."

Peter regarded him with pitying eyes. "Life has been unkind to you," he said. "The next time I go fishing I'll take you with me."

11

Syria: Preaching in the Back Country

PETER'S friendly disposition toward the Jews who adhered to the law of Moses came to the attention of
another Simon, an elderly Israelite who had prospered
as a merchant. He called on Peter at his house and requested him
to explain the teachings of the law of Jesus. When after several
meetings, Peter had concluded his dissertation, Simon said:
"You made a plausible case. But I am old. My habit of thinking
binds me. I cannot change. I hope your Master will not be offended."

"I cannot imagine his being offended with sincerity," Peter
said.

"I must concede that your religion has made just people of
many Gentiles. They believe in God. Some of them show good
will toward the Jews. And the Jews you have converted, on the
whole, have lost no respect for their ancient traditions. Yet, these
differences in religion . . ." The old man shook his head sadly —
"They stir up enmity, hatred for one another — in the name of
the God they adore — God must be very unhappy."

That same day he sent Peter a bag of silver coins for the
poor.

Peter now called upon Simon to ask his counsel about traveling in Syria. "I would go into the back country to visit the
churches there. You know the land. How shall I go about it?"

"How long will you be gone?"

"Six to eight months, possibly a year."

"You will face many hardships — poor lodging, and some-times no lodging, wretched food, bad water, the extremes of heat and cold, danger of accidents. You are no longer young. I advise you to send another in your place."

Peter spread his hands in a gesture of futility. "Send an-other? Who? Oh, if I could hire priests as easily as you can hire salesmen. I must go myself to the people and teach them and minister unto them; try to provide permanent services for them and choose young men who might become deacons and train them."

Simon raised a restraining hand. "Say no more. You must go, as the head of any other business. Let us plan for your jour-ney."

A week later with two young deacons, Daniel and Ignatius, Peter departed from Antioch riding sturdy donkeys, the property of Simon. They were accompanied by Levi, a servant of Simon's, an experienced traveler in Syria, who was leading two donkeys laden with food and equipment, likewise provided by the old merchant. In return for all this, he had received Peter's blessing, and a jovial, "What a good Christian you would make."

When they had come into the open country and settled in their pace Peter said to Ignatius, a delicate looking blond young man who had studied in Rome for some years, "I think this would be a good time for a Latin lesson."

For several months Ignatius had been teaching Peter to converse in Latin. In the beginning he had suggested that reading and writing be included but his pupil declined. "I am too dull of wit. But I have a fairly good memory, so we'll limit myself to conversations."

"You have an excellent memory, Master. Why you can recite most of the Scriptures . . ."

"A flattering exaggeration, my son," Peter had said. "A few of the Psalms and prophesies, some religious and patriotic songs . . ."

"And the Canticles," said Ignatius, "and Proverbs, the Book of Wisdom, the Lamentations, not to speak of the history of Israel and the Precepts of the Mosaic law . . ."

"How strange that I had to wait all these years for my talents to be discovered," laughed Peter.

Word by word Peter had progressed, repeating them over and over, joining them with other words, while Ignatius explained their meaning. And now, riding beside Peter, he continued his instructions, marveling the while that this aging man should so burden himself to teach God's word to people he would probably never meet.

Peter did not bestir his donkey from its slow, steady pace. Impetuous and impulsive by nature, he had disciplined himself to accept conditions with an air of patient resignation. Occasionally he would walk beside the animal, an arm draped affectionately over its blunt neck, thereby easing its burden and toning his own leg muscles.

In mid-afternoon Levi said he would go ahead of them into the village they were approaching and look for lodgings. When he met them as they entered the village he said, "There are no lodgings, but I found a hillside cave. I readied it for occupancy. It should be quite comfortable."

"Who am I to object to a cave?" said Peter.

Levi also had a fire going, over which simmered a kettle of stew. "You're a gift from God, Levi," Peter said. "Now I'll look around the place before darkness falls."

There were about a score of small stone houses grouped in a semicircle about a plot of ground with a well in the center. In the rear of these houses, in three stone huts were the forge and tools of an ironsmith, the wheel and looms of a weaver and a mart for the exchange of foods raised in the adjoining fields.

Peter went to the ironsmith's shop and with a respectful bow introduced himself to a beefy middle-aged man wearing a heavy leather apron. "I am Simon, a disciple of our Lord Jesus Christ. I would like to meet with the people here and tell them about him."

"They are at supper now," the ironsmith said. "I'm about to go to my supper. I'll notify the people to meet you at the well."

Peter and the two deacons were waiting in the public area when the first of the villagers arrived, a young man and his wife. He greeted them, introduced Ignatius and Daniel, and inquired about their family and means of livelihood. In like manner he greeted all who came, about a score, men and women. At his suggestion all sat upon the ground, he and the two deacons facing them. "We are disciples of the Lord Jesus Christ," he said. "Have any of you ever heard of him?"

About half of them had not heard of Jesus. Several had heard vaguely of his teachings. In a quiet conversational tone he told them of the life, works and death of Jesus, and of his claim to be the son of the true God. While Peter was speaking the ironsmith departed and returned with two lighted torches which he fixed in the ground.

"I fear I am keeping you from your rest," Peter said, "but if you are willing I will tell you more."

Their many questions was proof of their willingness, so he continued for about an hour.

Thanking them for their attention he said, "Let us meet again tomorrow evening. However during the day we would like to visit in your homes."

The friendly interest of the people was demonstrated in yet another way. They moved Peter and his companions into a small stone house in the village, first having cleansed it with lime wash and equipped it with sleeping mats, toilet facilities and stocked it with a supply of foodstuffs.

In the homes of the villagers Peter and his deacons instructed the women and children, and comforted the sick. In one home a ten-year-old boy was delirious from fever. In another an elderly man suffered from a bloated belly and prolonged constipation. With permission of the boy's parents he swathed his chest and back with hot sheep tallow, wrapped him in blankets and gave him hot water and pomegranate juice to drink. With ingredients taken from his pack, which he mixed with hot olive oil, he prepared a potion which he gave to the other patient. During the night and twice the following day he repeated this treatment. The boy sweated profusely — his fever broke. The old man became rid of his obstructions and left his pallet.

The villagers were so grateful that half of the period devoted to instructing them for the benefit of their souls was given to teaching them how to take care of their bodies. None of them however indicated any interest in conversion but they were dismayed when Peter announced his intention to leave. "We hoped you would remain with us."

"There are other sheep I must seek out," he replied.

"We want to be baptized," said the ironsmith.

He gazed at them for a few moments and said, "Your gratitude to me bids me say do not accept Baptism to please me; only to please God, and as a sign of your faith in him and love for him. I would give you more instruction about Baptism, its meaning and its effect upon one receiving it."

When he had concluded his instructions on the second day a score of adults, about half of the population were baptized.

"Now, let us meet in the morning for the breaking of bread," Peter said, "in one of your houses."

"Meet in my house," invited the ironsmith.

"Your questions about this ceremony indicated your awe

and wonder, perhaps even a plaguing doubt. So let us talk some more about it. I too was awed by its teachings. I asked myself how could bread and wine be changed into our Lord's body and blood? But I gave up trying to understand. No man could understand it. I accepted it on faith — faith without any doubt, a faith that bade me die rather than doubt. Then I was at peace. God had said it. Why should I question God? Dwell on this before you go to your rest. If you awaken during the night think about it. Let it be your first thought when you rise in the morning. Then when you partake of the consecrated species you, too, will be at peace."

At the morning service Peter gave them his final counsel. "Meet each day in prayer. Appoint one of your number at each meeting to lead you in prayer. I will give you a message for Evodius, the Bishop in Antioch, to send you a priest at least once a month for the breaking of bread. Prayer and the breaking of bread — they are the lines of communication between you and God. They will strengthen your faith and deepen your love."

From village, to town, to city, Peter and his deacons continued their journey, over mountains, across deserts and fertile fields, sweltering in heat and shivering in cold. They sat at tables laden with choice food and wines, and on the floors of houses sharing coarse bread, goat's cheese and tasteless vegetables with their generous hosts. They spoke to large crowds, to small groups, to one man or woman. Several women who firmly declared their faith had asked for Baptism; others wavered, Christian doctrine was persuasive but required much reflection; others were hostile. "Your Jesus would deprive us of our natural pleasures. We want none of him."

He met indifferent priests who were neglecting their people, and over-zealous priests who scolded them. In his gruff, kindly way he would say they were tired and frustrated by boredom and monotony and would personally relieve them or send another to substitute for them. He met uncomplaining, cheerful priests who sacrificed personal comfort to strengthen the faith and charity of their people. For them he had words of praise: "You are another Christ."

He revived the fervor of deacons, ordained them and sent them forth to preach and baptize. He appealed to young men, repeating the words of Christ: " 'The harvest is vast but the laborers are few.' He may be calling you. Listen attentively for the sound of his voice. If you hear it, do not turn away."

For all, priests, deacons and laity he stressed one counsel: "Our Lord made no distinction between master and slave, Jew and Gentile, rich and poor, white men and men who are not white. In his eyes, all men are equal; no man is preferred over another. Be ever mindful of this. God's imprint is in the soul of every person."

Almost a year after his departure Peter returned to Antioch, unaccompanied by the deacons Daniel and Ignatius. He had ordained them and assigned them to a large area "To sow and cultivate." When Ignatius inquired: "Master, what about your Latin?" he replied: "Far more important is your work here. If the Lord wants me to learn more Latin he will sharpen my mind."

But Peter and Levi were not alone. Six young men rode with them to receive instructions and training for work in the Lord's vineyard.

Levi had become fond of Peter. As they neared Antioch he said, "Rabbi, you have strengthened your Church in Syria."

"For the present," Peter agreed. "But for the time to come — the Church has strong competition — the lusts of the flesh, the coveting of power and wealth, the desire for popularity and ease and comfort. The Church needs priests — a legion of holy self-sacrificing priests."

"You ask too much of your priests," Levi said. "You were

not only priest to them but cook, physician and nurse, some of it most revolting."

"In sanitation and care of health we met some backward people, Levi. Should we have left them in their wretchedness?"

"And your severe hardships. All you got in return were some vague promises. Hardly worth the trouble, Rabbi."

"Sometimes I've questioned whether it was worthwhile," Peter acknowledged, "and contrasted my present life with the old. How good it was after a night of fishing to gather with a few friends and tell stories and laugh and sing over a cup of wine. But I would recall how he suffered for men's souls and when he bade us go and teach all men — I saw the trust in his eyes that we would be faithful until death, and the Spirit would revive in me and drive me on and on."

"You're a wanderer," Levi said, "a lonesome wanderer for your Jesus."

"A wanderer," said Peter smiling. "I like that. But I'm not a lonesome wanderer, for I hear his comforting words, "I am with you all days.""

12

Peter Sets Out for Rome

WHEN he returned to Antioch, Peter expected to find letters from Joseph. There were no letters. "I shall go to Rome," he declared, "as soon as I can clear the deck."

Evodius smiled at this expression, a heritage from Peter's life as a fisherman. "I'll get passage money for you," he said, "and living expenses for six months, at least."

"Thank you, my son, but go easy on the people, they are so poor. And do not ask Simon. It would be an imposition. Most of the money for our last journey came from him."

So pressing were his pastoral duties that twice he advanced the date for his departure, and then an unforeseen tragedy delayed him indefinitely. A fire broke out in Epiphana, the Jewish quarter, destroying or damaging more than half of the dwellings. Peter gave his passage money to a relief fund reserving only a small room to himself. He appointed a group of people to work with the Orthodox Jews in the solicitation of relief funds. With Evodius and two Rabbis he called on the city officials and urged them to erect temporary housing and to install a system of sanitation. They said to him, "You seem to know what is required. You direct it."

Peter did know, having observed the methods used for the thousands of people who visited Jerusalem on religious feast days. Under his guidance a system of sanitation was devised that conserved the health and comfort of the victims. After three months many of the damaged houses had been repaired; new houses were in the building: craftsmen among the Jews found steady employment. And one other result came from the fire which Peter mentioned to Evodius. "The Judaizers are at peace with us."

"It will be a short peace," Evodius said.

A portion of every day Peter could be seen mingling with his people giving them spiritual consolation, observing their living conditions and the distribution of food, clothing and water. This he did in a way that drew a comment from one of the deacons: "The Master knows how to get things done but he never gets in the way of those who are doing them."

Then the people realized that for several days they had not seen him and they inquired of one another, "What has become of the Master?"

*   *   *

The Captain of the cornship Tiber has turned from supervising the loading of a cargo to face a stranger who had unobtrusively approached him and said gruffly, "Work your passage to Rome? Why you're as old as the she wolf that suckled Romulus!"

"If you calculate by spirit and will," replied the man confidently, "you will find me as agile as a wolf whelp. If by years, half a century trails behind me."

"You'd be in the way aboard ship."

"Much of my life I've had an oar or a sail rope in my hand. I could handle that sail in a storm. I could man an oar and hold a true course with one of these steering oars. And if need be, I could cook a good meal for your crew."

The Captain exhaled gustily. "I never knew a Jew who thought ill of himself. Couldn't you also captain this ship?"

The Jew smiled. "I could, after a few lessons in navigation. I'll be content to carry sacks of corn on my Jew back."

The Captain shrugged, "How did I ever manage without such a jewel? What is your name?"

"Simon bar-Jonah. Native of Galilee."

The Captain looked at him appraisingly. "Let me see your back and legs," he said.

Peter removed his robe and tunic and exhibited his body.

"You're a better man than I thought," the Captain said. "You come from Galilee? Where is that? How did you learn to handle a sail?"

Peter told him of his life as a fisherman.

"Gennesaret? A handful of water. And you call yourself a seafaring man! But I'll take a chance. Bring your gear aboard."

"I must return to Antioch for it. When will you sail?"

"Tomorrow. At midday."

"I'll be here, God willing."

"God willing?" said the Captain, smiling. "What have the gods to do with it?"

"I didn't say gods," replied Peter amiably, "I said God."

Evodius cried out in consternation when Peter told him of his plans. "Work your way? As a common seaman?"

"That's what I was for twenty-five years, a common seaman."

"I'll get you money."

"Food and lodging money for a couple of weeks should be enough," Peter said.

"How imprudent! Take enough for at least six months."

"Make it a month and tell no one of my plans. I wish to go in peace."

Peter's continued absence bestirred his people to active concern. At a religious service conducted by Evodius, they said to him, "You are in the Master's confidence. Tell us where he is and when he will return."

"He is on his way to Rome," Evodius said. "Only God knows when he will return."

*   *   *

During his alternate four-hour deck watch at sea Peter manned one of the long heavy steering oars or trimmed the sails on the mizzenmast, often going aloft, even in stormy weather. In port from dawn to dusk, he carried sacks of corn and bales of freight aboard the ship. His fellow crewmen expected him to fall. They wagered he would fall. He did not fall. He plodded on, as durable as a camel in the desert. At mealtime he ate with them sitting on the deck. At night he lay there in the narrow portion allotted him, and slept like a dead man.

Several weeks after sailing the ship tied up to a long pier in the Italian port of Puteoli, and after carrying corn ashore for two days, Peter went to the Captain. "Worthy sire, my work is done," he said with that dignified courtesy characteristic of the Palestinian Jews. "I am grateful to you for giving me passage. Now, with your permission, I'll be on my way."

The Captain curiously regarded him. "I sweated you," he said, "purposely sweated you, to hear your whine, but you did not whine. Fifty is no age for a man to go to sea, but I'd make an exception with you. I offer you a permanent berth in my ship. Within three years I could almost guarantee you a ship of your own."

"I thank you, sir, but I am in command of a ship."

"Coming from another man I'd say he was a bit mad."

"I command the ship launched by our Lord, Jesus Christ, for the passage of men from this life to a life with him in heaven."

"So you're a Nazarene," said the Captain. "I've heard of your sect, and much of it was not good. Yes, I think you are a bit mad."

Peter spoke on a friendly tone. "My dear Captain, do you know why you can think? Because God gave you that power. Yet you use it to jeer at him."

Needle points glittered in the Captain's black eyes. "By the gods! You a crewman talking to me like that? I should have you flogged."

"A crewman receives a wage, sir. I did not."

The glitter yielded a stony smile. "You're in smooth water there. This god of yours — makes you sweat, doesn't he?"

Peter spoke of God with such fervor that some of the crew paused in their work to stare at him."

"How foolish to question a zealot about his God," muttered the Captain. Then a note of friendliness crept into his voice. "You've never been to Italy before, I suppose."

"This is my first journey, sir."

"Then beware! It's a dangerous place for a gullible old man. If the innkeepers don't poison you, they will rob you. And the serving wenches — don't be surprised if you wake up to find one in bed with you.

Again expressing his thanks, Peter turned to go. With a brusque, "wait!" the Captain stayed him, and inquired: "Have you enough money for a supper and a night's lodging?"

"For several nights' lodging," Peter said with a smile.

"You'll carry someone's pack for a shekel, I suppose," snorted the Captain. "Wait." Going below, he returned with a handful of coins which he put in Peter's palm. "Your wages," he grunted and turned away.

Peter gazed after him, muttering: "Lord, always you have provided for me in some unexpected way. I pray you, give this man the grace to believe."

The docks swarmed with people — passengers embarking and disembarking, laborers loading and unloading ships, shipping agents, police, hawkers of food and wine and clothing. Peter bought cheese and bread and grapes, filled his leather bottle with wine and water, and following the direction pointed by a brass arrow mounted on a red granite slab, he set out over the Appian Way.

Peter had heard numerous stories of this ancient Roman highway, yet, in some respects it was much like the road from Jerusalem to Damascus, broad enough for passing traffic, slightly convex to permit drainage into curbed gutters or ditches, paved footpaths on either side for pedestrians. All the world, it seemed was going to or coming from Rome. Sheiks from Persia, clad in rich silks and gaudy woolens, peasants from Arabia, their sinewy brown bodies visible through scant raiment; snake charmers from India, their heads wrapped in ponderous turbans, their backs bearing mysterious perforated boxes; black slaves from Numidia, dull and sad of countenance; blond slaves from Britannia, proud and defiant; cages of lions and tigers for the amphitheater; gladiators from many lands; some in the beauty of youth, others scarred by combat; squadrons of Roman cavalry; gold ornamented coaches with liveried outriders, their occupants dozing or amusing themselves at dice.

All this Peter beheld as he clipped off the miles, his wonder increasing with each mile. But there were disagreeable things, too. At sight of a man just ahead of him, he frowned, for on his back he carried a long leather bag from the open top of which an idol, an ivory figure with a man's head and a bull's body, leered grotesquely. But, upon overtaking the man, and discovering he was a Jew, he scowled. He suppressed his indignation, however and respectfully saluted the stranger. "Peace be to thee, my son. I am Simon bar-Jonah from Galilee."

"And peace be to you, my father," replied the young man,

courteously. "I am Ebulus, of the tribe of Judah. Often I gazed longingly toward the land of my fathers."

"It seems you have been to Antioch."

"No, I bought these baubles from a factor who imported them from Antioch."

Peter sighed. "I am grieved that an Israelite, a believer in the true God, should traffic in idols."

Ebulus smiled, the tolerant smile of a young man for an old one. "A dealer in idols is not necessarily an idolator. The pagans rave over these toys. Why should I not turn an honest profit?"

"You encourage men to worship things of wood and ivory. God is displeased."

"Calm yourself. The Romans have always worshipped base things. They always will. They are not the chosen of God."

Peter shook his head. The old Jewish heresy. But this young man should not be blamed. He himself had once believed the same. He spoke gently. "My son, all men are the chosen of God. Jews and Gentiles, believers and non-believers. And the Romans will not always worship idols. Some day they will know the Lord Jesus Christ."

"Jesus? Why you must be a Nazarene."

"I am an unworthy disciple of my Lord."

"You could pass for a Hebrew Patriarch! How can you worship a man as God?"

Peter told him straightway, for almost an hour, while Ebulus listened in amazement. "His enemies seemed to have more faith in him than his closest friends," he said finally.

"How wise you are," observed Peter. "What took me years to realize you grasp in an instant."

"Why should they want to kill a man like that?

Peter raised his arms. "How many men have asked that question! I will tell you later, my son, when you have considered well what I have already said."

The young Jew regarded him suspiciously. "I believe you're trying to make a Nazarene of me," he said.

"More than that. I would make a priest of you."

Ebulus paused and stared at him."

"You have the brow of a thinker, the jaw of a doer," said Peter, "and I sense in you a strong sympathy for my Lord. When you know him, you will love him."

"I could never believe that God would become man."

"The Greek Socrates was not favored by God's revelation as were we Jews, yet he said that God must become man; that if we are to know all of the truths necessary to our happiness, God must come down and teach us in his own words."

Ebulus shifted his pack. "All this is beyond me. Let the philosophers wrestle with it. I'm only a simple man of trade."

Peter told Ebulus about Jerusalem and the glory of the holy Temple. Toward evening, recalling the ship Captain's advice, Peter looked into several inns at a crossroad before choosing one he thought might offer his purse some protection against thieves and his sleeping mat security from prowling wenches. "If you know a better place," he said to Ebulus, "let us go there."

"One is no better than the other," said Ebulus. "All are dens of thieves."

As they supped together Peter asked many questions about Rome but spoke only briefly of his Lord. "I would leave you with one thought, my son. When you stand before God to give an account of your life and you tell him you sold idols to pagans, how do you think he will feel?"

"Not too bad," replied Ebulus, easily. "He will understand I had to make a living. I hope we'll have plenty of sleeping space tonight."

The sleeping space was a six-by-three-feet of floor area on a thin layer of stale straw. Ebulus was soon asleep but sleep avoided Peter. Projecting his thought far into the future he beheld a

Church triumphant over the pagan gods of Rome. Then the triumph of the future was obliterated by the actualities of the present — a crowded Italian inn, smelly snoring men sprawled all about him. Then remembering he had offered no prayer, he knelt and prayed in a low tone, "I thank you, O Lord, for giving me this day and protecting me from its dangers. I ask your protection while I sleep. Give me the strength to rise on the morrow, and the will to go forward with your work."

He welcomed the dawn and looked for Ebulus. He was gone. He inquired of a servant and was informed that Ebulus had departed an hour before dawn. "He is running from you, Lord," he muttered, "but we shall catch up with him." After a short breakfast Peter resumed his journey gazing about with interest.

About noon of the fourth day he saw looming out of the hills in the north a huge grayish-brown bulk, seemingly suspended in mid-air. "Rome!" he cried. "Rome, the oppressor of my people. I pray that God will give you the grace of faith in his Divinity."

About three hours later he passed under a stately granite archway, the Gate Capena, into an atmosphere of restless activity and ceaseless noise — the rumble of chariots, the clack of hoofs, the shouts of teamsters, the whirr of block and ropes raising building stones, the cries of street vendors, the shouts of laborers loading and unloading bales and casks. Above all this, from a huge stone structure close by, ebbed and flowed the raucous roar of human voices.

"This must be their great circus," he muttered, "the place of infamy, where men are forced to maim and kill their fellow men."

Passing around a hill crested with marble palaces he came upon a large open square, a marketplace, flanked by temples and government buildings, and crowded with people. There were men of seeming wealth and distinction, in serious discussion or reading bulletins fastened to a large board. There were idlers rolling dice on the lava pavement, screaming urchins chasing one another in play, hawkers crying their wares, orators haranguing into upturned faces.

What a vast field for sowing, he thought. Lord, send me many sowers.

Peter knew that most of the Jews lived in the Trastevere area on the west bank of the Tiber. He found it without difficulty, passing over a stone foot bridge. He knew, as well, that most of the Jews were poor, but he was shocked by the poverty in which he found himself — unbroken rows of tall, wretched tenements crowded into gloomy streets, cobblestone pavements littered with garbage, swarms of greenish flies, half-naked children scurrying from the threatening wheels of heavy drays. Over all hung a dank atmosphere of uncleanliness, so unlike the habitation of the Jews in Galilee. "My poor people," he sighed.

From the Roman Gallio he had learned the name of the man in whose house the Christians in Rome were accustomed to gather for Divine worship and this name he mentioned to the first Jew he met. "Could you direct me to the house of Nicodemus the weaver?"

"Go to the end of this street and turn right into the street of the weavers. You will see his sign."

"Simon bar-Jonah, a native of Galilee is grateful for your courtesy," Peter said.

He found the place without difficulty. When he announced himself the elderly Nicodemus knelt for his blessing. "Simon, the Lord's Rock," he cried joyfully. "In Rome! Now my eyes can close in peace."

After an exchange of personal greetings, Peter inquired about Joseph. Nicodemus sighed, "Would that I could give you tidings of joy, Master, but alas — Joseph is no longer one of us. He gave up his faith, abandoned his holy priesthood, took to

wife a beautiful rich pagan and now lives a life of luxury."
    Strength seemed to ooze from Peter's body. Sinking upon a
bench, hands clasped to his head he writhed in suffering. "Joseph! Joseph!" he moaned. "How could you turn from the holy
Son of God?"
    Nicodemus put a cup of wine into his hand. "Drink, Mas-
ter," he said. Peter drank, and said: "Tell me more — he is not
given to . . . to . . . idolatry?"
    "No, Master, not unless desire for wealth and social posi-
tion be idolatry. Joseph's father-in-law has extensive interests in
shipping, and mining. He took Joseph into the business. I hear
he is a capable executive."
    "Joseph is capable, I must go to him at once. Direct me."
    "No, Master, it would be best if you met him on the
street."
    "Perhaps that would be best. But tell me about yourself.
You are a Christian. How?"
    "My conversion came slowly. While en route from Damas-
cus to Jerusalem my caravan rested for a day at Capharnaum.
There was excited talk about a wonder-worker whom some said
was the Messiah. I was curious and followed them to a place outside the town where he was to speak. I stood where I could
clearly see his face and hear his words. Some of them I can
repeat. Upon returning to Crete where I then lived I began reading our sacred books that told of Messiah's coming.
    "I saw him again in the Temple grounds, when I returned
for the feast of the Pasch. He was teaching a group of people.
Suddenly he stopped to speak to a cripple who was being carried
in on a litter. He touched the cripple and straightway he got up
and walked. I gazed intently into his face, and I believe he looked
at me. I felt a sudden desire to speak to him, but I felt it might
not be appropriate. I've deeply regretted that I did not speak."
    "Oh, I wish you had spoken," cried Peter, "but I under-

stand your hesitancy to speak out, I too, had the same feeling."

"I was in Jerusalem again for the feast of Pentecost, after they had crucified him. Of course I heard it said he rose from the dead, but I doubted that."

"Oh I know how you felt!" cried Peter.

"Then I heard you preach that Pentecost day, Master, and I believed. I was baptized with a large group of people, by one of the Apostles but I did not know his name. Later the Apostle Barnabas came to Crete and I ate and drank of the bread and wine of thanksgiving. I came to Rome, about ten years ago and established my business. But I was disappointed. There were no Christians here, Jew or Gentile. Then one of our workmen happened to ask me about Jesus, and when I had told him he said he believed. So I baptized him, in the way Barnabas had instructed us to do. A few more came, including Gentiles, mostly slaves. We met about once a week for prayers and worship, but having no priest I offered them bread and wine and we partook of them in commemoration of him. I hope he was not displeased with us."

"Displeased with you!" cried Peter. "He loved you all the more for it."

"Our number slowly increased — to almost three hundred. Then the young priest Joseph came. He was zealous and devoted. We loved him. But after a few months he changed. He had other interests, and then he left us, with no word of explanation. So we went back to our old form of worship."

After a brief silence, Peter said, "It was fitting that you should act as priest. You brought Christianity to Rome. In your humble way you were our Lord's Apostle even as we, the Twelve, and Saul of Tarsus. You sowed the seed and nurtured the sprout into a healthy plant."

Nicodemus studied the Master's words, and replied, "I never thought of it that way."

"How soon could I meet with the brethren for the breaking of bread?"

"At dawn, if you wish, Master. I can assemble fifty or sixty of the brethren."

"That is well. And I would ask that you prepare yourself for something wholly unexpected. I would ordain you priest if you will consent."

Nicodemus bowed his gray head. "No greater honor could come to me, Master," he said, "but I cannot leave my wife and travel . . ."

"You will not be asked to leave her, nor to discontinue your business. Do as you have been doing. You have a large field for your labors."

In a storeroom connected with the weaving shop Peter conducted the service called the breaking of bread and ordained Nicodemus to the priesthood. Then he spoke to the worshippers.

"I ask your help. Be like our brother Nicodemus who established Christianity in Rome. Teach our Lord's message to your families and friends and working companions. Invite them to worship with us. Tell us of your sick and disabled so we may visit them. If any of you wish to counsel with me privately you will find me here, our brother Nicodemus having extended to me his gracious hospitality. Now I should like to meet each one of you personally."

13

Aventine Hill: Meeting with Joseph

A YOUNG MAN strode down Palatine Hill, his red-lined black velvet robe billowing in vagrant gusts of wind. Several times he raised his right hand in recognition of a greeting, but he did not stop. Nor did anyone attempt to detain him. His friends knew he was bound for the bath, the exclusive bath of the Princes, and mere acquaintances were repelled by his air of aloofness. But as he entered the Forum a man fell into step beside him and spoke, a man whose simple dress set him apart as a social inferior.

"Peace be to you, my son."

The young man's head jerked around. He stopped abruptly. "Rabbi!" he cried. "Rabbi Peter! In Rome!"

"Yes, Joseph. A hopeful Rabbi when I set out, a sorrowful Rabbi after I arrived."

Joseph braced himself. "Let fall your condemnation and have it over."

"Condemnation for the one who taught me Greek? Oh no, rather let fall my love." He took the young man to his heart in affectionate embrace.

Joseph lost his grand air. "Why should I be astonished?" he muttered. "I've been expecting you. Let us return to my house. I will tell you all."

"Some other time. You go to meet with friends . . ."

"I have no heart now for my friends. Come, let us turn back."

They walked in silence, Peter taking note of many things. Joseph had shaved his dignified Jewish beard; his hair was short and perfumed. His body, once lean from penitential fasting, was swathed in the torpid sleekness of easy living. But his eyes were not torpid. They were hard, restless, acquisitive. Half way up the Aventine Hill they entered a white limestone villa surrounded by trees and flowers.

Peter seated himself upon a sofa. Joseph stood before him, his sharp eyes unrelenting. "Say what's in your heart, Rabbi," he said. "Call me renegade!"

"What a terrible word," said Peter sadly. "No, my son, I will never call you that. You did not run away from Christ. You let yourself be gradually drawn away from him. I denied him, thrice denied him to the world, yet he did not call me renegade."

Joseph sat upon a stool facing Peter. "I could not go on," he blurted. "I no longer believed, and you would not have me pretend."

"No, no, my son. Our Lord doesn't like pretenders. You should have heard him denounce the Pharisees for pretending. But you might have confided your troubles to me. I would have come on the first ship."

Joseph went on the defensive: "I've had no troubles. I merely ceased to believe. So I glided into a new way of life. I am more Roman now than Jew."

After a brief silence Peter gently questioned Joseph. "You ceased to believe. Why, my son? Were you ensnared by a woman? Diverted by visions of power? Plagued by cravings for wealth?"

"A mixture of all that, I would say," replied Joseph. "I took a mistress, but cast her off upon meeting the woman I married. Perhaps the real worm in the apple — Rabbi, once while instructing us on the dangers to faith you spoke of our inclination to imitate other men in dress, amusements, social customs, even in our thinking. Here in Rome men of birth do not believe in gods, though they build temples to them. Influenced by my surroundings, I suppose my faith eroded away little by little until — I'm sure you understand what I'm trying to say, Rabbi."

Peter nodded. "I think I do. You got out of the habit of prayer; doubts gnawed at your foundation, like termites eating out the hold of a ship; you let the world crowd God out of your life until he was as unreal as the pagan gods."

Peter passed a hand over his brow. "I blame myself," he said. "You were too young for such a grave responsibility. Had I kept you close to me for a few more years . . ."

"I doubt if that would have helped, Rabbi. There's a vein in me you never discovered, a vein of self will, the desire to think things for myself. Pride, I guess you'd call it — I'm sorry for you, Rabbi. You trusted me and I betrayed you. You can't help but despise me."

Peter laid a gentle hand on Joseph's arm. "Let no such word pass between father and son," he chided gently. "Your faith is a matter between you and God. I will need a friend in this strange land — someone to counsel with. If my friendship would not be embarrassing."

Joseph looked down. "You are pouring salt into my wounds, Rabbi."

"Salt heals," mused Peter, "salt cleanses."

He gazed about, approvingly. "You have an elegant home, Joseph, and I am told, a beautiful, refined wife. I should like to meet her."

"You wouldn't be interested in her, Rabbi. She's a pagan."

"I assure you I'm much interested in pagans!"

"My lady is visiting her parents in the country."

"Some other time then. Now tell me about yourself."

Over a glass of wine Joseph told of the extensive mining and shipping business owned by his father-in-law, in which he was now an executive and partner.

Taking Joseph's hands, Peter said, "You are now a man of business. That is passing. You are also a priest of Christ's Church. That is eternal. 'Thou art a priest forever.' Your hands I anointed so they might hold God. And they did hold him! Keep them clean, my son. Never sin with them. The day may come when you will leave the marketplace and return to the altar."

Joseph looked at his hands. They were clean and mani- cured, the hands of a Roman noble. Then he hid them in the folds of his robe, as if moved by a sense of guilt.

"I am grateful for your kind forbearance, Master," he said. "I am really overwhelmed. I would like to do something for you — provide you a suitable house with servants and scribes . . ."

"I'll accept it!" cried Peter, "with pleasure. I've been won- dering about a place to live but let it be small . . ."

"Now, Master; I know your needs. Let me have my way — an humble house but one sufficient to accommodate your many visitors, and in which you will find some comfort and privacy."

Peter smiled. "How inviting that sounds. Again I thank you, my son, but let it be in the Jewish quarter."

Ever sensitive to the pressing need for priests Peter frequently spoke of it to the men of his flock. "Many of you could be priests. Nicodemus could teach you the doctrines of the old Law, and I the new Law. Ability to read and write is desira- ble but not necessary. For a long time my brother Apostles and I taught from memory. You would not be required to leave your homes or give up your livelihood. But I would not mislead you. A priest's life is hard and burdensome. It calls for sacrifice of per- sonal comforts; it demands that we discipline ourselves and give up many pleasures. We should pray many times a day and live lives that command the respect of all men, and elevate us to a high plane of holiness. And you will receive no worldly reward for your service. Often you will be criticized when you should be thanked. Even if the people supported you the most you could expect is plain food, a place to sleep, and clothing that will cover your nakedness but not much more. However, you will not be without reward. Our Lord has a grateful heart for those who serve him."

Two young men responded to his plea, Rufus, a married Jew who drove his own team hauling stones and other building material, and Junius, the slave of Capena who made wagons and drays. He had a black mother and an unknown white father. He conversed in Latin and could read and write that language with child-like immaturity. Peter sought Capena's permission for him to attend instructions.

Capena, a gruff, blunt man laughed scornfully. "Me give him time that is mine? To learn religion? You're out of your mind!"

"Sometimes I think it does wander a bit," Peter said, with a grin, and he gave a brief account of his former life and present work. Capena shook his head. "You gave up a good living and became a beggar? Just to please him?"

"Yes, I did. I realize it seems foolish but he was so kind and compassionate for men who suffered. Let me tell you some of his works."

For half an hour he proceeded to tell him. Capena interrupted with: "How could your teaching my slave benefit me?"

"He would become a contented happy man and this would make him a better servant. But if you should lose anything I'll work for you an hour a day without pay, to discharge his debt."

Capena stared at Peter, amazed. "If you want him that much take him," he said, "an hour a day. But I doubt if you'll keep him. He's too dreamy to learn the language of the gods."

Fearing that the conversion of Jews in a considerable number might bestir the Rabbis to indignation against him and the Church, Peter called on each of them to convey his respects and to assure them that in his missionary work there would be no detraction of the holy law of Moses, only honor and veneration, and no condemnation of the Jews who adhered to its teachings. Several of them were bitterly antagonistic. "The followers of the Nazarene were corrupting the children of Abraham," "Any Jew who taught his doctrine was deliberately misleading his brethren and endangering his salvation," "They would exert themselves against its baneful influence."

Peter pleaded with them. "How sad that worshippers of the true God should hold enmity for those who worship him in a different form and ritual." They rejected his plea. "You are the leader in this corruption. You welcome pagans into your worship. Every true Jew is horrified by your apostasy."

Others were cold but not bitter. "You are an apostate from the covenant God gave to Moses, but without ill will or condemnation of us. You do not call us Christ killers. Neither hold we enmity for you. We credit you with sincerity but we grieve over your departure and for the many brethren you continue to mislead. In good conscience we are bound to warn them against you."

Two were friendly and tolerant. "You are sincere. You make a strong case for the divinity of Christ. If you are right you have nothing to fear from God. If you are wrong your sincerity will be accepted by God. If any of our people wish to become Christians we shall caution them not to act hastily, without due consideration, but we shall not interfere. How one shall worship God is a matter between him and God."

"A God-like attitude," Peter said.

"There is another reason why we Jews should not quarrel,"

these Rabbis said. "We are barely tolerated here. Our religion is despised, our customs scorned. We are so emotional over religion that difference between us might result in public disorder. If that happened official Rome would let fall a heavy hand. Our liberty would be endangered, and possibly the lives of many of us."

Peter again visited Capena. "I hope you have lost nothing from our arrangement," he said amiably.

"No, he is a good workman. Will you drink a cup of wine with me?"

"It would be a pleasure, my friend."

Putting down his half empty wine cup, Peter said, "I like your slave. I presume to ask you for another favor — that he be permitted to sleep at my home, say three nights a week."

"I'm curious. Why do you ask this?"

"He is so eager to learn. And there is so much to learn. And I am learning from him." Capena stared at Peter, perplexed.

"I've discovered gold in him."

"Gold!"

"Spiritual gold."

"Why he's nothing but a slave! An animal — a black animal!"

"All of us are animals, my friend. And we're something else, too, that enables us to be compassionate and reverent. This seems to be potentially strong in him and he should be brought to full flower."

"I see no objection, Rabbi. But this talk bores me. Let us relax at a game of dice."

"I would like that, but I have no money."

"No money? Why you're the head of the Nazarenes."

"Not a lucrative position," Peter said, with a smile, "As you said at our first meeting, I'm a beggar."

"But you could put a yoke on your people and get what you should have."

"A Church that resorts to yokes will soon die, my friend. Only one built on freedom to give or not to give will survive."

As they were returning to Joseph's house, Peter said, "I am pleased with my Greek, now I must learn Latin. Could you find me a teacher?"

Levi, a grandson of Nicodemus, became Peter's instructor in Latin and his personal companion, as well.

14

Of Slaves and Senators

PETER inquired of his scribe Felix: "Could you get me a hundred sestertai? I have in mind an investment."

"An investment, Master?"

"Yes, in a slave."

"A slave?" gasped Felix.

"This is just between ourselves, so be discreet. My luck may not be good."

Felix shook his head, but the next day he gave Peter a purse of coins.

"Now tell me I may do as I please with them."

"Why, who knows that better than you, Master?"

"Let's not debate that. Tell me."

"To do with as you please, Master," Felix said almost mechanically.

That evening Peter went to Capena's house where he had frequently visited. "Would you care to play dice with me?" he asked with a taunting smile.

"Why yes!" said Capena, "But I thought . . ."

Peter rattled his bag of coins.

While they rolled the dice, Peter spoke in praise of Junius — his progress in speaking and reading Greek, his learning in the old and the new Law, his deep spirituality. The while, luck was favoring Capena who responded in half-intelligible grunts.

When Peter said he had no more money Capena inquired with a purr of satisfaction, "What is the good of all that?"

"I would ordain him a priest but there's an obstacle. He is your slave. My people would purchase his freedom."

"That would come high. He's a valuable slave."

"We could pay something every month or every quarter. Well, I'll be leaving now. Be generous with us, my friend."

As he started to put on his robe some coins fell out of its pocket. "Must have been a hole in my purse," he said, retrieving them, five in number. "Good for one more roll of the dice," he said gleefully.

In a short time Capena said, "I have no more money, but my promise to pay is as good as money. Fifty sestertai, or you name the amount."

More than fifteen-hundred sestertai lay heaped before Peter. "No, my friend," he said, pushing them across the table. "I return what you lost. This game is getting out of hand."

"A mere pittance!" laughed Capena.

"Their value is small. But I cannot keep them."

"Why there's nothing wrong in an honest game of chance!"

"Not in the game itself. But when it rouses one's sense of greed — I haven't been entirely honest with you. I proposed this game to please you, to win your favor as an agreeable companion, so you would yield to my plea and release Junius for a small price.

Capena laughed loudly. "There was no dishonesty in that, no deception, just natural Jewish shrewdness."

"There was trickery in it, unworthy of a friend toward another friend, even if the desired end was most praiseworthy."

"You are spinning too fine a web for me," Capena said."

"When I started winning — at first I thought I would keep them but as they grew I was in a quandary. I hesitated to return them lest I offend you, and I disliked keeping them for that would be compounding my trickery. Then suddenly I knew what I should do. Now I had better be going. It is long past my hour."

Capena rose and called a servant: "We shall go with you," he said.

Junius did not appear on the day scheduled for him to spend with Peter, nor on the following day. "I have offended Capena," Peter said in self-condemnation. "In my vanity I thought I was a skillful diplomat."

On the following day, however, Junius came to Peter's house and placed in his hand a sealed parchment. Peter scanned it and said, "I can't read Greek very well. What is it?"

"A certificate of my manumission from slavery," Junius said with a happy smile. "Capena went with me to a magistrate and filed a petition that I be freed." The smaller document attached to the other is my certificate that I am a Roman citizen."

That night Peter called on Capena. "How gracious of you!" he cried. "How magnanimous! Why you were truly God-like."

Capena shrugged. "That is what you wanted. But I don't understand how you could be so interested in a slave."

"A slave," repeated Peter. "You probably do not realize that a slave is a person, a human being like all other men, regardless of color or race or social position, and that all men bear God's likeness in their souls. But I would not realize this if God had not taught me. Slavery is a crime against men."

"If official Rome knew you were opposed to slavery you would be in grave danger."

"I am opposed to it and to all other forms of man's inhumanity to man but I would not advocate its rejection by force, only by education. My Lord has the remedy for slavery. 'Love your brother as yourself.' If I follow that teaching I will not make a slave of any man and by your generous action you in-stinctively followed that teaching. I cannot reward you but we would rejoice if you attended the ceremony of ordination."

"No, no, Rabbi, I wouldn't understand it. But if you are pleased I am pleased. Junius told me he wished to work for the conversion of slaves. Let him have his way. I wish him well. But I cannot imagine a more thankless work."

Many times Peter had said he would preach to the Romans, "When I can speak Greek well enough to be understood." One morning he was standing on the base of a statue in the Forum gazing into the upturned faces of Joseph and a score of friends who had come to draw an audience. With upraised arms he cried out in a loud voice: "Men of Rome! I stand before your god of war to tell you of my God! The God of Peace!"

Some men glanced at him but did not stop; others paused, and passed on. A few stopped and listened.

"He is the God of love and compassion. He healed the crip-ples, cured the sick and raised the dead to life!"

Several of his friends asked questions so he might develop his theme. One, a stranger said, "Your god became a man? You are an imposter."

"Learned men have believed it, one a Greek who stands high in the esteem of Romans, the philosopher Socrates. He said that God would have to become a man to instruct men in his law."

When Peter concluded his discourse he thanked the group for their attention, invited them to return in midafternoon and moved to a different place in the Forum to address another audi-ence.

In later appearances Peter recognized the faces of men who had heard him before. One in particular fixed his attention, a middle-aged man of dignified bearing, clothed in rich but simple raiment, accompanied by a servant. He stood apart from the group, asked no questions, but spoke frequently to his servant as if they were discussing Peter's utterances.

Peter always invited his hearers to come to his house for a more intimate discussion of his subject. One morning the stranger called upon him. "I am Adulus Pudens," he said. "This is my servant Marcus! We are interested in your religion."

"My master is a member of the Roman Senate," Marcus said.

"The noble Senator and his worthy servant honor me by your presence and by your invitation to explain my religion. But first let me tell you of the life and death and work of its holy founder."

When Pudens prepared to take his leave he invited Peter to call at his house to instruct his wife, Lady Claudia, his daughter Pudentia, his household, and some of his friends. That day Peter called on Joseph. "Once you readied me to look like a gentleman," he said. "I'd have you do it again."

Responding to Joseph's smile and look of inquiry Peter told him of Pudens' invitation.

"You are progressing, Rabbi, professionally and socially. I have just the men you need, and appropriate raiment, besides."

"How good to have the right friends in the right place," Peter said with a deep chuckle. "I would like a purple robe — a rich, dark purple."

The results of this teaching he discussed at a dinner with Joseph. "What an intelligent audience. What relevant questions. I could see I was reaching their hearts even though my Greek was faulty . . ."

"Why Senator Pudens told me your Greek was good, precise and direct to the point."

"Then let me thank you, my teacher. But I wondered if I was reaching their hearts. Then, one morning after almost three months, Senator Pudens said he and his family and his household wished to be baptized. Others promptly followed, about half of the group. What a joyous breaking of bread we celebrated after the Baptisms! Within a few days all of them, except two or three, were baptized — over fifty. Yes my son, I believe we are making encouraging progress."

This was also true in the Ghetto, where, during this time he and Nicodemus received almost two hundred into the Church. Among these were Aquila and Priscilla, moderately prosperous tentmakers, who gave the use of their house to the deacons, five in number, who were preparing for ordination to the priesthood. Being employed by day, instruction of these young men was limited to the evening hours, a slow process of development which delayed their ordination and roused in Peter a growing anxiety.

As was his custom when confronted with difficulties concerning the Church, Peter put them in the hands of his Lord. Going into the street one night where he could be alone, he walked in front of his house and spoke to him in that forthright informal way he had learned in Galilee, respectful, but not timid, even a bit insistent.

"Lord, you have given me priests to teach the poor, not nearly enough, by the way, and one, a former slave, to teach the slaves. Now I need a priest to teach the patricians, and minister to the recently converted, one of their own class, for men seem more likely to listen to such a man than to one of an inferior class. This is not a healthy condition, Lord, but it exists and it will take a long time to change it. I don't know where to find such a man so I am depending on you to send him to me and to help me recognize him."

In like manner he prayed for guidance in other matters, prayed until distracted by heavy cart wheels bumping over cobblestones into the dawn of another day. Going into his house he slept peacefully.

Dependent though he was on Divine aid, Peter did not underrate the value of human aid. That afternoon he called on Senator Pudens at his villa and requested him to suggest some of his friends who might be potential candidates for the priesthood. Pudens named several, and while comparing one against the others Peter suddenly interrupted him.

"Say no more, my friend. The man the Church needs sits beside me, the noble Senator Pudens."

"Me?" cried Pudens, amazed.

"You have strong faith; profound knowledge in the old and the new Law; you live a holy life, you are respected by men in high and low places. You could do much to help the Church."

Pudens' amiable countenance became grave, his intellectual brow furrowed with apprehension. "I am so unworthy," he murmured, "so unworthy!"

"None of us are worthy," Peter said. "I will not urge you. Pray to the Holy Spirit for guidance. Learn from Ecclesiasticus and the Psalms the great dignity of the priesthood and the important service a priest may render to God."

On the sixteenth day of the month Nisan by the Jewish calendar, the anniversary date of Christ's resurrection, before all of his household and many of his friends, Pudens was ordained into the priesthood. After placing of hands, Peter served as deacon while Pudens performed the blessing of bread and wine. At its conclusion he addressed Pudens:

"Sublime is the dignity the Lord has given you. He has chosen you to do as was done by him at the Last Supper. Everlasting is that dignity. Thou art a priest forever."

Some weeks later Peter had a visitor, a young man with thick bronze hair crowning a large head, the body of an athlete and the brow of a contemplative. "Your face seems familiar," Peter said. "I must have met you, yet in my dotage . . ."

"I am pleased I resemble one whom you highly esteem, my father Senator Pudens."

"Oh what joy!" cried Peter, embracing him. "Linus, the son of my beloved friend. He told me much about you."

"I have been in Greece. How amazed I was when I returned! That my practical judicious father should embrace this strange cult from Judea — it seemed incredible. He gave me to read the books of the old Jewish law and the sayings of Jesus you had written for him, and your account of his works. I began reading them, skeptically, in the spirit of a scornful adversary. When I had finished reading them I knew they spoke the truth. My father baptized me. From his hands I received the blessed bread. I would be a priest. I would give up all and follow him."

Tears stood in Peter's eyes. He kissed the young man's hands. "Oh what a blessed day!" he cried. "What a blessed day!"

15

Peter Speaks to Rome's Nobility

PETER confided to Joseph his desire to speak to the nobility of Rome.

"The Bath of the Princes would be a good place," Joseph replied. "Your audience will be idling in leisure and should be in a mood for such an unusual discussion. Let us go there tomorrow, in the early afternoon."

On the way, Joseph described the baths and their significance to Roman life. "You are a man of simple tastes, Rabbi, and you may be indignant at the love of luxury and sensual comfort afforded by the Roman baths. The Bath of the Princes is built around an open court, itself an object of beauty, with flowers and grass and fountains, in a series of rooms of stately architecture. In the first room the bather undresses, leaving his clothing in the care of a slave, passes into another room where he is rubbed with oil, and thence into a third where he may do gymnastics and other exercises. Next, he proceeds to a room where hot water is to be had, in sunken tubs or in showers, then to a steam room where he sweats heavily and slaves scrape him with instruments called strigils and massage his muscles. This done, he goes into a warm room where there is tepid water, then into the frigidarium for a swim in a pool of cold water, and last of all, he may rest in the lounging room, visit with friends and even hear lectures and the recitation of poetry. These various rooms are designed to please the eyes as well as to give comfort to the body, having marble floors and walls with paintings, mosaics and sculpture work."

"How do they heat such a large place?" asked Peter.

"Heat from underground furnaces and hot stones seeps through vents in the walls and floors. In the hot room the furnace is directly under the pool. All furnaces burn continuously giving off a steady heat."

"The expense must be enormous," said Peter.

"Who cares about expense when he gets what he desires?" Joseph said.

He conducted Peter into the lounging room and introduced him to a near score of his friends: "This is my friend Simon, a native of Galilee in Palestine, a philosopher, a teacher of Christianity who has brought peace to many men. He would tell you his message if you will grant him the privilege."

Joseph's request brought passive acceptance from the Romans. Peter laid off his robe and stood before them in sleeveless tunic, his stalwart body and dignified carriage changing their previous attitude of languid indifference to one of curiosity and even of respect.

Speaking in a conversational tone, he thanked them for their courtesy and gave a brief account of his personal life. Realizing that preaching would be unwise, and remembering Joseph's remarks concerning their love of luxury, he ventured on entirely new tactics. "On our way here, our friend Joseph seemed to fear I would be scandalized at what some might call your excessive love of luxury. I confess once I would have condemned it, unmindful that actuated by a similar desire, I had devised ways of easing my hard life by obtaining a hot bath, and having my back rubbed with oil by my patient brother Andrew. The only difference is you do it on a grander scale, amid more pleasant surroundings."

Some of his hearers smiled. Their aloofness gave way to an attitude of interested anticipation.

"I have learned a few things since those days, learned them in pain and travail. It ill becomes a man to criticize his brother, or for one people to judge another. Love of luxury has a deeper meaning than a craving in the hearts of every man. But, alas, all of us know that pleasure is not happiness, only its base counterfeit, and we grope for an after life of the spirit. If you have grasped that hope, however feebly, I would strengthen your grip upon it; if you have not, I would put it in your hand. For that hope I have from the one true eternal God!"

Encouraged by their attention, he told them of man's relationship with God, as revealed by the old Law and the Prophets, explained some of the teachings of Christ, and invited their questions.

One said: "Your claim of a virgin birth is not new. It has been asserted in favor of other gods."

"But never before asserted in favor of a man," Peter said. "Jesus as God could have had no birth at all. He always was. Jesus as man had to be born of woman. But he had no human father. God was his father and his conception and birth were foretold over four hundred years before, by the Prophet Isaiah who wrote: "A virgin (a virgin, mind you) shall conceive and bear a son.""

"A poetic fancy vinted from strong wine," one said.

"That might be said if there was only one prophecy, but not when the prophecies are numerous, and relate to the same subject and were spoken by men in different ages when there could have been no concert between them, when, in fact, the earlier Prophets could not know what later Prophets would write."

"You make a good case for your Prophets," one said, amiably.

Bowing to him in appreciation, Peter continued: "Every

event in the life of Jesus was foretold, and it came to pass as it was written. Together, they make history. In our search for truth we should carefully consider history for the germ of truth usually lies buried therein."

"You preach a cult of delusive hope," one said, "that has an appeal only to slaves and malcontents and the weak of mind."

"It is a religion of hope," Peter said, "and it has given comfort and peace to the rich and the powerful and the learned. You Romans have a high regard for the Greek philosophers. In Plato and Socrates and Aristotle you will read references to one god, an all-wise, all-powerful, all-pure, ever-existing God. But there is one much closer to you than these ancient Greeks, your own Senator Pudens . . ."

Several interrupted to say they knew about Pudens' conversion and voiced their reactions — critical, indifferent, commendatory.

"If you would inquire of him, the light of truth might open up to you, my friends. But let me say: I am not critical of your unbelief. Many times Jesus told us he would be crucified and would rise on the third day. But when he was crucified his promise of resurrection meant nothing to us. Dead men do not rise from the dead. Not until he appeared to us after his resurrection did we believe. So I repeat: 'Why should I be critical of you?' "

"Men of Rome, I thank you for your courteous attention. I expect to speak here again. I hope you will be present."

"You were as eloquent as Demosthenes," Joseph said, humorously. "Now we shall enjoy a Roman bath."

Two hours later, when Peter emerged from the bathing rooms and massage tables, he cried out jubilantly: "What an art the Romans have made of bathing! I haven't felt so clean and refreshed since the morning of my wedding day."

"Now you're coming home with me for supper and a night of undisturbed rest."

"How accurately you read my thoughts," Peter said, with a smile.

He had frequently been an overnight guest at Joseph's villa. Between him and Joseph's wife and his two children had grown a bond of strong affection. This bond had strengthened when, a few months before, Joseph had said: "Rabbi, I have returned to the faith of my fathers. I have returned to the synagogue, and my wife and children have joined me."

"Oh Joseph, my son!" Peter had cried joyfully. "God is blessing your house!"

After dinner Peter told Joseph of matters that were troubling him — the shortage of priests, the inadequate facilities for educating the neophytes, the lack of money for Church support, the need of places where the brethren could meet for worship. "You have a good business head, my son. How should I manage the growing business of the Church?"

After some thought Joseph said, "You should not try to do so many things, Rabbi. Choose the one apparently most capable of doing a certain work and tell him to do it. Instruct your priests to remind the people that the Church is dependent on them for support. Linus is a man of wide learning, a logical thinker. He should instruct the neophytes, and when your seminary is ready he should be its administrator. And it would be well if all of your priests met together once in a while socially as well to discuss Church affairs."

"Oh that I had the daring and confidence of youth," said Peter. "You have helped me more than you know."

In response to Peter's call all of his priests met together at Senator Pudens' villa. In social rank they ranged from the nobility of Rome, Pudens and Linus, to a former Roman black slave, Junius. In between there were Jews of the laboring class — Nicodemus, a weaver, Jonas, a saddle and harness maker; Silas a truck gardener, and Samuel, who owned a small interest in a tannery. There were also Gentiles; Marcus, a former servant of Senator Pudens, now a full-time priest; Philo, a Greek slave who served as an instructor of his master's children, and the Ruffalo brothers, builders of houses and pavers of roads.

Peter related his conversation with Joseph and invited them to offer suggestions. Out of the ensuing discussion came a definite policy. On land north of Rome owned by Senator Pudens a seminary would be founded, necessary housing would be built by Joseph. Linus would be chief instructor and administrator. Neophytes for the priesthood would live there and could be partially self-supporting by raising vegetables, grapes, fowls, sheep and fruit. Each of them gave an account of his priestly work, the economic status and number of his people and spoke of the need of a place where all could meet at one service. But it was the report of Junius that drew the closest attention. He worked only among slaves. His people, more than four hundred in number, worshiped in an abandoned stable owned by Capena. While marriage of slaves were discouraged by their masters, he had performed more than a hundred marriages. "When they understood that the Christian religion recognizes the dignity of men and the sacredness of human life, they embraced it with joy. Abortions were abandoned and every precaution is exerted to preserve life."

In commenting upon these reports Peter said, "More than three thousand converts to our Lord. Many more eager to be converts. Only eleven priests, and most of them are limited in their service to a few hours a day. Oh Lord, send more workers into this vineyard."

He praised all of his priests for their zeal and self-sacrifice, but for Junius he had a special commendation.

"My son, Junius, I would say in your presence what all of us have said when you could not hear. You love the poor and all who are in sorrow. To help them you give of yourself until your strong young body is bent in weariness. And you do it with a tenderness, a compassion, that is more Godlike than I have ever seen in any other man. All of us would be like you in humility, in holiness and in love of God and men. It is our wish that you now perform for us the holy rite of the breaking of bread."

After this act of worship Pudens addressed the gathering: "My brothers, for a long time we have been grave and serious. Now let us be festive and cheerful. Sit with us at table. May the food be savory and give you delight. May the wine part your lips in laughter."

16

Rome: Journey to North Country

IN ANTIOCH Peter had often looked toward Rome. Now he turned his gaze to the country north of Rome. On horses furnished by Joseph, accompanied by Linus and Antonio, students for the priesthood, and two servants from Pudens' household who were leading horses laden with food and water, he set out for the North country.

After a four-day journey they were cordially received in a village of about a hundred inhabitants. Appicus, one of the leaders of the place, lodged them in a comfortable cottage and appointed one of his servants to attend them.

Within an hour after their arrival Peter spoke about God to a group of about twenty. He spoke twice each day thereafter. In between speeches he talked in private homes. In the third month he baptized Appicus. In the sixth month a fourth of the population had been baptized and Appicus had been ordained a priest. Peter earnestly praised them. "You are a fruitful harvest."

In discussing Peter's method of instruction with Pudens, his father, Linus said he seemed able to make God a real person. He read to them from Genesis of man's creation and fall. This he followed with reading all of the prophecies of the coming of the Holy Redeemer. Then he would ask a question. "Why did God do all that? God didn't need us to make him happy." Then he would answer the question. "He did it because of love. He was eager for us to share in his divine happiness. Forever, forever, forever."

"There is only one Simon Peter," said Pudens, reflectively.

"One man questioned God's power," Peter said. "Only God could create a crocodile and a hummingbird. Only God could create a boa constrictor and a dove. Only God could create a man after his own image and likeness."

Reluctantly Peter quitted the peace and quiet of the country for the turmoil and cross currents of Rome. Foremost of his anxieties was the enmity of the Orthodox Jews for Christian Jews. In spite of the efforts to preserve peace one sensed that anytime there could be an outbreak of violence. Nicodemus confirmed this when Peter talked with him on the morning after his return. "Only last week several of our worshipers were assaulted as they were entering the Temple. I talked with Rabbi Humber about it. He is not friendly to us but he realizes the danger to all Jews and assures me he would make every effort to quiet those who would do us injury."

Several weeks passed. Peter decided to undertake his long deferred visit to the Church in Hispania. On a ship furnished by Joseph, accompanied by two neophytes, he sailed from Ostia to a port in the East coast of Hispania.

The moment he put foot on deck he ceased being Peter the churchman and became Simon the waterman. He surveyed the rigging and the sails; he gazed at the sea to its western horizon; in measured pace he walked the decks the while taking deep draughts of air and slowly exhaling them. For an hour at a time he would stand in the bow and gaze down at a squad of porpoises escorting the ship on its course. While he had the privilege of dining with the Captain of the ship he frequently ate with members of the crew.

As the ship neared port, Peter began thinking of the work ahead. Where would he find the Church? Of the names James

had mentioned he remembered only one — Sebastian — probably a Bishop.

As they were being conveyed from the pier to an inn Joseph
had recommended, Peter's searching eyes fell upon a small building on high ground. A building with a spire which supported a
cross. "Therein we see the handiwork of our brother James," he
said in a tone of prayerful rejoicing.

In a modest dwelling near the church he found Sebastian, a
middle-aged Bishop of subdued dignity, who graciously welcomed him. "The Rock of Christ's Church. I am deeply honored."

Within a three-month period Peter had visited the twelve
churches and the eight chapels in Sebastian's extensive diocese.
Without exception he was received with enthusiastic cordiality.
"Here was the man who lived with God for three years. The
man God chose to be the foundation stone of his Church."

To this glorification Peter had one comment: "James, the
master builder, the great thinker, the profound teacher. Why did
God choose me and not James?"

Before his departure to another diocese most of the priests
and students for the priesthood met with Peter to receive his
counsel and his blessing.

During their discussion of the most effective way to preserve the Church from injury he emphasized the virtue of humility. "Rigorously shun all customs and habits that would tend to
set you apart as a person of superior social caste. The crosier is
the symbol of shepherds. Let yours be a simple crozier not
daubed with gold nor studded with jewels. Let your vestments
be colored according to the season but devoid of gilding, laces, or
other ornamentations. Rings and head ornamentation should
likewise be shunned. Keep in mind you are not princes or nobles.
You are servants of the servants of God."

Peter's welcome in the two other Bishoprics was a close

duplication of the first. But there were pleasant surprises. One of a number of persons who came to him privately introduced himself as "Cadiz, a slave," who said, "Tell me more about your Jesus."

For three days Peter told him about Jesus and he learned something about Cadiz. He was born in slavery. In his youth he attended his master's sheep and cattle. An elderly slave had taught him to read and write and cipher. He had a white father and a black mother. When Cadiz asked to be baptized Peter baptized him without hesitation. When he said he wished to be a priest, Peter said, "Take me to your master."

For three hours they rode to the farm of Pizzaro, owner of Cadiz. After the usual social amenities Peter said, "Most noble Don Pizzaro, on behalf of your servant Cadiz, I beg of you a most generous favor. That you give him his freedom so he might be ordained a priest and give his life to the service of Our Holy Lord Jesus Christ."

Pizzaro's black eyes lighted up, but were not unfriendly. "A priest," he said. "Is he capable of being a priest?"

"Not until after a year of study would we know that. He would be taught in our seminary in Rome."

"Where would he work if he were ordained?"

"Most likely he would be assigned to this diocese."

"This is where I would like to serve," Cadiz said. "Among the people who have been kind to me."

"He's a black man," Pizzaro said. "Would people . . ."

"Christ's religion is for all men regardless of color or social rank or wealth or poverty or high or low places. Senator Pudens of Rome is an ardent Christian."

"A Roman Senator, a Christian? That is hard. . . . What if Cadiz is not ordained?"

"If I am not freed I shall return to you," said Cadiz. "If I am freed I shall return to serve you if you wish my service."

Pizzaro stared at him. "Do you mean that? It was not made up?"

"I never thought of it until I said it."

"I was as much surprised as you were," Peter said. "He spoke from the heart."

"Who will provide for him while he is preparing himself?"

"The generous people who contribute to support the Church."

"Perhaps you?"

Peter smiled. "This robe and tunic and sandals is all the property I own, and they were gifts."

"He may have his freedom," said Pizzaro, "I will pay for his support."

"How generous you are. We shall leave for Rome in about a week."

When Peter stepped upon the pier at Putola, Joseph greeted him affectionately. Then he said, "That black boy should make you a good servant, master."

Peter laughed. "Clement will do much better than that. He will make for God a great saint."

As Joseph drove Peter to Rome he acquainted him with recent events. Incited by two Rabbis from the East, the Orthodox Jews renewed their quarrel with the Christian Jews. Public riots resulted, so often and with such intense emotion that three hundred of them had been imprisoned. These Rabbis were specially bitter against Peter. Nicodemus feared the Emperor might banish all Jews from Rome.

"I fear that," Peter said. "Something must be done at once."

To Senator Pudens he outlined a simple plan. For the Christian Jews the Priests would be permitted to conduct the rite of the breaking of bread. For the Mosaic Jews Rabbis would have the privilege of conducting an orthodox service. Permission would be asked to bring the prisoners some fruit and at least one hot meal a day.

"I'll introduce you to Favius, the Minister of Justice," Pudens said, "but be not surprised if he thinks you're mad and orders you to be confined."

Peter had said that he lacked social graces. He had even confessed to being "something of a boor." But he had been heard to boast that after three-years' association with "the only perfect gentleman ever born," he could "rise to an occasion and comfort myself with the grace and dignity of a prince."

It was this Simon Peter, garbed and barbered with excellent taste, whom Pudens introduced to Fabius. He bowed with ceremonial Hebrew courtesy and prayed "your excellency's pardon for beseeching such an unusual favor."

In a low, quiet voice, he acquainted Fabius with the religious differences among the Jews and the "sad effects sometimes flowing from those differences." He suggested that some of the prisoners "might be innocent, for in the excitement of a public affray it is sometimes difficult to distinguish the innocent from the guilty." But he assured the minister that he was not "complaining of Roman Justice. Public disorder must be suppressed." All he asked was permission to bring the Christian prisoners "the comforts of their religion." This would give them "peace of soul and banish any ill feeling they might have for their jailers or for one another. Then they could be released without . . ."

"Ridiculous!" growled Fabius. "Within a week they would be guilty of even more dangerous rioting!"

"We Jews love liberty," your excellency. We have lost so much of it. These prisoners realize that further public disorder would probably result in life imprisonment. They would not again risk this great loss. Moreover the men who incited them to this disorder have departed from Rome and they are wise enough not to return."

"As I understand," said Fabius, "you are speaking for the Christian Jews."

"For them and for the Jews of the old Law, your excellency."

"Why I thought they had injured your people."

"Some of them did. But if word of mine could bring them comfort and I refused to speak that word I would violate the cardinal principle of my creed. Love God above all things and your neighbor as yourself."

Fabius stared at Peter. "Love your neighbor as yourself," he murmured. "Love your neighbor. . . . It shall be as you request."

Joseph informed the Rabbis what had occurred. There followed what Senator Pudens declared to be a miracle. Men were adoring God in Roman prisons. Men of the Law of Moses and of the new Law of Jesus of Nazareth.

Every day some prisoners were released. Within a fortnight all had been freed. For the present at least the Jews were at peace. Several Rabbis publicly thanked Peter for his God-like generosity.

17

Peter Fights Heresy

SENATOR PUDENS expressed astonishment when Linus told him the results of their journey. "Over three hundred converts! What is his secret?"

"He has no secret, Father, unless it be his friendly childlike candor. To the first group of about thirty he introduced himself: 'I am Simon, a native of Galilee in Israel. My brother Andrew and I were fishermen on the Lake of Gennesaret. We made a good living. One day, while we were casting our nets, a man on shore called us to follow him and said he would make us fishers of men. We rowed to the shore, left our nets and followed him. This man was Jesus of Nazareth, a carpenter. Why did we abandon our good living to follow a carpenter who had no steady employment to make beggars of ourselves?"

After a pause, he continued: "I know what you are thinking. I often thought the same. But this man is the only man I ever knew who had a deep compassion for people who were suffering. For all people, the poor, the sick, the afflicted. Hungry people, people without a robe or a place to sleep. People too weak to work. He helped these people — thousands of them. Having been given a miraculous power He gave some of that power to us, even to me. One day I met a boy rotting with leprosy. I touched him and he was cured. So grateful was he that he cried out in joy and covered my hand with kisses. Never in all

my life did I feel so good. I trusted him, he is all truth!"
   "I would tell you more about Jesus. He is the only man I
ever knew who respected all men as equals before God. Slaves as
well as masters; paupers as well as princes; black men as well as
white men; pagans as well as believers. In every person he saw a
creation after God's own image and likeness who could become
a saint if properly instructed.
   "He is the only man who ever taught men to love their
neighbor as themselves. By neighbor he meant the classes of men
I just mentioned.
   "After another pause Peter continued. 'Some of you may
not believe that Jesus rose from the dead. I would not censure
you for that. Several times he told us, his Apostles, that he would
be crucified to death and would rise from death on the third day.
We did not believe him. We did not understand him. When he
died we said among ourselves: 'This is the end. So final is death
that we never once thought he would rise to life.'
   " 'But he did rise. John and I saw his empty tomb. That
night as we supped behind locked doors, he entered the room,
having passed through the walls.'
   "After a short pause he told them of the other appearances
made by Jesus, and related in detail all that was said and done by
him on those occasions. Then he said: 'This should help your
unbelief. Every event incident to the conception and birth of
Jesus, his life and death and resurrection, were foretold by the
holy Prophets. Hundreds of years ago Isaiah wrote. "Behold, a
virgin shall conceive and bear a son and his name shall be called
Emmanuel!" '
   "Then he quoted from all of the other prophecies and narrated the events that had fulfilled them. An impregnable fabric of
truth did he weave for them. They listened, enraptured."
   "I wish I could have heard him," said Senator Pudens.
   Linus quoted more from Peter's sayings. "There is some-

thing more you should know. I was so angered by Jesus' refusal
to subdue his foes, for what appeared to be a cowardly surrender,
I was ashamed to have people know that I knew him. So I
publicly denied knowing him. Three times did I deny him. Yet
he did not cast me out. Three times he gave me the opportunity
to declare my love for him. And three times he bade me feed his
lambs and his sheep. What gentle mercy! This is the man I
would make known to you."

"A Jew fisherman," murmured Senator Pudens. "Unable
to read or write, yet a strong leader; an accurate teacher, by word
and example. God knew his strength and faith and love."

"He explained how man rejected God and why God
wished to be reconciled with man. He made them understand
that God was not a tyrant seeking revenge for this rejection but
was a loving Father eager to forgive and restore them to his holy
grace."

After a three-month journey in the North Country, Peter
and his two companions set out for Rome. The weather was
good but upon reaching a point about six hours' distant from the
city a cold heavy rain steadily fell upon them. Their clothing was
soaked. Their horses slowed to a cautious walk to maintain their
footing. They looked in vain for shelter. Cassius, one of his
young companions, said, "Master, I've heard wonderful tales of
your miraculous power. Couldn't you make the sun shine upon
us?"

Peter smiles. "No, I can't control the weather. It's all I can
do to control myself."

"The rain doesn't seem to bother you, Master," said the
other companion. "I suppose you are used to it from your life as
a fisherman."

To distract them from their discomfort, Peter related some
of his adventures on Lake Gennesaret: "Scarcely a day passed
that we were not drenched with rain or lake water. It became a

part of our way of life. But I'm no longer young. Notice how my teeth chatter from the cold."

Coming to a crossroad Peter said, "The road to your right will take you to our seminary, an hour's ride. Go there and get some dry clothes and a hot meal. I'll follow the other road to my house in the city. I would invite you to go with me but I couldn't take care of your needs."

It was dark when Peter entered his house. His "house companions," as he called those who served him, promptly got him to bed and gave him a cup of hot wine to drink. "I'll go for a physician," said one, hurrying out. "Get Deborrah," said Peter to the others.

When Deborrah, the wife of Nicodemus, learned of Peter's illness she bade the messenger purchase some mutton tallow and onions and bring them to her at Peter's house. She melted the tallow, cut the onions into small pieces and heated them. Making a poultice of the tallow and onions she applied it to Peter's chest and back and bound him in a blanket. "Jewish mothers," muttered Peter, "the great physicians."

As she finished a Gentile doctor arrived. After looking at the sick man, he said, "I must bleed him."

"Bleed him!" shrieked Deborrah, thrusting her formidable bulk between him and the bed. "Blood is his life! I'll not permit you to spill it on the ground!"

"Mother is right," Peter said. "I'll keep my blood. I thank you for coming. My scribe will pay you your fee."

"There's no charge," the physician said and departed.

Peter became delirious. He fought strong winds and heavy seas on Lake Gennesaret. He boasted about a huge catch of fish. He taunted Andrew for saying he had met the Messiah: "How many soldiers has he got?" He cried out angrily: "I tell you I never heard of the fellow you speak about. For the third time I tell you I don't know the man!" The shrill crow of a cock shredded his dream world. He flayed his arms. He sat up in bed. "That damned cock!" he shrieked. "That demon out of hell!"

Deborrah thrust a bottle into his mouth. "Drink," she bade him. He gulped in self defense. Soon he was in a deep sleep.

Deborrah told her husband of Peter's dreams.

"I knew of his trouble," he said. "In agonizing sorrow he said to me. 'Adam disobeyed God. Judas sold him to the Sanhedrin. But I denied knowing him. I was ashamed of God! Ashamed to have people know that I knew him! The most heinous of sins! God forgave me but I cannot forgive myself.'

"I shook him roughly by the shoulders. 'You are not bad,' I yelled at him. 'You are distraught. God's forgiveness is enough, even for Simon Peter.' This seemed to console him, but not entirely. 'That damned cock,' he muttered. 'How he enjoys feeding on my heart.' "

On the third day the fever broke. The chill left him. "I feel good," he said. "I'll get up now."

"Not for five more days," Deborrah said, "except for short walks about the house. No visitors. No talking. Eat all that we give you."

Peter simulated a reluctant obedience and quoted Jesus: "When you are old another shall gird you and lead you about." Then, with a smile, "What a comfortable present you give me, Mother Deborrah. I ask only one favor. Will you let me have my kinnar?"

Peter's mother taught him to play this ancient Jewish harp. When he came to Rome Joseph gave him one. Deborrah brought him the harp and asked him to sing a lamentation of the Jews when they were captive in Babylon.

Peter strummed the strings. And his resonant baritone voice chanted the ancient song, "By the waters of Babylon we sat and wept, O Zion, whenever we thought of thee."

During his convalescence Deborrah provided Peter with

something he had not enjoyed since he abandoned his fish nets to become a disciple of the Man from Nazareth — a flavor of home life. Several times a day some members of his household and Nicodemus and other friends would join him in song while he played the harp. And over a cup of wine they would draw from him stories of exciting and humorous adventures of his youth and young manhood. But she forbade visitors speaking to him of events that might cause him anxiety. "There will be plenty of that later. Let him enjoy these few days in peace."

In secret glee Peter cooperated with her — considerably past the time when his role as an invalid could have been abandoned. How comforting it was to withdraw for awhile from the burdens of his office. But the day arrived when the nettles of conscience became irksome, and he said to Deborrah, "As much as I would like to remain there I must come out from under your protective wing. I think Joseph has something serious to tell me. Let him know I can probably bear hearing it."

In the reign of Tiberius there had come to Rome from Alexandria one Apion who became notorious for his hatred of the Jews. In his stentorian voice he publicly charged them with ritual murder, cannibalism, and worshiping the head of an ass. Tiberius scoffed at these lies and denounced Apion, calling him a "tinkling cymbal," and he departed from Rome discredited.

When Joseph visited Peter he referred to Apion's campaign of slander.

"Those old slanders are being widely circulated, Master, revived by the recent disorders among the Jews. Men in high places are advocating that the Emperor take severe action against all Jews, the innocent as well as the guilty."

"I have been fearing that," Peter said. "Have there been any disturbances during my absence?"

"Frequent private fights, some public hooting and jeering, but nothing that called for palace intervention. But the jeering is

now sounding a more provocative note. The Christians — the
Gentile Christians — are directing a terrible epithet at the Mosaic Jews — 'Christ killers' — not realizing that the Christian Jews
are included in their condemnation. This is rousing bitter hatred,
and disunity among the Christians which might suddenly erupt
into public disorder. How much suffering that will bring to our
people."

While Joseph talked Peter strode the floor, head thrust forward, hands firmly clasped at his back, as if he were gathering
strength for an assault upon a wily adversary.

"Heresy," he muttered. "The most insidious form of
heresy, for it hides its face behind the mask of hypocrisy. It subtly
teaches that God did not love the man who persecuted and
reviled him. And slander. Perhaps more evil than murder — the
slander of an entire race for the sin of perhaps no more than a
score. But what can I do to stamp it out? I have nothing but
words, words, words."

"And example, Master," Joseph said, "words and example.
That is all Moses had, and David, and the Prophets. Jesus
seemed to depend more on words than his great works."

Peter stopped and faced Joseph. "You are right, my son,"
he said, reflectively stroking his beard. "Words are instruments
for the conveyance of thought, for probing the mind, for igniting
the fire of the intellect, and the teaching of truth — and untruth.
Oh Lord, give me words that will reveal the injustice of their
words."

When he spoke to the Gentile Christians in their places of
worship, grave was his manner, stern were his words.

"It has come to me that some of you have given a slander-
ous name to the Jewish people — Christ killers. I assure myself
that you spoke not in malice, but carelessly, without consideration of the facts.

"The Jews directly responsible for the death of Jesus were

the members of the Sanhedrin, less than the full body, who condemned him, and their servants who instigated the people to cry out for his crucifixion — although probably about a score. Pilate who gave judgment and his actual executioners were not Jews. For the actions of these few men you condemn all of the Jewish people, even those who were born after Jesus' death. Oh the injustice of it! The sadness of it! I pray you, in Christian charity do not condemn even those who actively participated in his death. Leave their judgment to him. It will be more merciful than yours. I urge you to be messengers of this truth — to your children, to your relatives, to your friends. Yes and to all men. And I have another reason for asking this, one that might deeply concern you. The Jews in Rome are in grave danger. The recent disorders have revived old slanders against the Jewish people and influential men are urging the Emperor to take severe action against them. Should he do this hostile sentiment might rise against Jews and Christians, Roman and Jewish Christians, and result in the suppression of your religious freedom, and a bloody persecution should you not renounce your faith. So, my children, if you cherish your faith, if you love men as it teaches you to love, you will venerate the Law of Moses and respect the Jewish people who worship God according to its rituals. Hold no enmity for the Jew who does not become Christian. In this, too, leave their judgment to God. Live with them in peace and good will."

From the priests and their people Peter received numerous assurances that his counsel would be followed. Rabbi Salathiel called to express his gratitude for Peter's "public avowal of respect for the law of Moses and your good will for the Jewish people who worship God in that law."

"They are my people!" declared Peter. "I am proud to be one of them! I love them!"

"But many of them do not love you, Simon. They regard

you as a traitor of the Holy Law."

Peter nodded understandingly. "Jew and Christian" he said in a musing tone. "Religions of love, yet for each other they bear hatred. A sad paradox."

"All the world seems steeped in hatred, Salathiel said, with a sign, "or in cold selfish indifference. Will this be forever?"

"It will be for so long a time it will seem like forever," Peter replied. "Yet there will be improvement — slow, scarcely noticeable improvement, persistent, yet far from perfect."

"Through the merits of Christianity you mean."

"Largely through the merits of Christianity, for it will become the religion of the Gentiles. But the merits of Jewry will bear an important part, for it, too, came from God. It was the first major step toward God."

"That is true," Salathiel agreed.

"And another factor will have its effect in this regeneration of men — the merits of the Divine Image God impressed upon every man of all races and all colors. Even in primitive pagans I have seen love and compassion and self-sacrifice most edifying — not restricted to one of their own family or their own tribe or their own country, but for strangers. I have in mind a pagan who is typical of those who are influenced by this Divine imprint — Socrates, the Greek philosopher. He oppressed no man, deceived no man, slandered no man. He consorted with prince and slave and freeman as if he were brother to them all. He urged men to seek truth, not wealth and power, taught them how to find truth and asked no fee. He suffered death for his teachings but he expressed no animosity for his executioners, only kindness and understanding. And so sensitive was he to justice between men that in his death agony he remembered a small debt, and bade one of his friends pay it in his name. He never heard of God, unless one of our holy books chanced to come into his hand, yet he spoke of God with reverence and faith."

After a brief silence he continued: "Yes, my friend, some-day, I believe, man will be sensible of his brother's hunger and his thirst and his nakedness and the injustices that are heaped upon him and will make some provision to relieve his suffering."

"One day," murmured Salathiel, "a far, far distant day. Oh, if we could have something like that good will this day between Christian Jew and Mosaic Jew."

"Many of them do have good will," Peter said, "a compar-atively small group of extremists, emotionally unstable men, are responsible for these disturbances. But in spite of our pleadings they persist, like that public brawl a few days ago. I thought they would be arrested."

"That puzzled me," Salathiel said, "Rome is not a tolerant master. I believe some sinister policy is in the making."

When another public disturbance was ignored by the po-lice, this view was shared by numerous people. And when the rioters who had been imprisoned were released even Senator Pudens could offer no explanation.

"This is without precedent, Master," he said to Peter. "I spoke to the Minister of Justice but he would not, or could not give me any information. But his face lacked frankness. I feel cer-tain he knows what is in the wind."

But the prisoners and their friends were jubilant. "What care we for reasons why? The prison gates opened wide for us and we are free!"

Their freedom was restricted to one condition. Heralds rode about the Jewish quarter announcing that by decree of his Imperial Majesty Claudius, all Jews not citizens of Rome were expelled from the city of Rome and the country of Italy. Ships would be provided to transport them to destinations of their choice. Any person not obeying the decree would be imprisoned and his property confiscated.

18

Comforting the Suffering Jews

" ' ' A VOICE was heard in Rama, weeping and loud lamentation; Rachel weeping for her children, and she would not be comforted.' "

In these poetic words of Jeremiah the Prophet, Peter compared the anguished consternation of the Jewish people in Rome. In the crisp practical words of Simon bar-Jonah he described their plight to a group of friends in the home of Senator Pudens, whom he had gathered to formulate plans for their relief.

"Economic disasters threaten many of these people. Some own their dwelling places in whole or in part, and furniture and bedding and cooking utensils. They own shops and tools and material from which they earn their livelihood. Probably none of them have any money to establish themselves in another dwelling place or a new business in a strange land. I suggest that we raise a fund to be held in trust for the purchase of this property at a fair price, giving the contributors the privilege of receiving property of equivalent value, or the return of their contributions, or most of them, when the property is sold. If this is not done they will be obliged to sell at great loss. May we expect contributions on such terms?"

All assured him that his plan was practical, and "most humane." Senator Pudens and Joseph and several others, themselves men of property, volunteered to solicit contributions.

142

He thanked them, and continued: "Because of advanced age and sickness and other disabilities, some of these people would be subject to severe suffering and possible loss of their lives if they are compelled to leave Rome. We should petition the Emperor to exclude them from his decree. Senator Pudens, could you obtain for us an audience with the Emperor?"

"I regret to say that such an attempt would be futile, Master. In fact it would be resented."

"He might not object to one," persisted Peter. "Would you ask him to see me?"

"That will not be necessary, Master. Within a few days he will hold his monthly public court, when any man, regardless of his social position, may ask his favor. Few take advantage of this opportunity, however. They find the imperial light too strong for their eyes."

A reminiscent gleam shone in Peter's eyes. "Once I looked at a Light," he said, "and fell upon my face blinded by its splendor. But I shall not fall before this light. Teach me the ways of a courtier, my friend, so that I may approach him in the respectful way to which he is accustomed."

"You need no such instruction, Master. The innate dignity and respect of the Palestinian Jew will strike from him a kindred spark of respect for you. But I shall be pleased to introduce you."

Garbed in an unadorned purple robe, his hair and beard barbered, but unoiled, Peter went to his knee before the small, pale faced, low-browed man named Claudius, Rome's Emperor. At the word "Rise," spoken by a guard, Peter stood and Pudens introduced him.

"Your most gracious Majesty, Simon bar-Jonah, a Jew from Galilee in Palestine, presumes to address you. As head of the Christian religious cult he is known as the Rock."

Claudius regarded Peter with some curiosity. Then, as if it were his intention to intimidate or humiliate him he said, with a thin smile, "You are wearing purple. Are you of royal blood?"

Peter was not intimidated. In a low, but respectful tone he replied, "Sire, for Simon the Galilean fisherman, purple would be vanity. For Peter, the head of Christ's Church it is fitting."

Claudius looked astonished, then severe. "Your Jewish cult," he said, "it invites the Jews to hatred of one another, and to rebellion against the state."

"Oh your Majesty! Blame not my Lord's teaching for the wickedness of those who say they love him. He taught us to have love and good will for all men. *All* men. He bade us have respect for all lawful authority. He said to us, 'Render unto Caesar the things that are Caesar's and to God the things that are God's.' "

Claudius smiled, "What excellent poetry. A Galilean Virgil, would you say?"

"A divine poet, your Majesty!" cried Peter, his face aglow. "Another time he said, 'Behold the lilies of the field; they toil not, neither do they spin, yet I say to thee, Solomon in all his glory was not arrayed as one of these.' "

"Quite fanciful," Claudius said.

"But there was more than beauty in his poetry, sire. There was wisdom, and majesty." Another time he said:

"Blessed are the poor in spirit for theirs is the kingdom of heaven.

"Blessed are the meek for they shall possess the land.

"Blessed are those who mourn for they shall be comforted.

"Blessed are the clean of heart for they shall see God.

"Blessed are the merciful for they shall obtain mercy." And that is why I presume to approach your Majesty "to obtain mercy. . . ."

Claudius frowned. He waved his hand in dismissal. "Our decree shall not be withdrawn," he said tersely.

"I pray only that it be slightly modified, your Majesty. That you let fall your gentle mercy on the aged, the invalid and the infirm. They would suffer much and some of them probably would die."

Claudius stared at Peter, the while tapping his right toe. "How many?" he inquired.

"About fifty among my people. Perhaps three to four times that many among the Jews of the old Law."

"You plead also for your enemies?" asked Claudius, in a tone of surprise.

"They are not our enemies, your Majesty. They are our brothers before God. If you give them mercy, Sire, I pray you extend it to those upon whose care they are dependent — a father, a mother, a son, a daughter, a friend. We shall not abuse your clemency by including one not actively so engaged."

Claudius had ceased tapping his toe. His foot held firmly to the floor and again he looked into Peter's face. "Most unusual," he said, "I never before heard the like. It shall be done as you request."

This unexpected favor thrust upon the Church leaders corresponding responsibilities, which Peter laid before them at Pudens' house.

"The conditions of this reprieve should be explained to our people so they will not abuse them and be exiled in punishment. Their names and places of residence and their affliction should be given to the authorities without delay. I have suggested to Rabbi Salathiel that this be done to protect our other unfortunate brothers."

After some discussion he mentioned the plight of the deportees.

"We should make provision for the transportation of the women and children to the ports of embarkation, and for elderly men. They will be bearing heavy packs of their possessions. Likewise, for their food and shelter and sanitation while waiting to board ship. Having had some experience, I shall attend to that.

"Now, there's something else — the ships. The proper official should instruct the ship Captains to store ample wholesome food and clean water, and not to overcrowd them. This is very important — no overcrowding. Joseph, I am sure you can bring that about."

Joseph's efforts to accomplish this resulted in the assignment of an official to supervise the embarkations, who accompanied Peter to Ostia in a carriage furnished by Joseph. Discovering upon arrival there that no preparations had been made to accommodate the departees, he cried out in dismay: "No tents! No food! No water!" Then, addressing the official, a personable young man, he said, "My dear Marcus Antonio, I pray you forgive my unseemly outburst of emotion. But the women and children — I fear there will be much suffering. May I ask your help? Would you say a word to the port authority in their behalf?"

Early the following morning army tents were being erected upon high ground. Later in the day water tanks were being installed and wagonloads of food were being stored. Julius, an old friend of Peter's who had driven him to Ostia, said, "Master, you should be on the stage. Your acting was most effective."

"All of us are on a stage," Peter said reflectively, "the vast stage of life. But I was not acting, at least, I was not pretending. Experience has taught me that if I need the assistance of another I must communicate to him that need and my reason for it, in such a way that he, too, will feel the need. In short, my son, I must be sincere. I must be aflame with sincerity."

Peter now turned to another need — sanitation. Discovering that the Romans had little experience in this matter, he obtained permission to create a system in "the old Jewish way." When the first refugees arrived they were assigned to a camp which some of the veteran soldiers declared was "the cleanest and the most comfortable" they had ever seen.

When the first ship was ready for passengers, Peter conducted his people aboard. He showed them how to secure their packs and arrange their bedding on the deck. Half an hour before sailing time he blessed them and heartily assured them: "Give yourselves into the hands of the Lord, and he will lead you to a haven of peace."

For over two months, alternating between Ostia and Puteoli, Peter was constantly engaged. Every day from dawn until late at night he could be seen moving among the refugees, Christian and the followers of Moses alike, in camp and aboard ship, cooking and eating a meal with them, ministering to their physical ills, contriving in many ways to soothe the irritations of Roman officialdom with the balm of Jewish compassion and making of himself a legendary figure.

"A meddlesome old Jew," some of the Romans called him. "Like Moses leading his people through the wilderness," said his own people. "Every time we turn around we are looking into his huge black beard," grumbled some of the port officials. "With soft words and mournful brown eyes, he pleads with you until he gets what he wants for his people."

In the deserted camp at Ostia, Peter stood gazing at the ship bearing the last of his people out to sea. When it had merged with sky and the water he turned a sad countenance toward the man at his side and said, "Julius, forty thousand innocent people banished from home and country for the wrongdoing of only a few. The fruits of tyranny: the capricious whim of a weak man in power."

"We see this everywhere, Master."

"Yes, yes, we do. And it will continue until the leaven of our Lord's teaching, 'Do unto others as you would have them do unto you' works its way into the hearts of men."

Coming out of his contemplative mood, he said, "We have done what it was given us to do. Let us return to Rome."

Entering the carriage he removed his sandals, and squirmed and twisted, seeking a comfortable position and finally thrust one leg through an opening in the door. Within a few minutes his sonorous, rhythmic breathing let it be known that he was asleep.

Julius was fascinated by that foot and muscular calf. "Plexes, the wrestler, could not boast of such a foot or leg," he mused. "Tough as bull's hide. He could climb the Alps barefooted and not suffer a stone bruise."

In midafternoon the foot disappeared inside. "I must have fallen asleep," mumbled Peter in a tone of mild astonishment.

"Yes, Master," Julius said, smiling. "You slept fully four hours."

"With my mouth open, I suppose. I'm very thirsty. Stop at the first respectable looking inn."

Julius stopped at an inn with a brass dolphin over the door where they were served wine. Peter drank leisurely; his body relaxed — a weary man subsiding into a posture of ease and comfort. He gazed about, indolently observing the patrons. Suddenly he stiffened in astonishment. Rising, he strode to a table where a man was eating alone, a large leather bag beside him. "Ebulus," he said amiably. "I've finally caught up with you."

"Rabbi!" gasped Ebulus. "Rabbi! I thought you had long ago been gathered to Abraham's bosom! Sit with me. Let me pour you some wine."

As Peter seated himself he said with simulated guilessness, "I'm sure there are no idols in your bag."

Ebulus spread his hands. "Rabbi," he said, "you wouldn't snatch bread from a poor man's mouth. Let me think — you were — ah, yes, you were preaching — yes, you are a Nazarene. Have you been here all this time?"

Peter briefly acquainted him with his work and said, "I am concerned about you, my son. You are a Jew, a believer in the true God. Yet you traffic in idols. Don't be surprised if God lays a heavy hand upon you." Peter scolded the merchant.

Ebulus smiled. Taking from his pack an ivory figure with a man's torso and a ram's head and horns, he inquired, "Could there be any evil in exchanging this work of art for a few pieces of silver? Why this man-goat is laughing at you."

Peter was patient with adulterers and drunkards and thieves, but for idolators, and above all for a Jew who flippantly encouraged idolatry — suppressing an angry roar, lest he draw attention to himself, he said in a low, tense voice, "You seem to be so fond of it. You should have it with you all of the time. You shall not be able to let go of it!"

His blunt forefinger stabbed at the object in a gesture of malediction.

Ebulus paled. His fingers tightened about the object like the talons of a hawk clutching a hare. "I can't open my hand!" he gasped. "You put a curse on me! Take it off! Take it off!"

Peter sat unmoved. Striving to compose himself, Ebulus said, "Rabbi, you have great power — even raising the dead to life . . ."

"Only God has power."

"True, Rabbi, but God works through his servants."

"If God wills, your hand will be opened."

"If God wills — when will he . . .'?"

"Who can read the mind of God?"

"He might never open it!"

"He might not."

"How can I go through life with this thing in my hand?"

"You shouldn't object. You have profited much from idols."

Ebulus cried out in desperation: "I'll not leave you until you rid me of this thing."

"You're welcome to ride with us, but not your sack of idols."

"Why I have a fortune in them!"

"Burn them, and sprinkle the ashes on your head."

Ebulus talked with the innkeeper. When he had arranged to put the idols in his care, for a fee, Peter invited him to enter the carriage.

He moaned continuously of his plight. "People will scoff at me. I'll lose my business. It gets heavier and heavier!"

"Rest your hand in your lap," Peter said.

"I'll not be able to eat or to bathe, or to . . ."

"One-armed men manage to eat and bathe."

"One-armed men?" shrieked Ebulus. "You mean I should cut off my hand?"

"That is for you alone to decide."

After a long silence, Ebulus cried out, "Rabbi, ask God to open my hand!"

"I think he would like it more if you asked him."

When Ebulus alighted from the coach Peter said, "If you have forgotten how to pray, go to Rabbi Salathiel" and directed him where the Rabbi might be found. "I'll be here for about a week. Come to see me if you feel the need."

Midway in the week Ebulus came to Peter's house, his right hand wrapped in a white cloth, and said, "Come with me to the river." Peter rose from the table where he had been dictating to a scribe, and they departed. Ebulus was in a state of high tension. He walked so rapidly that Peter, a sturdy walker, could scarcely keep pace with him. Suddenly he cried out, "You bade me pray. I did pray, hour after hour. I begged God to open my hand. I promised to change my life. He did not. I grew desperate. I decided to have my hand cut off."

After a brief silence he continued in a quieter tone. "Last night I woke out from a dream about my older brother who was a cripple. He was always complaining about his condition. Suddenly I remembered him asking the Rabbi why the Lord didn't cure him. The Rabbi said perhaps he could serve the Lord better as a cripple. I remembered I disliked the Rabbi for saying that, it seemed so cruel. But when I was fully awake I began to understand what he meant, and I wondered if I could serve God better holding this thing in my hand. So I began talking to him, like you said. I told him I had pushed him out of my life and that I hardly knew him and that sometimes I doubted if he really existed. I said I wished to spend the rest of my life doing something for him, without this thing, but holding on to it if I could serve him best that way."

"A very good prayer," Peter said. "Like a wayward son talking to his father."

Ebulus stopped on a low hill overlooking the Tiber, and removed the covering from his hand. "Rabbi," he said, "I do this not to draw attention to myself but as proof of my faith in the power and majesty of God. At your word, he closed my fingers about this object. At your word I believe he will open them if my faith is sincere and if I can best serve him that way. But if he does not — I shall submit to his will in complete resignation. I beseech you speak that word."

His arm swept out and down. Peter cried out, "Depart from him!" Soaring upward in a wide arc the idol plunged into the river.

Peter embraced Ebulus. "What joy, my son! What joy. Your faith has made you free. But I beg you do not mention this to any person."

"How good God is!" cried Ebulus. "He worked a miracle! To help me — to help me."

As they returned to Peter's house Ebulus looked at his benefactor with troubled eyes. "Rabbi," he said, "I have heard much of the man called the Rock, some of it good and some of it bad. I was dumbfounded when I learned from you that you were that man. You are hated by many of our people."

"So I have been told," Peter said.

"I fear your life is in danger. There is a secret society of criminals here who extort money from wealthy Jews and Gentiles by threats and intimidation. No one knows who they are, but since they are known by the name Goliath, it is believed they are Jews, but I am told there are Gentiles in it."

"Why are you telling me this, my son? I have no wealth."

"They blame you for the banishment of our people, for it removed a number of prospective victims from their operations. Others, as you well know, were sentimentally attached to the old Law, though they never entered a synagogue, and they deeply resent your conversion of so many Jews to the Christian religion. They would imprison you, even slay you."

"How did you learn this?"

"From men who seem to know the leaders. They trust me. They have got me buyers of my toys, and I paid them. Of course some of their talk is idle gossip, but I feel sure there are men who would injure you."

"Since I don't know them, how can I protect myself?"

"You can be less trustful of strangers, Rabbi. When you board ship, avoid all strangers. They might try to throw you into the sea. Perhaps you should hire a couple of stout men to guard you."

Peter smiled. "I am grateful for your concern, my son, but I have a guard. He will suffice. And he will serve without pay. Now tell me about yourself — your plans for employment. I would like you to meet Nicodemus, the weaver. He has prospered in a small way, but he is getting old."

"I don't know the trade, Rabbi."

"You might consider whether it is worth learning. The expulsion of the Jews hurt his business, but he said it could be revived among the Romans. You know many of them, and you are young and energetic, and — personable."

Ebulus smiled. "What an idol salesman you could have been," he said. "You make me anxious to know Nicodemus."

Knowing Peter's intention to obey the decree of expulsion, Pudens and Linus, who had been recalled from Hispania, urged him to remain in Rome. But he did not yield. "It would be much more comfortable here," he agreed. "I could easily persuade myself that I would better serve the Lord by not risking the hazards of travel. But the Church is in its formative period. Her Bishops and priests look to me for counsel — you have seen many of their letters — face-to-face discussion is far more effective than my writings — I am not a Paul or a John and I have many dear friends in the East whom I wish to visit before I am taken to Abraham's bosom."

"At least put off your departure for a while," Pudens said. "I have something in mind for you."

In response to Pudens' invitation, priests of Rome and within a fifty-mile radius of the city gathered at his home to honor Peter at a farewell breakfast which would follow the dawn service of the blessing of bread to be celebrated by him.

In a jovial spirit of comradeship they greeted one another, paid tribute to "Our beloved father, the Rock of the Church," exchanged narrations of some unusual experience and discussed policies calculated to strengthen the Church and improve their priestly ministrations.

When all had spoken Peter addressed them. "You have graciously referred to me as the head of the Church. Humbly accepting that to be true I am concerned about who shall be my successor. To preserve the purity of her doctrines and the unity of her purpose this Church must have continuous orderly succession in the one who is designated her head. After much prayer I propose to you our brother Linus . . ."

"Why Master!" cried Linus in consternation.

Peter continued: "You know his virtues and his qualifications as teacher and administrator. Usually I urge the people of a district to elect one to be their priest, but for the head of the Church that would be impractical. The people, the whole people, could not know his capabilities. His election must be limited to those who do know — the priests and the Bishops, and perhaps the people of the city or the district where he has been serving. I hereby appoint Linus to act for me in my absence. Should I die, he will notify all of the priests and Bishops so they may come here and elect my successor. I would not ask your pledge to support Linus. I ask only that you give him thoughtful consideration and pray to the Holy Spirit for guidance.

Nicodemus, the frail, aging priest spoke to his brethren. "Orderly succession in the head of the Church! How important! In this fisherman from Lake Gennesaret we see another Daniel. Another Moses."

That night Peter slept at Joseph's house and early next morning he was driven by his host to the Port Ostia. He spoke of Ebulus. "He ceased selling idols and has returned to the synagogue. He will need encouragement. Watch over him."

"I will do that, Rabbi."

"He warned me of a secret criminal society, Goliath, he called it, that was a threat to my life. Surely he is in error."

"I have heard of it," Joseph said. "It is said that men of wealth were imprisoned by some of its members until they paid large ransoms. But no one can say this for certain. But this I can say, Rabbi. Many of the Jews blame you for the expulsion of our people. They hate you. Some of my friends believe they might attempt to kill you. I am greatly relieved that you are leaving Rome."

"If that is their intent the deck of a ship might be helpful to them."

"True, Master. The ship has a full quota of passengers, so avoid strangers. Do not trust anyone."

They boarded the *King David,* one of a fleet of ships in which Joseph's father-in-law had an interest. When Peter learned he had been assigned a private cabin he exclaimed joyously: "I am rising in the world! I came to Rome as a deck hand. I leave like a prince!"

As the hour approached for visitors to go ashore Peter spoke of personal matters. "Joseph, my son, The Lord has blessed our relationship. You have been my devoted son. Your home was always open to me. I have enjoyed the cheerful companionship of your wife and children. Your generous contributions of money and personal services have enabled us to broaden our charities. And your aid to our exiled people! You saved many of them from heavy losses. How grateful they should be."

"Rabbi, you disregard your guiding thought and your guiding word, you forbearance under vexation and trial, and particularly what was your most severe disappointment — my betrayal of your trust. But not once in all this time have you censured me — not even a frown. You have never suggested how I should worship God. You recognized that I alone must make that decision."

"Every man is entitled to that consideration," Peter replied, "a truth I was slow to recognize in my impetuous zeal. I was at fault. I pushed you into the priesthood before you were ready. While I did not dwell upon my fault I was not indifferent. With all of my sins I offered it to God with my sincere sorrow. So be not critical of yourself. You will find peace in prayer to the Holy Spirit."

The shrill blast of the mate's horn signaled the final warning for the departure of visitors. Peter and Joseph affectionately embraced. "I believe we shall see each other again," Peter said confidently.

19

Askar: Friend or Foe?

WHEN the ship had cleared the harbor Peter retired to his cabin to rest, but before he could lie down, a man entered bearing towels and a basin of hot water. "Why, Lucan," he cried, recognizing one of Joseph's servants. "What are you doing here?"

"Joseph bade me serve you on this journey," replied Lucan, smiling at Peter's astonishment. "I shall prepare your meals and arrange for your comfort. When you have washed, sleep for a while and then I will bring your supper."

Peter shook his head. "This is something I'm not accustomed to, but I like the idea. We shall drink a toast to Joseph's kindness while we sup."

"Oh Master, it would never do for me to eat with you."

"Would you have me eat alone? And talk to myself? No, Lucan, we shall eat together. I'm sure we have much chaff to toss into the wind."

"Whatever pleases you, Master," Lucan said, bowing.

Peter enjoyed conversation at meals as much as he relished bread and cheese and wine. Before the end of the supper, Lucan had shed his cloak of formality and was eagerly telling Peter about his life in Rome and inquiring into Peter's life in Galilee, and he spoke of Joseph's deep concern for Peter's safety. "He fears some of these fanatics may be among the passengers. He bade me guard you constantly, and to keep you from becoming too friendly with any of the passengers."

"A most difficult task for you, my son," Peter said, smiling. "But I'll try to be obedient."

But he favored himself in this regard and excluded the ship's crew from the interdict. They are not passengers, he reasoned, with self-satisfaction. He mingled with them freely, expressed admiration for their skill and agility and, to win their respect, subtly let it be known that he, too, was a man of the sea.

Accustomed to walking, Peter began walking the deck at certain times, striding vigorously and taking deep draughts of air into his lungs and expelling it with long drawn-out exhalations. One evening after supper a man fell into step beside him and inquired, a note of raillery in his voice, "Rabbi, are you scheming to corrupt the ship's crew?"

Abruptly halting, Peter gazed into the red-bearded face of a stalwart man in his middle thirties. Even in the dusk he could see a glint of derisive humor in the deep-set dark eyes. "I did think I might save some of them from corruption," he replied amiably, "but how could that interest you, a son of Abraham?"

"There are sons of Abraham in the crew. I might resent your corrupting them as you have corrupted so many others."

"If you have ever corrupted a son or daughter of Abraham you should not resent me."

The man chuckled. "What a quick wit for a Galilean fisherman. I understand how you have worked yourself into the leadership of the Nazarenes."

"Since you know me so well," Peter said, taking his arm and resuming his walk, "give me the privilege of knowing you."

"Privilege? You'll probably regard it as a leprous affliction. I am Askar, son of Jacob, of the tribe of Judah, who has come out of bondage to be a man of the world."

"Of course you have a wife."

"Many wives, but none that the law of Moses would recognize."

"And children?"

"Many children, from Hispania to Arabia." After a pause he added. "And all are provided for by Askar."

"I feel sure of that. So you have outgrown the synagogue. I understand. There was a time when the synagogue seemed stuffy and boring to me."

Their conversation was gruffly cut off by one of the crewmen. "Don't you see we're shipping water? Off the deck! Both of you!"

At breakfast next morning Peter told Lucan of meeting a red-bearded Jew who reminded him "of a dear friend, the Apostle Simon the zealot."

"I have noticed him, Master. A hard face and a sneering smile . . ."

"He is cynical, and a renegade from his religion, but he has an interesting personality."

"He might be one of the Goliath! You were in grave danger walking with him!"

"We were never far from some of the crew. I'd like to invite him to dinner — I'll be safe with you being so close."

When Askar sat at table with Peter, he said with a jeering smile, "What a change from your hovel in the ghetto, a luxurious cabin, a trained servant, excellent food and wine. . . ."

"You know more about me than I suspected."

"Oh you are very well known. Last night you said you had wearied of the synagogue. Many men have, but they didn't seem to better themselves except in one particular: they became free. But you — you founded a synagogue of your own. You preach a philosophy of self-denial and sacrifice. And you live by it. I thought you were in your dotage, but I was wrong. All the while you have been scheming to rise in the world."

"Isn't everybody trying to do that? Even you?"

"I have made far less progress than I dreamed of. Yes, I was wrong about you, Rabbi. You're not mad. You're a pious old fraud. You're as subtle as a serpent. You put out a story of a prison rescue by an angel who conducted you through iron bars and stone walls."

"Yes, yes, I did," confessed Peter.

"That was a master stroke. I admire the way you have deluded so many people into believing you are another Moses. I am not above trickery myself, but I am far below you. You are called the Rock of this new religion. They obey your slightest wish. You are more powerful than Caesar — except in one respect — you have no wealth, no lands, no vineyards, no herds, no palaces. But you could have them. Your people could clothe you in gold. I could not have thought of anything so original, so daring as you. I have wealth, not idle words of idle flattery and adulation — gold and mines and lands. That is the source of power, Rabbi — wealth."

"Moses had no lands or gold or palaces," Peter said, with a satisfied smile and suggested that they walk for a while on the deck.

"You're taking a risk, Rabbi. I might cast you overboard."

"Then both of us would find ourselves in the sea."

Askar laughed enigmatically. "Surely you have heard of Goliath. I might be one of them hired by your enemies to slay you for causing the exile of the Jews."

"You might be, if Goliath is not a fiction to frighten people."

They went on deck. Askar resumed the conversation. "You don't seem to be the least bit disturbed. Don't you fear death?"

"Not in the sense you mean, but I would put it off — for a long time. Life has been good to me. And there are so many good things to see — the heavens at night, the mountains, the forests, and the sea. And people. People are the most interesting of all."

"I am fascinated by your rescue story," Askar said. "I'd like to test you. If I lunged my dagger at your breast could an angel suddenly turn it into straw?"

"He could if God gave him the power."

A heavy sea rocked the ship. Legs spread, they braced themselves. "And I suppose he could suddenly make a bowl of water out of this sea," jeered Askar.

"I saw Jesus do just that," Peter replied.

"You are under a spell," Askar said impatiently, and began telling of his adventures.

"You have had a fascinating life," Peter said. "You are bold and daring. And fearless save for one thing. You will not face truth."

Lucan remained unreconciled to Peter's association with Askar. "I am sure he would have harmed you if we had been off our guard."

"I doubt that. He seems to be avoiding me. When we meet he soon goes his way. I think I have touched a sore spot. I told him he lacked courage to face truth."

When Peter went ashore at Joppa he gazed about in rapture. "Bless this day!" he cried. After years of absence a lonely wanderer returns to the land of his fathers!"

He and some of the other passengers rode donkeys up to Jerusalem, but Askar rode a horse that had been awaiting him, attended by a servant. After entering the city he rode up beside Peter and said, with that same enigmatic smile: "Sleep with one eye open, Rabbi. I'll be lurking in the shadows."

"You look much better in the sunlight," Peter said. "Now that you are in the holy city, go up to the Temple and offer a sacrifice for your sins."

Hearing the voices of men and the scraping of hooves before his house, the Apostle James looked out the door, exclaimed in amazement, "It is Simon!" and rushing out embraced a man who had alighted from a donkey. When he disengaged himself he gazed admiringly at Simon. "You are as lean as a reed, your face is thin, your eyes glow with a strong healthy light. An ascetic! That's what you have become — an ascetic!"

Peter laughed. "An ascetic who enjoys laughter and good food and cheerful companions. Ask Lucan. He will tell you."

For several days Peter rested, visited old friends and heard reports concerning the Church in Palestine and Antioch. "The Judaizers are still brewing trouble," James said. "I fear they will cause an irreparable rift in the Church."

"I should go to Antioch," Peter said, "even though my presence is more of an irritant than a balm."

"The time is not right, Simon," James said. "The issue has not been definitely formed. It might be well to wait until then."

"You are right, James," Peter agreed. "I shall visit the Churches in the North Country."

"They need your help. Due to the shortage of priests the old fervor is becoming weak."

Accompanied by Samuel, a young priest, and Jonas, an experienced traveler, riding donkeys, Peter set out for Samaria over the Jerusalem-Damascus highway. He rode leisurely, for one in a hurry would lose much of the beauty of crag and hill and tree. How often he had traveled this way. What memories it revived. The chant of pilgrims journeying to the Holy City for the sacred feasts; the jovial banter of his companions. Proud were they of the religious history of Jerusalem, astonished at the magnificence of her palaces, awed by the grandeur of the holy Temple. A flock of cranes swooped gracefully out of the north, their silver breasts and gray plumage contrasting harmoniously the green and brown and yellow of the landscape.

"Would that I had your wisdom," mused Peter. "You fly

162 UPON THIS ROCK

unerringly to your heaven. I am often plagued by doubts and un-
certainties of the course I should follow. Lord, your Church is
torn by internal strife: Jews suspicious of Gentiles; Gentiles
despising Jews, all unmindful that they are brothers. Teach me
how to cure these wounds."

Upon entering a village or a town he would introduce himself in a loud voice, "I am Simon bar-Jonah, a disciple of our
Lord Jesus Christ," and invite the people to meet with him in the
synagogue or in the marketplace if there was no synagogue, at a
time most suitable to their convenience. He would proceed to
the marketplace where he was most likely to meet some of the
people and repeat his name and his desire to meet them. If there
was a priest serving the village he would visit him, ask his assistance in assembling the people, and would accept his hospitality.
If there were no priest he would inform the people that he and
his companions would accept bread and bed for themselves and
feed for their donkeys from anyone who could give it without in-
convenience or sacrifice. If there was an inn they would lodge
there, unless the brethren insisted on taking them into their
homes.

At a time most convenient to the greatest number he, and
then the young priest Samuel, would perform "the holy rite of
the breaking of bread," the name given the rite by the Jews, and
he would urge all to prepare themselves spiritually to partake of
the consecrated bread and wine. He preached a simple theme:
"Thank God for his gift of faith. Guard it well. Live by it and
you will surely die in it. Thank him for his gift of love, for when
you love you will take food from your table and give it to the
poor. You will share with them your robes and your tunics. You
will nurse them when they are ill and console them when they
are without hope. When you give them of these things you will
be giving to God." Then he would emphasize the benefits of
prayer.

"Pray many times a day. Ask God for the things you need. Thank him for the things he gives you. Praise him for his goodness and holiness. Compose your own prayers, even as you would compose conversation were he talking to you face-to-face."

He received encouraging response. Many who were lax became fervent; unbelievers professed their faith and asked to be baptized. When Samuel mentioned this and compared Peter's "burning zeal" with the "sluggish indifference" of many priests, Peter rose to their defense.

"They are not indifferent. They are weary. They are so poor in this country and in most other countries, they labor from dawn to dusk in order to provide for their families. When they meet for worship on the day of the sun their zeal has no vitality to sustain it. And their training for the priesthood is woefully inadequate. It is difficult for them to rouse the people to fervor for they are as weary and as poor as the priest."

"You and the other Apostles lived celibate lives," Samuel said. "It might be best if all priests were celibate."

"That would be very difficult for most men, my son. But if the people ever rise above their oppressive poverty they may be able to provide for their priests so that their apostolic work will not be neglected."

"Even so, I believe it would be best if all priests were strictly celibate."

"Oh, it would be best. And the day may come when celibacy will be a rule of the Church. But at this time it should be voluntary — entirely voluntary. But their training — that is all-important now. We must plan to have seminaries in every country like we have in Rome."

In this fashion Peter worked his way from village to village to town, passing through Judea and Samaria. When he entered Galilee, he said with deep emotion:

"Galilee! God's own country. Here Jesus lived for a quarter of a century. And my country. Here was I born and grew to manhood. Honored should be the land which God chose to be his earthly home."

Upon his arrival at Capharnaum, Peter rested from his labors and went fishing with Andrew's sons. When his traveling companions inquired if he had enjoyed himself he regarded them with incredulous amazement and cried out: "Enjoy myself? Why I lived again in my youth! The feel of the nets — the dash of spray in my face — the chug of the oars — sails billowing in the wind — what memories they revive. Yet it wasn't entirely like the old days. Andrew wasn't there; John wasn't there; James wasn't there. Perhaps James was there, his valiant spirit shielding us from harm."

In the synagogue, at Capharnaum, Peter spoke to the people. "Keep the faith," you have been told. Did it help you? Did you ask yourselves, how did I get it? How do I lose it?

"You got it from God, a free gift from him. Why it weakened, why you lost it, is not so simple. In this synagogue Jesus said he would give us — give all people — his flesh to eat and his blood to drink. Many of them turned away and walked with him no more. They lost faith in him. Be not severe in your judgment of them. All of us are prone to believe what we prefer to believe, even though it is not true. We refuse to believe that which is contrary to our habit of thought, or contrary to human experience.

"Once I undertook to walk upon Lake Gennesaret to meet our Lord who was walking on the water to our boat. I had faith that he would sustain me. But it weakened under the knowledge I received from human experience, that we cannot walk upon water and I began to sink. So weakened the faith of the people who turned from Jesus. Their human instincts were outraged by the thought of eating human flesh and drinking human blood. They did not consider that he also said, "the bread that I will give you is my flesh." They would not believe he would give them his flesh and blood under all of the appearances of bread and wine. Their habit of thinking, their knowledge of human experience blinded them to this concept.

"Oh, how compulsive are these facets of our nature! Many times we Apostles heard Jesus say he would rise from the dead. But we could not believe he had risen. We did not scoff. Our habit of thought, our knowledge of human experience had convinced us that dead men do not rise. They had crushed our faith in our Lord's promise.

"I would mention one other enemy of faith — pride. I have heard men say they would not believe Jesus had risen from the dead even if they had seen him come out of his tomb. They were scoffers. They believe only that which pride and rebellion makes palatable. For such men I have no word. They scoff at God. They would scoff at me.

"How, then, shall we keep our faith in God and in all of his teachings? I emphasize all of his teachings, for it would be a profanation to say, God, I believe in you but I cannot accept certain things you teach.

"In substance, this is what a Roman convert said to me recently. His sickly wife became pregnant. He chanced to tell me he had consulted a physician to produce an abortion as he had several children and wanted no more. When he observed my dismay he inquired the reason. I said he would be destroying human life, which was no less than murder. He said that life was not a person until it was born into the world. I tried to reason with him, but he remained adamant. I told him he could not receive the Rites of the Church unless he repented, but he became angry, saying he would not be dictated to by the Church in his personal life. Oh how many of us distort God's law to conform to our desires.

"How shall we keep our faith? By frequent prayers of

thanks to God for grace to strengthen it. By frequent reception of our Lord's body and blood. By an humble submission to his truth. Say to him, Lord, you can speak only what is true. I believe what you say, even though I do not understand."

A message came from James by one of the brethren who had returned to Galilee, informing him that delegations of Judaizers and Christian Jews would arrive in Jerusalem from Antioch to submit their dispute to him for final decision. He requested Samuel to continue teaching, bade Jonas remain with Samuel and set out alone for Jerusalem over the Jordan road.

Near Betharabah in Perea he overtook an elderly man hobbling along on a crippled leg. Halting, he introduced himself and inquired: "Whither art thou bound?"

"I am Nathan bar-Simeon," the man said. "I go up to Jerusalem."

Peter dismounted. "Ride this donkey," he said, and assisted him into the saddle. "Deliver it to James, Bishop of Jerusalem."

20

Jerusalem: The Rock of Authority

B Y THE ANCIENT Ford Betharabah, where Joshuah led the Israelites over the Jordan into Canaan, Peter crossed the river and, over the Jericho-Jerusalem road, set out for the holy city. His iron-pointed staff bit vigorously into the soil, vagrant gusts switched the bottom of his blue robe, exposing his muscular calves. He strode sturdily, his face grave, his eyes set in preoccupation.

"Submitting their dispute to the Church," he murmured. "I sense the guiding counsel of Paul and Barnabas. I must be the mind and the voice of the Church. I shall pray to the Holy Spirit, and he will guide me to decide according to truth and to speak courageously. The Church will be strengthened, but I fear it will not be at peace. The inflamed emotions of biased, disappointed men will not be quieted. There will be resentment and sullen rebellion. Our Lord warned us that false teachers would persist in misleading the people."

Taking a donkey at Jericho, he rode in a convoy of travelers up to Jerusalem.

That evening, as he and James supped together, they discussed the impending meeting. "There is no need for all of this," Peter said. "The burdens of travel, and the expense. Paul's decision would have been sufficient."

"Paul is not the final voice of the Church," James said.

"This dispute involves a matter of faith for all Christians. Christ's teachings must be interpreted. By his appointment this responsibility falls upon you. The disputants have the right to ask that."

"I do not question their right."

"It will not be the first time. You decided that we Apostles were erroneously excluding the Gentiles from the Church, even though none of us asked for your decision."

"I am surprised that the Judaizers would submit anything to me for decision. They disliked me in Antioch, said I favored the Gentiles. The Jews in Rome blamed me for their expulsion. Surely the Judaizers have heard that."

"It is also known that you saved many of them from financial ruin and that you rescued the sick and the aged from deportation. You still have a few friends among our people."

Peter smiled dubiously.

On the eve of the scheduled meeting Peter said to James: "I've been giving much thought to this. I'll go out for a while and walk off some of my perplexities."

He walked leisurely, along quiet streets, following no route, and finally found himself in a crowded marketplace. He stopped to look at some fish represented to be only four hours out of the sea. A low voice spoke into his ear, "Rabbi, one of your exalted position should leave the buying of fish to your steward."

"I trust no man to select my fish," he replied without turning his head. "Have you been up to the Temple to make your peace with God, as I counseled you?"

"I have had no quarrel with God. No need for me to make peace with him."

"Askar, the prince of scoffers," sighed Peter, facing him. "Do you not fear he will cleave your tongue to the roof of your mouth?"

"Oh, he would not do that, Rabbi. I don't weary him asking for favors he doesn't care to give me. I do for myself. He appreciates self-reliant men. But let us move on from here," he added, taking Peter's arm. "Smells bad."

"I never expected to see you again," Peter said. "How long . . .?"

"Chance, mere chance. We like to walk. Why shouldn't we meet?"

"Not chance, Askar. I have a feeling it is more significant than chance."

"You talk like a superstitious old woman," snorted Askar. "I learned by chance you had gone to the North Country. I knew you would return. My business detained me here, and I like it here, for a change. By the roll of the dice we should meet again, in time."

"I would like further talk with you," Peter said. "Have supper with me."

"You'll be too busy. When you were expelled from Rome I thought that would be the end of you as a leader. Instead, the Jews in Antioch send representatives asking your decision on some religious question."

"So you've heard of that?"

"Why, you are the talk of the city! How you manage to keep hold of power and influence! Never do you come out of that shell of mystery and pretense. You are superior to me. Occasionally I unwind with a friend and we have a good laugh."

"So you, too, are not always what you seem," Peter said in a tone of wonderment. "I did not know — but I am so dull — so lacking in imagination."

"Oh, you fraud!" jeered Askar, with a smile. "I wish I had met you fifteen years ago. To what heights could we not have risen! But even now you have a good opportunity to improve yourself. A decision favorable to the Judaizers would win innumerable converts to your sect. It would grow in power and influence and you would be regarded as another Moses."

"I didn't realize you were so interested," Peter said.

"Rabbi, I don't care how you decide. The dispute seems utterly childish to me. I have given you the opinion of Jews of reputed wisdom. I question their wisdom. I think they are fools, but I pass it on to you. I would like to hear you spoken of as another Moses."

"Another Moses," mused Peter. "I am touched by your solicitude."

Interrupted by Askar's laugh, he continued: "I'll confide to you a secret. I don't care to be regarded as another Moses. To the sect known as Christians I am Simon the Rock. A distinctive name, wouldn't you say? And that is all I care about — to be a rock in all that the name implies. How firm a Rock I shall be my decision will probably determine. I wish you would attend the debates. You might learn something to your benefit."

Askar shook his head in apparent disappointment. "You are chasing a phantom, Rabbi. You could be a monumental figure among the Jews, but you pursue a phantom."

"Come to the debates," Peter said again. "In the synagogue nearest the Temple."

This synagogue, one of the larger places of worship, was filled with spectators. Standing on the rostrum Peter spoke words of greeting to all and of special welcome "To our beloved brothers from Antioch who have come to lay before us the merits of their controversy." Then he gave place to the first advocate for the Judaizers, a dignified elderly Rabbi, and sat beside James, the only other Apostle then in Jerusalem.

The Rabbi spoke with much fervor. In substance, he said that the Judaizers were faithfully obeying the commandments of the Law given to the world by Jesus, the Christ. But they had not abandoned the Law of Moses. They were observing all of its rights and rituals. They felt obliged to do this because Jesus said he had come to fulfill the old Law, not to destroy it.

Jesus had given them an example. He had reverently submitted to the old Law, had observed all its sacred feasts and had offered doves in sacrifice. He had been circumcised. "If our Gentile brothers loved him they would humbly follow him in these observances. The Church, speaking through Simon Peter, whom he chose to be its head, should declare that all believers in Christ should observe the Mosaic law in all respects."

Then he added, gravely, solemnly:

"And the Church should declare that these are matters of faith. And that their observance is as necessary for salvation as were the other doctrines so taught by our Divine Lord."

Several speakers followed the Rabbi, each enlarging his argument and supporting it with arguments of their own.

During the recess declared by Peter, the audience of Christian Jews and Judaizers and friendly Jews of the old Law separated into groups. From their animated conversation and emphatic gestures it was evident that many of them were gravely impressed by what they had heard.

When the session was resumed James introduced the first speaker for the opposition, a young Jewish priest, who spoke calmly with no attempt to bestir emotions.

What his brothers in Christ had said of Jesus was true. He was a Jewish man reared in a Jewish home. He reverenced the Jewish religion. During his private or hidden life he worshiped God according to its precepts, rites, and rituals. He offered sacrifices in honor of God.

But when he entered upon his public life and began teaching the doctrines which were to be the fabric of his Church he no longer observed the forms of worship of the old Law. He did not teach the people to be circumcised. He taught them to be baptized with water and the Holy Spirit. He did not offer the sacrifices of the old Law. He taught that his body and blood under the appearances of bread and wine would be the offering to God, the unbloody offering as foretold by the prophet Malachi.

The speakers who followed him argued that many of the rites and ceremonies now practiced by the Jews were the laws of men, not of God, which had been added to the Mosaic law through the centuries. Illustrative of this were the interpretations of the commandment to keep holy the Sabbath day. Many burdensome and impractical restrictions were being imposed — limiting the distance a man might walk, or the limit of the weight he might lift. Jesus was criticized by the Pharisees for his works on the Sabbath, and he confounded them by asking if a man's ox had fallen into a pit on the Sabbath should he not lift it out? The foundations of the old Law, which came from God in the Ten Commandments, had been taken into the law taught by Jesus. Being God, he would not and could not exclude the teaching of the Father. He and the Father were one. The law given by them was one law — a complete law — one that could not be added to or taken from.

The speakers expressed deep respect for the sincerity of the Judaizers and for the spirit of tolerance and good will shown by them in the presentation of their views.

When all had spoken, Peter stood, his head bowed, his shoulders bent. He looked upward and then into the anxious faces looking up at him and said in a low, clear tone: "My brothers in Christ: It has become known to you that God commanded me to teach the Gentiles. He sent to them the Holy Spirit as he did to us, making no distinction between us, and purified their hearts with the gift of faith."

Many Judaizers expected Peter to waver, to compromise to try to please both parties in an effort to restore harmony, as he had appeared to do in Antioch. But he did not waver. He did not compromise. At Antioch he had spoken as Simon bar-Jonah. Now he was speaking as Peter the Rock, the head of the Church, for the Church, for the integrity of Christ's doctrine, as he believed Christ himself would speak were he present in the flesh.

"Why do you question the act of God by placing a yoke upon the necks of our brothers which neither our fathers nor we were able to bear?"

They did not answer him. The whole assembly remained silent.

Observing the disappointment and anger in the faces of the Judaizers on the rostrum, James, the gentle peacemaker, the tactful harmonizer, engaged them in conversation. They appeared to be appeased by what he said, for in a tone of voice and by looks that included the opposing delegates, he proposed that the Christian Gentiles be counseled to abstain from the defilement of idols, from fornication, from what is strangled and from blood.

Abstinence from the first two practices was not a concession to the Judaizers. They were grave sins forbidden by the Church. The other two referred to Jewish prohibitions against eating the flesh of animals that had been strangled in a certain way. "Counseling" the Gentiles not to eat such meat could not be construed as a concession or a compromise, for they did not slay animals in this manner, except perhaps in isolated instances, when converted pagans adhered to a tribal custom.

But out of respect for the Judaizers, to show his good will for them, James singled out these observances hoping they would be pacified and reconciled to the Church. It was clear to all that while the Gentiles would be counseled to abstain, out of respect for the Jews, they would not be required to do so as a matter of faith or as a condition for remaining in the Church.

Peter so construed it, for he agreed with James, and at his direction a document was written to the brethren, informing them that "The Holy Spirit and we have decided to lay upon them no further burden."

After the meeting, to a gathering of friends in James' home, Peter gave voice to his sadness.

"Our sacred synagogue. It was my hope and prayer that it would be absorbed into Christ's Church and become one of its strong branches. Alas, this will not be, in my time. Today I spoke words that probably separate it even further from us. They may even direct against us the breath of enmity. If there is — if there is enmity — may it give way to understanding and good will. May the synagogue be one with the Church."

In the quiet of his house James forecasted the consequences of Peter's decision on him and on the Church. "Henceforth you will be outcast from our people, a traitor, a renegade. Many who might be disposed to be Christian will turn away. Most of the Judaizers will persist in their heresy."

"Oh, if I were the only casualty!" murmured Peter. "But I will have much company. All the people you mention who might be Christian but for me will be hurt. Yet I do not despair for them. The synagogue has been standing for centuries. Men cling to it with passionate veneration. It is true that we can be blinded by passion, but in this — God will understand and be merciful."

James rose and brought a jug and two cups from a cupboard. "Yes, you are a casualty," he said, proudly filling a cup with wine. "Soldiers must expect that. But the Church — and she is your foremost concern — the Church will be strengthened. You have placed a firm rock in her foundation — the rock of final authority in matters of faith and morals. Of course it was there from the beginning. Christ put it there. To be precise, you discovered it, guided by the Holy Spirit, and made it plain to us.

"In the years to come, when other heresies will beset the Church, when her doctrines are questioned, when the Divinity and Person of our Lord will be attacked, your decision will be noted by your successors, and they will do likewise. Of course they would act under the Holy Spirit without a precedent, but your action will give them confidence to speak out boldly."

"You remind me of the older James," Peter said, musingly. "You are a thinker, a reasoner, a logician. But you have grown into it. Formerly you seemed, well, a bit uncertain. . . ."

James smiled. "It was James who stood me on my feet," he said. "What an intellect God gave him. Christ said there would be false teachers, and he said he would always be with the Church. To me that meant he will direct someone to speak and act as the occasion demands."

"And not only her head," Peter said. "There will be others, like yourself, who will point the way. And that recalls what I have had in mind for some time — my successor. Orderly succession in the head of the Church will be an important stone in her structure."

"So you too have been thinking," James said, smiling. "I confess I never thought of that. You seem so rugged, so durable."

"Yes, even I must die," Peter said, putting down his cup with a feigned gesture of regret. "I have in mind Linus, son of Pudens. . . ."

At some length he told of Linus' virtues and capabilities and the growth of the Church in Rome, and added, "She is more accessible to more people than any other large city. As the Church grows, the more people will be having business with her head. He should be there. I would not dictate Linus' election, but I think it would be best for the Church. Make him known to all your people and to your priests."

"I hope your successor must wait a long, long time, Simon," James said.

After a short silence, he went on: "What are your plans? I hoped you might remain here. . . ."

"I thought so too, but I believe it would not be wise. The people would not receive me well. I shall go once more into Galilee. There are places there of hallowed memory — Mount

Tabor, Nazareth, Cana, Bethsaida, Capharnaum. I would see them once more. I shall not pass this way again."

"And there are no Judaizers there," James said. "May the Lord bless your work."

Months later Peter returned to Jerusalem. "The Lord did bless our work," he reported. "Over three hundred were baptized. I ordained twelve priests, ardent young men learned in the old Law and the new. I was surprised and gratified by the response of the people."

"I am not surprised," James said. "Spiritually you have grown very much. There is a concentration of spirituality in you that cannot be contained. It pours out from you with such intensity that it inflames the hearts of men of good will."

"Oh you exaggerate!" said Peter. "I have never been aware of anything like that. I am just the same rough fellow you first met twenty years ago."

21

Seleucia and Other Ports

ACCOMPANIED by Silas, a young priest, riding donkeys, Peter went down from Jerusalem to Joppa, where they boarded a ship bound for Seleucia and other northern ports. As he walked the deck the first evening at sea he observed a man standing by the ship's rail gazing out over the water. Approaching him, he inquired: "Could you be sorrowing for your sins?"

"So you're leaving Jerusalem," replied the other, facing him. "It's about time. You've been in constant danger."

"Were you at the meeting?"

"For awhile. It was so dull, so senseless, Jews trying to impose ridiculous Jewish customs on Gentiles. What tyrants religion can make of people. You decided sensibly, but you were too mild. You should have put down your heel on their stiff necks."

"Shouldn't authority be exercised gently my dear Askar?"

"Authority?" rasped Askar. "It is the enemy of religion! It corrupted the Jewish religion and it is whirling you to destruction."

Peter smiled. "You are talking to gratify your ego," he said, "like one having authority. Let us walk for a while. What a pleasure to meet you again. God's providence, I'm sure."

"Chance! I was prepared to leave a week ago, but my servant suddenly became ill. Mere chance."

177

Peter looked skyward. Askar went on. "How men delude themselves chasing phantoms. You could unite the Jews — be their leader, political and religous. But I've told you that before and you ignore me. I'm wasting my breath. Instead, you go about like — like that madman John the Baptist, with no more clothes on your back, with no more money in your purse."

Peter smiled. "You'll not believe me, but once I thought John the Baptist was mad."

Askar stared at him, doubtingly, and shook his head. "All the while I thought you were scheming to be a famous religious leader. And that your piety and poverty were disguises, a means to that end. I misjudged you. You are sincere . . . impractical, but sincere."

Peter laughed loudly. "At last I am unmasked! By Askar, the astute reader of the human heart!"

"Yes, you are impractical. People are not drawn to the bowed head and the timid word. The spectacular, the dramatic, are their magnets, the loud voice and the flashing eye."

"How true that is," Peter said reflectively. "When our Lord fed five thousand men with five loaves and two fishes the people were so affected they wished to make him king. But when he said he would give them his flesh and blood to eat under the appearance of bread and wine they turned away and walked with him no more."

"He should have become king!" Askar declared. "The people would have rallied to him. He could have expeled the invader and raised Israel to glory. But he was too timid, a dreamer, too impractical. Thought he could do by words what only the sword could accomplish. He meekly submitted to his enemies and his grand plans collapsed."

"That is precisely what I thought the night they seized him in Gethsemane," Peter said.

"It was?" cried Askar, in deep astonishment. "Then why

did you give up everything to preach in his name?"

"I saw his empty tomb."

"You believe he rose from the dead? Incredible! Impossible!"

"I recalled him saying he would rise from the dead, and I believed. That night he appeared to us at supper and showed us the wounds, in his hands and his feet."

"He did not die," Askar said with adamant conviction. "On your word, I believe he appeared to you, but he did not die. Dead men do not rise from the tomb."

Peter looked closely at Askar. "You'll scoff at this," he said. "I have the feeling that some day you will retract those words."

Askar smiled. "Thinking we have the gift of prophecy is a trait of most Jews. But suppose we think of the present. Let us go below for some meat and wine."

"Have you a cabin?"

"Of course, else I would not have sailed on this ship. If you have not, I'll share mine with you."

"I thank you, my son, but the night is fair and there's a cool breeze, and the deck is not harder than the ground. But I'll be pleased to partake of your meat and wine."

Under Askar's questioning Peter said he intended to visit all of the countries on the Middle Sea where there were Christian churches. These visits, Askar learned, would not be relaxed convivial associations with the local priest or Bishop or some affluent convert. They would require traveling into the back country, teaching the people, instructing neophytes for the priesthood, soliciting alms for building churches and seminaries, and to aid the poor.

"A stupendous undertaking for a Galilean fisherman," Askar said. "So exclusively dedicated to one work, you turned from everything worthwhile in life — wealth, power, fame, refined leisure. You sacrificed personal comfort, endured innumerable hardships and discomforts. For what? Economic insecurity, even poverty, the indifference of the people you served, criticism, contempt for your Jewish customs and thinking and, finally, total obscurity. Future generations will not know you ever lived."

Peter smiled. "You almost make me feel sorry for myself, but life hasn't been quite so burdensome and unrewarding. I have felt hunger and thirst, cold and heat, but I never suffered from them. In fact I enjoyed food and wine, and warmth and coolness all the more. I have been weary of mind and body, but always I could sleep and wake up refreshed. Never have I been bored — too many challenges to meet. I am too unsettled to have a fine house. I have no property but never has my purse been without at least a few coins — some of them as precious as the widow's mite, spoken of in praise by my Lord. Some people have been indifferent, even ungrateful, but others — what gratification to sit by a dying man you have helped to be at peace with God. I could be robbed of property but this joy no man can take from me. Fame — a phantom, to use your word. In life it might flatter my vanity. After life — you'll not find it written in God's scroll. I am concerned about many things, my son, but my main concern is the account I shall render to God of my stewardship."

"How differently we see things," Askar said, after a brief silence. "To me your life has been a scourge. What drives you on and on?"

"A restless spirit you might say," Peter replied. "The restless Holy Spirit."

At this and other meetings Askar spoke sketchily of matters personal to himself — of a silver mine in Arabia, "copper diggings" near Alexandria, vineyards in southern Italy and Macedonia, forests and marble quarries in northern Italy, a "small interest in some ships on the Middle Sea."

Concerning this, Peter once remarked casually. "You are

subject to the laws and administrators of many nations."

"In some minor respects," Askar replied. "In all others, I am a law unto myself."

Noting Peter's look of astonishment he explained: "Many administrators of the law are tyrants, others are derelict. Most of them can be bribed so I enforce the law. If my legal rights are violated, I exact my own justice. If one cheats or steals from me, I inflict punishment."

"With mercy, I trust," Peter said.

"With justice. A business associate broke his agreement, causing me loss. When he refused to pay what I lost, I had him seized and held him prisoner until he had discharged his obligation. Another associate betrayed my trust and stole a large sum of money. He could not repay me, so I imprisoned him on an island I own. A mild imprisonment — works out in the open, eats wholesome food, a clean place to sleep."

"You spoke of tyrannical magistrates," Peter said. "Were you including yourself?"

Askar smiled. "He is fortunate. Had I taken him before a magistrate he would have been executed or at least cast into a dungeon."

"How long did you hold him prisoner?"

"I am still holding him. I credit him with a fair wage each day. When the debt has been balanced I'll release him."

"How difficult for an injured party to judge justly," said Peter.

"This is a harsh world, Rabbi. When one deliberately treads on your foot and you do not object, he will knock you down and walk all over you."

"In one of our sacred books," Peter said, "Sirach, it is written: 'If your neighbor injures you, forgive him and your sins will be forgiven when you pray therefor.' "

As the ship put into the harbor of Seleucia, Peter and Askar were drinking a farewell cup of wine. "You are about to resume your wanderings, Rabbi," Askar said, a note of regretful resignation in his voice, "over deserts and mountains preaching your idealistic but impractical doctrine. Not only is your head in the clouds, but also your feet. I would like to see you sink them firmly to the ground, and I know a place where you could do that, a little island I own, a day's sail from Rhodes. It's an enchanting haven with vineyards and gardens, and herds and fowls, streams teeming with fish, a comfortable house and servants to wait on you. Go there and rest as long as it pleases you."

"Could that be your island prison?" inquired Peter with a sly smile.

Askar laughed loudly. "So Goliath still lurks in the back of your mind!" he taunted.

"I have been warned so often about him. Your generous offer is tempting, my son. What luxury to be rid of perplexities and responsibilities; to walk over the hills at night, to swim on a sandy beach, to put out to sea under sail. But I hear a voice, a voice speaking words of hope to a desolate world: 'Go and teach my word to all nations.' So, as you say, I must continue on my way."

"Years of wayfaring," mused Askar, "in distant lands. I'll not see you again. I regret that, Rabbi."

"Oh, I think we shall meet. Probably in Rome. I anticipate that meeting with much joy."

Askar shook his head. "The risks of travel," he said, "the advance of age — how you prosper on hope, Rabbi. At times you are actually childlike."

"What a charming compliment," said Peter.

Askar accompanied Peter from the ship to the pier. "Safe traveling, Rabbi," he said lightly, "Take good care of him, Silas."

But Peter did not part lightly. Embracing Askar, he bestowed upon him the ancient Jewish blessing:

"May the Lord bless thee and keep thee; the Lord make his face to shine upon thee and give thee peace."

Shortly after his arrival in Antioch the bitter feelings against him for his decision at Jerusalem were again demonstrated. Salathiel, a former Rabbi, learned in the old Law and the Prophets, a convert of Barnabas' and ordained by him to the priesthood, called at Peter's house and berated him for his "infidelity," challenged his authority to speak for the Church in a matter so vital to salvation and charged him having so "gravely sundered" the Church that her "mission to preach the word of Christ could be destroyed."

Peter listened calmly, closely attentive, but spoke no word. Nonplussed by this attitude, Salathiel broke off his tirade and indignantly inquired, "Have you nothing to say?"

"Yes, I have," Peter rejoined in a low tone. "I understand how you feel and why you feel as you do."

"Then you could the more readily remedy this tragic situation and withdraw your decision."

Peter gazed at him with friendly eyes and inquired: "Will you drink a cup of wine with me?"

"Drinking wine together is a mark of friendship. I cannot pretend a friendliness I do not feel. You have caused me and my people deep distress."

"Your people," murmured Peter. "They are my people, too, children of Abraham. I would like — in your charity would you permit me to speak to them?"

That the man he recognized to be the head of the Church should make such a request, so humbly, astonished Salathiel. He stared at Peter and cried out, "Why certainly, Master!"

"You are kind. We shall talk to them together."

To a gathering that filled the place of worship Peter addressed himself:

"As you know, I decided that the rites and rituals of the Mosaic law were not binding on Christians and that their observance was not necessary for salvation.

"Our brother Salathiel, with deep sincerity, has decided to the contrary. For this I bear him no enmity, no ill will. I pray that you bear no enmity or ill will for me or your brothers in Christ who are in accord with me. We, too, are sincere."

Peter had spoken quietly, but from the vibrance of his voice, from his deep-set eyes and his commanding countenance, from his posture of leaning toward the people, arms extended in supplication, the spirituality of which James had spoken radiated from him with such intensity that they gazed at him in awe.

"One of us is in error, but it is an honest error. So judge calmly, judiciously. Do not let anger or indignation or hatred unseat your reason.

"In judging which one of us was guided by the Holy Spirit consider this: All of you believe that Jesus is God, the second person of the Holy Trinity. You have been baptized in his Church. If these things were necessary for salvation, why did he not tell us? He taught us many other things, but not these. Pray over this, my children. If you conclude that God could not neglect us, could not deceive us, you will know who spoke with Divine authority, my brother Salathiel or Simon bar-Jonah."

He turned toward Salathiel to embrace him in parting. Salathiel accepted this mark of affection by embracing Peter, but would not part with him. Facing the people, he said: "We have just witnessed the work of the Holy Spirit. He has made known to us that our father Simon Peter spoke in truth and wisdom and that I spoke in error. I pray that all of you will purge yourselves of this false teaching."

A voice cried out: "Blessed is Simon Peter!"

Immediately the entire congregation joined him in unison. Then they crowded about Peter with assurances of loyalty. Not until he had greeted every person individually did he set out for his house escorted by a half score, led by Salathiel.

To Silas his scribe, in a tone of wonder, he described the meeting: "I don't understand it. I spoke but briefly, my words were not inspiring but how they responded! The joy in their faces as if suddenly relieved of a depressing burden. The soothing hand of the Eternal Comforter, the Holy Spirit. Oh, if our other dissident brothers would let themselves be comforted. But they will not. They will not."

Peter spoke from experience, not in prophecy. His "dissident brothers" spoke out in opposition. "Simon Peter is a usurper of power. The Church does not have the authority to command our blind obedience. Neither does any Bishop nor any priest. This attempted exercise of authority in the name of the Church must be resisted."

When some of his people expressed alarm at their defiance, Peter drew upon his knowledge of men to assure them.

"All of us are rebellious against authority. We are self-confident. We declare that no man shall tell us what we can or cannot do. We cry out: he speaks falsely. Look to me for the truth. Now, that is not always bad. We are justified in rebelling against tyranny and exposing what is false, and in some instances force should be used. But we should not degrade a man for differing with us and that is particularly true of religion. We should not scoff at a pagan for worshiping an idol. Have respect and tolerance for his sincerity. When you explain to him why you believe differently, speak with calm reason. Do not try to force your belief on him. Remember the words of Holy Writ: 'The soft word disarms wrath.' "

Of the many activities in the Church at Antioch, Peter gave most attention to the training of priests. At a conference with Church leaders it was decided to remove the seminary to a

country place near the city, as in Rome, where the neophytes
could partially support themselves raising fruits and vegetables,
sheep and fowls, and engage in healthy exercise. He began teaching neophytes, not philosophy or dogma, not from the old Law
or the new (that he left to others), but from what he called the
"essence of the priesthood" — personal holiness, the habit of
prayer, fervor, self-dedication, the art of communicating with
people beset by spiritual and material difficulties. Above all else
he emphasized: "You will be the servant of the people, the comforter of the afflicted, the guardian of the orphan, the visitor of
those in prison. You will be a priest forever."

Ever mindful that the Church was not of one region or one
country, but of the world, Peter began thinking of a journey into
the "Syrian back country," but for lack of money his thinking
had not matured into action. His old friend Simon was reposing
in the bosom of Abraham. He should have at least two traveling
companions, including one to tend the donkeys and act as guard,
but his people were so poor he could not ask them to contribute
except in very small amounts.

"How I miss my dear friend Simon," he said to Silas, who
would accompany him on this journey. "He did not believe as
we do, but in many ways he was more Christian than many of
us."

"Perhaps the Lord will send us another Simon," Silas said,
hopefully. Peter smiled. "He could," he said, "but I think he ex-
pects us to do a little hustling ourselves."

"Even so, I think I'll pray with that intention."

"A good idea, my son. And while you pray I'll ply my blan-
dishments on Lystra the merchant. It wouldn't hurt him to give
at least a third of what Simon gave, as a Christian it is his obligation to be generous."

Peter returned empty-handed. "You should have heard him
squeal," he said, "as if I had put a hot branding iron to his back-

side." Debts are piling up on him. Debtors will not pay him. Competitors are stealing his customers. He was most convincing. Against my shrewder instincts I felt sorry for him."

While they were voicing their disappointment and their hopes Peter observed two men approaching his house. Rising he opened the door, and one of them inquired: "Are you Simon bar-Jonah, sometimes known as Simon the Rock?"

Peter acknowledged his identity and invited the visitors to enter. The speaker entered, a hefty middle-aged beardless man, who spoke unceremoniously and directly, and introduced himself as Sinus of the banking house of Derbe, which "transfers to you three hundred silver coins." He placed a bulging leather purse in Peter's palm.

Peter gasped. So overwhelming was his astonishment that his inert fingers permitted the purse to fall to the floor, from whence Silas quickly retrieved it.

Anticipating Peter's inquiries, Sinus said, "This money is delivered to you upon order of a banking house in Alexandria. If you should journey in Syria, we are instructed to give you bills upon certain banking houses in Aleppo, Hanath and Honis where you may receive money in exchange. Will you please acknowledge its receipt?"

He laid a sheet of parchment upon Peter's table. Silas put a quill into his hand, and he scrawled a heavy meandering Simon bar-Jonah. Pocketing the receipt. Sinus said, "We do not know the source of the money," and with a stiff nod, departed.

Peter sagged onto a bench.

"Manna from heaven!" cried Silas joyfully.

Peter silently regarded the young man. After a long silence he said, "That could be. And it might be the spoils of violence or trickery by a lovable scoundrel, a blasphemous, scoffing lovable son of Abraham."

Silas stared at him in amazement. Peter told him about

Askar. "I don't know he did this," he said, "but I know of no other person who would be so generous to me or who has the ingenuity to bring it about."

Silas had plunged from elation to chagrin. "But Master! It is tainted money! We must return it!"

"I am not so sure about that," Peter replied. "Many other circumstances should be considered. But why condemn the criminal before his guilt is proven? We don't know this money is tainted; or if tainted in part, how large a part, so let us presume it is clean money."

"Since it is justifiably under suspicion wouldn't we be guilty of — of subterfuge? Duplicity?"

"I don't think so," Peter smilingly assured him. "Even if some of the coins have a bad odor, that should disappear from the worthy use we shall make of them. Let us prepare for our journey."

Knowing the need of an experienced guide, Peter sought Levi, who had accompanied him on his previous travels, but he would not leave his work and family. However, he offered to furnish the donkeys and equipment and suggested his nephew, Moses, as a guide. "He knows the country, Rabbi. He is strong and active and has no family ties to keep him here. Come to dinner tonight. He'll be here so you can talk to him."

While they supped Peter appraised Moses to be a jovial, amiable young man given more to song and laughter than the serious things of life. He learned that he could play the flute and other reed instruments. "That is well," he said. "I can play the harp. We should have some pleasant hours." It was agreed they should leave Antioch early the second morning hence.

But when Peter and Silas arrived at the place of departure, Moses was not present. A half an hour later he had not appeared. Peter paced impatiently, muttering against "sluggards." "He'll be here soon," Levi assured him.

"Until then come in and have a cup of wine with me."
Peter went in, but not with good grace. He barely sipped
the wine and answered his host in grunts. Suddenly, he stiffened.
A man's voice was heard, singing. "Sounds like Moses," Levi
said.

Peter rushed out before him. It was Moses, happily drunk.
He inquired blandly why everybody was in such a hurry. Noticing Peter, he said, "I remember now. I'm not going, Rabbi. I
couldn't bear your preaching religion to me all that time."

Bristling with indignation, Peter said to Levi, "We must
find another guide!" and strode away.

Silas tried to quiet him. "It may be for the best, Master."

"For the best?" retorted Peter. "Consider the time we'll
lose, My time is running out! That irresponsible whelp! How I
would have enjoyed lashing his back!"

Peter's quest for a guide became generally known and several men sought the employment. One of these was a middle-
aged man, named Cyrus, a native of Syria, familiar with the
country and experienced in travel. His fifteen-year-old son
named Ignat, would go with them to Alleppo where he would
resume his studies. This was so unusual that Peter questioned
Ignat about his studies and was informed that he hoped to found
a school of philosophy in Syria.

"A worthy ambition," Peter said. "I wish you well. It will
be a pleasure to have you for a companion."

Silas seemed dubious about Cyrus. "You know nothing of
him, Master. Shouldn't he be asked for credentials vouching for
his good character?"

"His son vouches for him," Peter said. "Didn't you notice
the spirituality in his face? Its strength? Its firmness? He thinks
noble thoughts. And how respectful he is. A man who has reared
such a son must be a good man."

22

Eastern Coast of Aegean Sea

"I THINK, therefore I know," said Ignat, as he explained to Peter some of the philosophic principles he had been taught.

"And I might also add," Peter replied: "I feel, therefore I know. I have experience, therefore I know."

They were riding side-by-side at the time. The young man regarded his elderly companion, astonished. Many times while traveling or resting in camp or in a village house, Peter had talked with Ignat about his studies, but never before had he voiced a thought.

"Why, Rabbi," he said, "these are the basic principles of philosophy. What school did you attend?"

Peter smiled. "I picked up a few crumbs of philosophy from Linus, one of our Bishops, and Plato and Aristotle. I have read the Hebrew philosophers David, Daniel, Isaiah and others. And for three years I was taught philosophy by Jesus of Nazareth."

"Did he not suffer death for his teaching? Like Socrates?"

"Yes, he did."

"I never heard of any of his writings."

"He never wrote anything."

"That is strange. Perhaps he did not expect his teachings to become known!"

"Oh yes, he did. He bade his disciples teach others as he

had also taught them," Peter quickly reminded Ignat.
"Was that not wholly inadequate? The meaning of speech
suffers continual misconstruction when repeated by others."

"He said he would protect his doctrine from corruption.
But that leads us into his religion. You are not quite ready for
that, my son."

Ignat looked displeased, as if this remark was an affront to
his maturity. Peter hastily added: "Matthew, one of his disciples,
recorded some of his teachings in Aramaic, our Galilean dialect.
But few people speak it. I hope it will be translated into Greek.
If you wish to learn something of Jesus' philosophy, my son,
come to our meetings when we teach the people."

Ignat attended several meetings but instead of discussing
with Peter what he had taught, he said, "I heard one of the people say you were a fisherman from Galilee. Surely he must be
mistaken."

"I was a fisherman until I was about thirty-four years old,"
Peter replied, smiling.

Ignat seemed disappointed.

"And Jesus of Nazareth was a carpenter until he was about
thirty. But I am not surprised at your wonderment. One of his
friends was at first far more dubious about him. He asked if anything good could come out of Nazareth."

"Then he never studied philosophy?"

"I doubt if he ever heard of the Greek philosophers, but he
was learned in all of the Hebrew teachings."

"Yet you say his philosophy was his own."

"His own, with some blending with the old. I think you
would be interested in his teachings."

Ignat's scholarship was not an impediment to practical matters. He became skillful in packing the donkeys, making camp,
erecting a tent and igniting a fire. He even competed with Peter
in cooking meals.

"You are a man of many talents," Peter said. "You should rise to a high place in the world."

"Aristotle said that only the educated are free," replied Ignat.

"Jesus of Nazareth expressed the same thought in almost the same words: 'The truth shall make you free.' "

"I would be educated to think as well as to do. Then I would teach other men to be free."

"A praiseworthy ambition, my son. May you realize it to the full."

In discussing this conversation with Silas, Peter spoke hopefully of Ignat. "He would make a worthy priest, an exceptionally able priest. But I have not told him lest it appear I was urging him. To my sorrow, I once made that mistake."

Later he did venture a step in that direction. "My son, so that you might widen your education in philosophy, I would gladly instruct you in the philosophy of Jesus of Nazareth — that portion of his teachings that may be distinguished from his religion."

"I would like that, Rabbi. The little that you have told me I find most interesting — and appealing."

Upon their arrival in the city of Aleppo, where Peter planned to remain for a time, Cyrus and Ignat parted company with him, the father to take other employment, the son to resume his studies. After three months, as Peter prepared to continue his journey — with Cyrus, he hosted the father and son for a farewell dinner, during which he gave Ignat a package wrapped in parchment.

"There being no Rabbi available," he explained, "I was requested to give spiritual comfort to a dying Israelite, an aged man and a strong adherent to the Law of Moses. We became friends, and to show his gratitude, he gave me two scrolls, very precious to him, one called Genesis, the other Exodus, or Beresith and Velle Semoth, respectively, in Hebrew. Therein is written the early history of my people. He would be pleased to know I had passed them into such worthy hands. Scholars of every nation should know them well for they record the first relationships between God and man."

"I am grateful to you, Rabbi," Ignat said. "I shall study them reverently. You are justly proud of being a Hebrew."

"Not because I am a Hebrew, my son. God could have chosen any other people. But I do feel honored that he chose us; and gratitude, yes, and humility too. How awesome it is to speak to the true God!"

When Peter returned to Aleppo on his way to Cilicia, a country adjoining Syria on the North, he again met Ignat, who said that he intended to go to Athens and continue his studies. Cyrus, his father, offered to remain with Peter, but he declined.

"It would be a joy to have you, my friend, but your son will need your counsel and companionship. Go with him to Athens."

To Ignat he said: "God willing, we shall meet again in Athens. But before that day I have many hills to climb and many plains to cross."

"And many weary hearts to uplift," said Silas, "and many dark minds to enlighten and many straying sheep to gather into the fold."

Peter smiled. "That is what a shepherd is entrusted to do," he said. "Round up the straggling sheep."

With another guide, Salma, a Syrian, a convert to the faith, and Amir, a young candidate for the priesthood, Peter and Silas passed over into Cilicia, thence into Galacia and Phrygia and Cappadocia.

"We are treading in the footprints of a giant," Peter said, "the dynamic Paul, the Apostle of the Gentiles. We shall see many monuments of his great work."

This proved to be true. In the cities of Tarsus, Derbe,

Ionium and Antioch in Phrygia, they found flourishing churches and fervent churchgoers. The priests Paul had ordained, the Bishops he had consecrated, and the people he had taught received Peter with manifestations of sincere respect and affection. But there were some crevices and shaky foundations and leaky roofs and indifferent religious practices. In his quiet way so different from Paul's burning and sometimes abrasive zeal, he set about correcting them. He sought counsel from the Bishops and priests and elders of the people and frequently conformed his policy and his methods to their views. They, in turn, evinced deep satisfaction in having so decisive a voice in Church affairs. In particular, they were in unanimous accord with his desire to strengthen the priesthood and in every bishopric they assisted in founding a seminary for the education of priests.

Time, the element which Peter so often said was running out on him, brought an unexpected change in his immediate "household." While serving in an isolated village where the priest was elderly and in frail health, Silas said, "Master, you have been instructing me for three years. I would like to be ordained and appointed to assist this good man."

"You fill me with joy!" cried Peter. "I have been thinking of that. But I would remind you, life will be lonesome here for a young man."

"I have heard you say that a busy priest is seldom a lonesome priest."

"That is not always true, my son. How often I have been lonely and depressed. In Gethsemane our dear Lord cried out in pain from loneliness. In preparation for this holy ceremony abstain from all work. Seclude yourself for several days in prayer and meditation. Then I will elevate you to the altar of God."

As he had done so many times, Peter humbly served Silas as acolyte as he celebrated the breaking of bread immediately after his ordination.

With some reluctance, Peter decided he must end his so-journ in what he called "Paul's country." Before leaving he gave Silas three gifts: the donkey he had been riding, a purse of fifty silver coins from the mysterious treasury attributed to Askar, and his blessing.

He proceeded northward into Pontus and Bethynia, sparse-ly settled regions on the whole, that had scarcely felt "the life-giving breath of the Holy Spirit."

While the harvest was not bountiful and time was fleeting, and there were other fields that "offered more wheat" for his "reaping," Peter plied himself with his accustomed vigor. "These people must be given an opportunity to believe," he said to Amir.

"If I were a priest, Master, we might increase our harvest," replied Amir.

Peter studied the young man's face "You have grown in grace and learning," he said, "but it might be well to wait a while, and pray. My brother Andrew, when last I heard of him, was teaching somewhere near the Black Sea. I would like to counsel with him about this."

Amir seemed surprised that the head of the Church should counsel with another about such a routine function. Peter ex-plained. "Andrew has the gift of wisdom. Since our boyhood I depended on him to keep me on a straight course. Let us go in search of him."

While crossing a plain in Bethynia the travelers observed a herd of sheep grazing. Peter rode toward the shepherd, an elderly black-bearded man and asked him the distance to the Black Sea. He was informed that it was a two days' journey. As he turned about, he noticed that the shepherd's staff did not have the usual curve or hook at the top, but a cross. Stopping abruptly he point-ed to it and inquired "Christos?"

"Christos," replied the shepherd.

Remembering Andrew's deep veneration for the cross as the sign of man's redemption, he inquired, speculatively, "Did the Lord's Apostle Andrew teach you to venerate the cross?"

"The holy Apostle Andrew taught us many great truths. He baptized me and my family into the Church of our Lord Jesus Christ."

"I am Simon, Andrew's brother. I am seeking him."

"He lives for a while in one city or village and then in another. I think he is now near the sea, two days' ride from here."

He directed the shortest route and mentioned "running water coming from under a large red rock on the west side of the trail" where the travelers might rest for the night and find pasturage for their donkeys.

"You're a gift from God!" cried Peter, embracing the amazed shepherd. "The brother of the holy Apostle Andrew is grateful for your courtesy and kindness."

In mid-afternoon Peter halted on a low hill overlooking the Black Sea. Below him, in a sheltering cove, sprawled a village of perhaps a hundred houses. Fishing nets were drying on the beach; boats idled at anchor; others were skimming the surface of the sea under sail. Rounding a blunt arm of land, two boats were entering the cove under oars, fishing nets dragging in their wake. "How like Gennesaret," murmured Peter, under a surge of nostalgia.

Dismounting, he gazed about, comforted by the peaceful atmosphere of the scene, then fixed his attention on the two boats. In one of them a man stood and raised an arm, as if giving directions to his companions. Peter started. That stature — that gesture — he hurried down into the village. As the first boat nosed onto the beach the man stepped out — into the eager outstretched arms of Peter, who cried out joyfully: "Andrew! Andrew?"

When they had disengaged themselves Andrew inquired with reproachful solicitude: "What are you doing here? Rome is your bishopric!"

"The whole world is my bishopric," Peter replied.

Andrew was living with the local priest, occupying two small rooms of his house. Here he and Peter ate supper which they had cooked together. After eating they strolled on the beach — strolled until a pale quarter-moon — a two-hour advance messenger of the sun — appeared in the sky. "Let us rest," said Andrew.

"I shall lay my bed on the beach," Peter said. "How soothing is the flow of the surf."

A carved wooden cross hung on the wall at the foot of Andrew's bed. "So it will be the last thing I see upon retiring and the first thing when awakening." After gazing at it Peter said, "You have always loved the cross. But it seemed to have such a vital part in our Lord's cruel death, I hated it. But you are right. It is the symbol of our salvation. But I think it should be complete. The figure of a man in great agony should be affixed to it. We should constantly be reminded of how he suffered for us."

After a fortnight Andrew invited Peter to visit some of the churches in the "back country," but he declined. "I am weary of preaching and weary of traveling. And besides, I could not improve on your ministrations. So, unless a grave emergency arises, let us rest here and fish and talk over old times."

Three months passed. Peter prepared to resume his journey. Their mounts were replaced by younger mules. Amir was ordained to the priesthood and accepted Andrew's invitation to serve a while with him. One of Andrew's neophytes, Conus, agreed to accompany Peter.

The light in Andrew's room burned far into the night. Eavesdroppers might have heard words of sadness as he and Peter talked of parents, relatives and friends; and soft laughter as they recalled humorous events. They would have heard declarations of confidence in the growth and glory of the Church, and mutterings of awe as they spoke of their Lord, "the gentle man from Nazareth." And they would have witnessed a solemn ceremonial of farewell.

Andrew filled a cup with wine, held it up before him, murmured "to the day" and gave it to Peter. Peter drank of it, said "to the day" and returned it to his brother. Andrew drank, and again gave the cup to Peter. He drank all that remained. Andrew then rinsed the cup with water and thoroughly dried it with a towel. No other person would share in their pledge of love and devotion.

Leaving Bethynia, Peter passed through southern Thracia, thence down the Eastern coast of the Aegean Sea, visiting in turn the populous cities from Troas, to Ephesus. This, too, was "Paul's country," and everywhere were signs of his vigorous evangelizing. At Ephesus Peter sold his donkeys, bade farewell to his guide Salma, who returned to Syria, and with Conus took ship for Greece.

Upon his arrival in Athens he began looking for Ignat, calling at a popular philosophical school, or lyceum. Neither lecturers nor pupils had ever heard of Ignat. Nor could they identify him from the description given them. He inquired at another lyceum with the same result, but at the third he was asked, "Are you Simon bar-Jonah, otherwise known as Simon Peter?"

When Peter acknowledged his identity he was informed that "For four years this young man attended our lectures. And then he became a tutor to the children of Somas the merchant. He was expecting you."

"Somas?" inquired Peter. "Where might I find him?"

He was directed to "an estate in the hills north of the city."

Peter talked with Ignat in a cottage on the estate provided for his exclusive use. In age he was only six years older than when he and Peter had parted, but in maturity he seemed twice that age. He had studied all of the books of the Mosaic law, the Prophesies, the Psalms of David, the history of the Jewish people, and the Gospel of the Apostle Matthew. He had written the teachings of the philosopher Jesus as he remembered them from Peter. They appeared not to contradict the old Law. Rather they clarified those teachings and brought them into fulfillment. "As you so often said, Rabbi, one might not understand all of Jesus' teachings unless he knew the teaching of the old Law."

"You have done well, my son," Peter said. "I marvel at the extent of your learning, and even more at your eagerness to learn. That is a priceless gift. But may I offer you a thought, a thought born in the travail of a struggling dull mind, and the abrasions of harsh experience? Learning is not an end in itself. It is only the means to an end, and its highest end is the attainment of spiritual and moral growth — a way of superior life. I have never suggested that you be a Christian. Nor do I suggest it now. But I do suggest that you consider whether it is the end for which your learning could be preparing you."

Ignat smiled upon Peter. "Knowing your zeal for converts, Rabbi, I admire your restraints. I have doubts about some tenets of the Mosaic Law — the commandments against killing and stealing and adultery. They are forbidden by natural law. Even the pagan instinctively knows that, for he will use force to save his property and to protect life and the honor of his women."

"Who made the natural law?" asked Peter. After a brief silence he continued. "It might be well to consider another law, the law by which a man believes even though he does not understand. Faith we call it. Now let us talk of other things, my son. Tell me about your dear father and your prospects for becoming a teacher."

When telling Conus of his conversation with Ignat, Peter said, "The Church needs him. He should be a priest, perhaps even a Bishop. Pray that he will obey God's call."

"Of all the cities in the world, past, present and those that will be, Athens is the most important to man. When all the world lay sunk in ignorance and slavery, and groveled under the tyranny of prince and priest, there was born in Athens the concepts of human liberty, government by the people or through their chosen representatives, and recognition of the dignity of man as a person. Here arts and sciences and philosophy have flourished for over five hundred years. A miracle, Rabbi, the greatest miracle in the history of the human race."

So spoke Ignat as he and Peter strolled about Athens. It was one of a series of panegyrics delivered by him in praise of Athens during his meetings with the Apostle.

Peter nodded in qualified agreement. "Much of this I have learned from the history and literature you have given me to read," he said, "and from your explanation of her philosophy. But in your enthusiasm, you have excluded my country from the high place it deserves in the esteem of man. Long before Athens gave birth to these concepts they were vital principles among the Hebrews. Slavery was not sanctioned. We had kings, but no artificial class distinctions, and no royal oppression of the people. Save in the Rabbinical schools, education was not fostered by the state, but it was given in the home and the synagogue. Even though a man could not read or write, he knew his rights as a citizen and his obligation to God. You might say that the two complement each other. Athens clarified man's relationship with man, the Hebrew man's relationship with God, which necessarily includes his relationship with man. But man is slow to learn, and he has been without means of communication when he did learn. After five hundred years the teachings of Athens have not been accepted beyond its limits. Only after fifteen hundred years are men beginning to accept the philosophy of the Hebrew."

The conversation took a personal turn. "Athens is a most

interesting city," Peter said, "but I must move on — to Crete, to Malta, to Sicily, and finally to Rome. I lack words to tell you how much I have enjoyed our association. "I'll probably not see you again unless you visit Rome."

"Seeing you again, Rabbi, should be sufficient incentive for me to visit Rome," Ignat said, smiling.

On the day before Peter's departure Ignat called at his house and in his forthright manner said, "Rabbi, for some time my reason has accepted the religion of Jesus Christ as the religion of God. Last night I awoke from sleep and I remembered what you once said, that reason would convince one of its truth but only by grace would he accept it into his heart. At that moment I took it into my heart. I arose and read again the Gospel of Matthew. I have faith in its truth and in what you have told me. I ask you to receive me into the Church."

Peter embraced the young man. "You give me great joy!" he cried. "And I am sure our dear Lord is joyous, too. I would ask from you a privilege. When I baptize you may I Christen you Ignatius? It is more soothing to the ear and has a significant meaning; God-bearer. You are worthy of that title, my son."

23

Rome: Linus, the Successor

JOSEPH disengaged himself from a long, affectionate embrace of Peter and gazed at him in awe. He beheld a gaunt face seamed by trials and frustrations and blotched by excessive heat and cold; disheveled hair and beard filmed with gray; eyes that trickled water and shoulders that sagged.

"Eight years!" he cried. "Eight long years trudging the highways and the by-trails of the world!"

"I had no idea the world was so large," Peter said, sinking onto a couch. "How are you, Joseph, and your dear family?"

"We are quite well, thank you, but let us not talk until you are rested," and he gave him into the care of a servant.

The following morning Peter emerged from his room in a new robe and tunic, his hair and beard expertly barbered. "If I had any wealth," he said, smiling broadly, "I would leave it to your servant Marco. For two hours he rubbed and massaged me, from my neck to my toes and dipped me alternately in hot and cold water. A great sleeper I have always been, but never did I sleep so well. I am ready to engage in a gladiatorial combat. But Conus? Where is he?"

"We gave him a similar treatment," Joseph said. "He rose early and went out to see the city."

As they breakfasted, Joseph told Peter of events in Rome since his departure. Many of the Jews who were expelled had returned. Others had come so that the Jewish population was larger than before. Some Jews were bitter against him, not only for their expulsion but for his decision in Jerusalem, which had "dishonored the holy Law of Moses and defamed the synagogue." But this unfriendly attitude had been softened by the work of Nicodemus, who had become a full-time priest and had made numerous converts among the Jews.

"Nicodemus," murmured Peter. "One of God's saints, an honor to Israel."

"The former ill feeling between Christian and Mosaic Jew has largely subsided," Joseph said. "And the Gentiles seem to have a more tolerant attitude for the Jews. I attribute this in most part, to your teachings, Rabbi."

"Credit for that, if credit there be, should be divided a thousandfold," Peter said.

Joseph's encouraging report was clouded by Senator Pudens and Linus when Peter dined with them that night at the Senator's villa.

"A new obstacle has risen to the growth of the Church," Pudens said — "our government, our Emperor Nero. He is mad. He craves to be worshiped as a god. While he probably would not condemn worship of the mythical gods, he could easily be turned against the worship of one who is scoffingly referred to as a Jewish carpenter, who was executed for sedition against the lawful rulers of Judea. He is surrounded by courtiers who pander to his vanity. At their instigation he has seized the property of several wealthy Romans who seemed reluctant to worship him as a god.

"Some Romans of property who were thinking of accepting the faith urged me not to speak of it in the presence of others and even suggested that I sever social relations with them, lest they become suspect. Nero is so emotionally unstable that some insignificant incident could initiate a persecution of the Chris-

204 UPON THIS ROCK

tians. So let us practice our religion quietly, so we shall not attract attention."

"I agree with you, my friend," Peter said. "During the persecution in Jerusalem under Herod we met in the homes of the faithful in small numbers, frequently in the dark hours of the morning. We might try that for a while. Let all of the faithful be cautioned not to create any incident and I think it would be well if we discontinued all public preaching. Let every person become a private teacher as the opportunity arises."

Peter then spoke of a matter which he deemed to be of vital concern . . . orderly succession in the head of the Church. "I discussed this with James and Andrew, and John, with all the Bishops and priests of the countries I visited, and with most of the people. All were in agreement that it would be well for the Church if my successor were a Roman and that the seat of Church government should be in Rome. Since our brother Linus is a Roman and is the assistant Bishop of Rome, it seemed appropriate to them that he should succeed me. And this judgment was their judgment," he added with a smile. "They knew I would not have it otherwise."

"Excluding my son Linus from consideration," Pudens said, "I would say it was a wise judgment, but not as free from your domination as you suggest."

"I did stress my views," Peter admitted. "In a matter so vital I was obliged to speak forthrightly. And I do so now. My son, if you should be living when I die or become unable to serve, I trust you will not hesitate to take up that cross. The Church will need your learning, your wisdom and your holiness. And she will need your strength. You will not compromise her teachings. Strong will be the temptations to compromise — the threat of persecution, the loss of members, even of entire provinces, the hatred of rulers. But you will not yield to them. You will put down your heel upon them! You will know that the compromise of even one of Christ's teachings will topple the entire structure."

Without hesitation, in a firm quiet tone Linus said, "Guided, I believe, by the Holy Spirit, I will accept that cross."

From a pocket in his robe Peter removed a wooden cross with the figure of a man impaled thereon and held it up for them to see. "I have hated the cross," he said. "I regarded it as an emblem of the degradation, of the dishonor, inflicted upon our Divine Lord. I have rejected that feeling."

He told them of his meeting with the shepherd whose staff bore a cross.

"Then I began to realize how much at fault I was and how inspired was my brother Andrew, who always venerated the cross. I suggested to him that a figure of a crucified man should be affixed, and he was in full accord. I think the people would be spiritually exalted if they were taught to hold it in veneration. What do you think, my friends?"

"What a holy thought!" cried Senator Pudens. "What an edifying practice! All followers of our Lord should be grateful to your good brother Andrew."

"Then let a cross be exhibited in every place of worship, above the altar. Let the cross be possessed by every priest and Bishop. Encourage the people to expose the cross in their homes."

After a brief silence Peter added: "May it be our constant reminder of how Christ suffered and died out of love for men."

With Nicodemus, Peter visited all of the "Temples" where the Christian Jews worshiped and narrated for them the growth and development of the churches in the Eastern countries. Among his new acquaintances were Aquilla and Priscilla, converts of the Apostle Paul, who gave him the use of their house on the lower Aventine Hill. Here he could live comfortably and have ample room to consult with visitors and administer the functions of his bishopric. Peter was well-pleased.

Many old friends visited Peter, but he looked in vain for one he was particularly anxious to meet. So he went to him, in the weaving shop formerly operated by Nicodemus, and surprised him, so occupied was he with his work. "Ebulus," he said cheerily, "this appears to be more prosperous than selling idols."

"Rabbi!" cried Ebulus turning from his work bench. "You come to me?"

Taking Peter by the arm he led him into a room out of the hearing of his fellow workers. "You come to me? I should have come to you, but I — I was afraid to come."

"Afraid? What nonsense is this you are telling me?"

"I am not a Christian."

"Do you think I'd love you less on that account?"

Ebulus shook his head. "We can't talk here," he said. "Come to my house."

In the short walk to his house Ebulus strove to make himself clear. "Rabbi, you are the head Christos — you did so much — you worked a miracle — two miracles . . ."

"Calm yourself, my son. We'll talk about this over a cup of wine."

Peter was in no hurry to talk about it. He complimented Mariam, the wife of Ebulus, for her "grace and beauty of spirit," and her name, "made memorable by a most holy woman," fondled their three children, and praised Ebulus for his accomplishments. "Nicodemus told me how earnestly you worked to learn the weaver's art, and how you prospered the business and yourself. I am proud of you, my son."

Taking a deep drink of the wine, he added. "I am not the head Christos. I am the servant of all the Christos."

More at ease, Ebulus said, "I was afraid to meet you, Rabbi. I knew you wanted me to be a Christian."

"Want is a misleading word. It is a form of coercion. I

would like it if you and the whole world were Christian, but your choice must be entirely your own, free from the slightest tinge of constraint."

"Christians have told me I must be one or lose my salvation."

"They judged, even though only God has the power to judge," Peter said. "One who scoffs at God, or who ignores him or is indifferent to him, is in grave danger of losing his salvation but none of us should say that a particular person is doomed."

"Then, Rabbi," persisted Ebulus, "the Jews will not be lost because they are not Christian."

"I was asked to give spiritual consolation to a dying Jew," Peter said, "a just man, who was plagued by that question. I think he found the answer. He cried out in prayer: 'Oh God of Abraham and Isaac and Jacob if I am at fault for not believing, please forgive my unbelief.' "

To strengthen the improved relationship between the Christian and Mosaic Jews, Peter visited all of the Rabbis, a few of whom were old acquaintances, and commended them for their efforts in this regard. They received him courteously and some invited him to address their people. For all he had the same text: "Do not judge lest we be judged."

"The differences between Christian and Mosaic Jews over how God should be worshiped led us to unjust judgments of each other. The Jews of the old Law condemned the Christian Jews for worshiping a man as God. The Christian Jews convicted you of obstinate pride and of profaning the one they believe to be the Son of God. Neither should have judged the other. Such judgments are reserved by God, for only He can judge justly. For the disorder resulting from those false judgments, thousands of people were exiled and suffered severely in mind and body. Some of you were victims.

"Those differences will continue for they spring from sincere convictions. But let us have no more enmity, only love and mutual respect. To the Romans we are an alien people committed to a strange Eastern religious cult. They look upon us with suspicion and ill will. Let us not give them pretext for other forms of persecution. Let us refrain from judgments and leave judgment to God."

Peter sometimes questioned the reasonableness of his fears for the Jews and mentioned it to Nicodemus. The old Patriarch supported him. "We were in bondage to the Egyptian and the Babylonian. Even now Israel is under the Roman heel — largely because of our religious beliefs. No, my friend, you are not overly apprehensive. Nero acclaims himself to be a god. When a madman is in power, sane men must be constantly on guard."

They had further evidence of Nero's instability as they walked together on a street leading into the Forum. They and their fellow travelers were met by a squad of the Praetorian guard crying out, "Make way for Imperial Caesar!" Following them were other guardsmen holding aloft brass Roman eagles and gilded busts of Nero. Courtiers trailed them riding in chariots and litters, and behind them rumbled cages of tigers and lions and other animals for the gladiatorial games. Clowns and buffoons capered in the wake of the cages and vied with the musicians blowing horns and reeds for the plaudits of the people.

Behind these, drawn by six black Arabian stallions shod with gold, rolled an ivory chariot, and upon its black plush covered deck Nero reclined, a turquoise toga rakishly draped over a white silk tunic and a laurel wreath playing grotesque homage to his flabby pasty face.

"Hail to Nero! God of Rome!" cried out the people. With a nod and an indolent wave of a hand he acknowledged their tribute.

"A loathsome beast," muttered Nicodemus, "yet, but for the grace of God so be I."

"A truth we are inclined to overlook," Peter said. "What mystery is God's grace. It could make of him another Dismas, another Stephen."

Knowing of Peter's friendly overtures to the Rabbis, Nicodemus frequently spoke of incidents concerning them. One of these was the grave illness of Rabbi Abraham, aged father of Rabbi Josephus. Later he informed Peter the Rabbi had died "about midday."

After a brief reflection Peter said, "The burial will probably be in the morning from the synagogue. I shall attend, Will you go with me?

"Josephus felt bitterness for you in the past," he said, "and he was not cordial when you recently visited him. But when one is in grief — it would be well. I will go with you."

Peter stood by the bier, head bowed and murmured a prayer for the soul of the deceased. Then, giving way to others, he moved on, bowed gravely to Rabbi Josephus and the other mourners and took an inconspicuous seat in the rear of the synagogue. Nicodemus, who had followed him, whispered, "How startled was Josephus when he saw you. And pleased, too. I could read it in his eyes."

"May this mustard seed grow into a tree of good will," Peter said.

Yielding to the urging of his friends Peter agreed to "curtail his activities for a while." He lectured two or three days a week at the seminary, worked in the garden or in the vineyard and found an hour a day for secluded meditation. A portion of the other days was given to private consultation in his house, and this gradually increased to full days and even into the night. One day Linus came to his house and found a half dozen people waiting to see him. "Why Master!" he cried. "I did not realize you were so burdened. You should not make yourself so accessible."

"That's what I've been thinking," Peter replied wearily.

"My feet have been itching. I think I'll go upon a little journey."

"Any particular place in mind?"

"Several places, Sicily, Gaul, Hispania."

"At your age, Master? Why that would be even more burdensome!"

"Oh, I could easily sympathize with myself," Peter said, smiling faintly, "but traveling has some advantages. When the load gets too heavy I mount my donkey and seek relief amid mountains and valleys and plains. But I must talk with these people, my son. A few have been waiting a long time. Suppose we continue our discussion."

"At my house. While we have supper together," Linus decided.

"What an excellent idea," the Apostle said with a smile.

When they sat down to supper Peter promptly resumed his theme. "The Church . . . my brother Apostles said I was to be the builder of the Church — not the architect; our dear Lord was the architect — I was to lay the stones and mortar them in place. I was bewildered, like a man who had never laid a stone, attempting to build a house. I thought of our holy Temple, the greatest, the grandest house of worship in the world. How was I to build such a structure? What vast wealth I would need. What a large army of skilled craftsmen. Surely our Lord had something else in mind — something not of stone and marble. Gradually I came to understand. People would be the Church, men and women and children of all nations who have a covenant with God. A covenant by which they would believe all that he taught and would worship him according to his form and plan and be blessed by him in this life and in the life to come."

Linus gazed into Peter's face. "Master," he said, "Never before did I clearly understand the nature of the Church. Yet it is so simple! So true! The Church is something more. It is organization. It is order. It is harmony."

Peter smiled. "I wish I could speak as clearly as you. So in spite of burdens we must keep in mind that the Church is in her swaddling clothes. She needs the same attentive care a mother gives to her infant child. I lack the persuasive guidance of a mother, but what I have I must give without stint. I must give all."

"By giving all, an humble fisherman has become a great teacher of Divine truth," Linus said.

Peter shook his head. "What a teacher!" he ejaculated disparingly. "Crude, impatient, domineering. A ranter. I taught as I had been taught in my youth. Fear God! He is stern, inexorable! He hates sin and will cast the sinner into eternal fire! I frightened the people. But John and Andrew helped me change my style of preaching. I emphasized God's love and mercy, and patience. How the people loved it."

"You learned from experience," Linus said. "Perhaps the greatest of all teachers."

"And from thinking," added Peter. "I am a slow ponderous thinker, but gradually I perceived another aspect of the Church. While the Church is people it is not a Church of isolated groups — Jews, Romans, Greeks — it is one — the Church of all people, of all colors, and all races and all nationalities, the rich and the poor, the prince and the slave, the learned and the ignorant."

"Distinctions in social and economic classes," Linus said, reflectively. "They should never be tolerated."

"Tolerance of them will be difficult to abolish, so deeply rooted is this concept in the minds of men. But the Church should never yield. The dignity of the human person! The imprint of God's image in the souls of men! These are truths that must displace the man-created class distinctions!"

Drinking a draught of wine, he put down the cup and inquired: "Am I boring you with my ravings?"

Linus smiled. "Master, for me you are laying a stone upon a stone."

"But we must be practical and recognize a distinction between those who believe in Christ and those who do not. Not a discriminatory distinction, one of classification only. It is the believers who are the Church — those who worship God according to her forms and endeavor to live by her teachings. They are so pleasing to our Lord that they are a chosen race, a royal priesthood, a holy nation, a people purchased by the sufferings and death of our Divine Lord."

Linus gripped Peter's arm. "Magnificent!" he cried. "An inspiration from the Holy Spirit!"

"They have been rendered capable of constant mutual charity, a blessed virtue, for charity covers a multitude of sins."

"Charity covers a multitude of sins," repeated Linus in an awed tone. "What a rich treasury is charity. What a hope for sinners. Your words should live forever."

"Thank you, my son, but I see nothing spectacular in them. Just a truth simply spoken."

"A truth simply spoken," repeated Linus. "That is the heart of wisdom, like 'pride goeth before the fall' in Proverbs; like 'the root of wisdom is to fear the Lord,' in Sirach. All you have said here should be written on parchment so that it will not be lost, so that those who live after you may be lifted up in spirit."

Peter smiled. "I appreciate your compliment, my son. In fact I feel a bit proud. Andrew and James urged me to write. I may get around to it some day. But let us continue our reflections. We have said the believing people are the Church. Is there nothing more to say? Jesus is a person — a Divine and human person. What is his relationship with the Church?"

"Why, he was its founder."

"True. But standing alone, that seems to imply that they are separate. Surely that could not be true. He is intimately related — he said he was the Vine and we were its branches — a beautiful figure of speech. Would it not be true to say that the Church is Christ? That as the Church he is carrying on his earthly mission, teaching, inviting the people to be united with him? To be one with him? To be his branches?"

After a long silence Linus said, "Master, I — am — convinced — it is — true. I am confident that the Holy Spirit prompted you to make that truth known to me. Our Lord told Paul that his persecution of the Church was persecution of him."

"I wish we could make that known to all the people," Peter said. "For many it might be difficult to understand, but if we used our Lord's figure of speech, 'I am the Vine, you are the branches,' their minds might be opened."

"The Lord taught in parables," Linus said. "Surely this truth could be illustrated by a parable, like the story of the Good Samaritan to show the meaning of charity, or our Lord's figure of speech, 'I am the Vine, you are the branches.' "

"A good idea. Suppose you have your priests try it. I find that the people are deeply interested in the human nature of our Lord. They question me about his looks, his manners and moods, the sound of his voice, his personal habits. Did he ever laugh or seem cheerful? I should not complain if they weary me, I was privileged actually to see and hear him. They are limited by their imaginations. That which I received I should be willing to share with them and not keep it shut up in my memory."

"I wish we could persuade you not to make this journey," Linus said.

"Be not troubled, my son. I enjoy traveling. It is an adventure. Our priests cannot come to me, and communication by letter is unsatisfactory. So I shall go to them."

With three companions, one of them a servant from Senator Pudens' household skilled in cooking food and treating wounds, Peter sailed for Gaul.

24

Gaul, Hispania and Islands

AFTER VISITING the churches in the coastal cities, Peter journeyed into the back country where no missionary had penetrated. Profiting by his experience in similar regions, he was able to avoid many hardships and even to contrive some comforts. His simple speech and friendly manner won him a warm reception. In introducing himself he would say:

"I am Simon bar-Jonah, a Jew from Galilee in Palestine. I earned my living fishing in Lake Gennesaret. I would tell you about another Jew, from the city of Nazareth in Galilee, Jesus bar-Joseph, a carpenter, who left his workbench to teach men how to love God and love one another so they would find happiness in this life and in the life to come."

These people were illiterate. Their language was a mixture of Greek and the local dialect. Even with the aid of a priest who could interpret his meaning Peter spoke with considerable labor. Nevertheless, the people understood him and exhibited lively interest in the carpenter who had devoted his life to teaching happiness to men.

When they had heard the full story of his life and death they would cry out in grief for him and in anger at his persecutors. Peter would explain the meaning of his suffering and death.

"This was not something that happened by chance. God the Son became man to atone for our sins and open the way for our salvation. He knew how he would suffer and die. Do not regret his sacrifice. That would be ingratitude. Be thankful. Show your grief for him by obeying his commandments, by professing your faith in him, by praying to him, by repenting your sins, by loving the beggar who tramps his way through your village."

When one expressed a desire to be "a Christos," he would say, "Be patient. Wait until your feelings are under control. A Christos must give up many enjoyable things because they are evil. He should sacrifice his comfort and give of himself and his substance to help those who are in need. Do not become a Christos until you are resolved to do these things cheerfully, in the name of our Lord. Pray for strength to sacrifice yourself. I shall journey into the neighboring country to teach, but I shall return. While I am gone, meet every day and pray together and discuss what I have told you. The men should lead you in these discussions, taking turns, so that all may have an opportunity. We may discover one whom the Lord is calling to be his priest."

After a time he would return, and those who were firm in their desire to be a Christos were reminded of his former teaching — that a Christos must not only believe in Divine truths, he must live by them. "Faith without morals is a mockery. Unless you are willing to live by God's truth and his code of morals, do not accept Baptism. On the other hand, do not hesitate over some imaginary difficulty. All of you are simple, unlearned people, but God has given you intelligence. None of his truths are beyond your belief, beyond your capacity for faith. We cannot understand how there could be three Persons in one God, but we can believe it because he said it is true. This is a mystery. But Christ is not a mystery. He died to redeem us, rose from the dead and returned to his Father. Is his work done? No. He has been continually at work, offering himself to the Father, that all men, individually, may receive the redemption he won for us. Work with him and you may be assured his offering for you will not be in vain."

When he had received the new Christos into the Church he began planning for their spiritual care. Of the men who had acted as leaders he nominated those who most closely conformed to his standards of qualification, but left the choice to the people. If those who were chosen were willing to accept the responsibility of the priesthood, he would give them a period of concentrated instruction, apprise them of the disappointments and frustrations they should expect, and ordain them. Usually they were given jurisdiction over an area that would leave them "very little time for leisure."

Holding aloft his crucifix, Peter would urge the people to expose a crucifix in their homes and in their places of worship; that when they became despondent over hardship and suffering they were to gaze upon it, "and they will receive the grace from the Divine sufferer to endure them with peaceful resignation."

In this manner, with variations adapted to conditions and circumstances, he evangelized village after village in Gaul, Hispania and the islands of Corsica and Sicily. After an absence of two years he returned to Rome.

While dining with Senator Pudens at his villa, along with Linus and other Church leaders, Peter gave an account of his work.

"So many people became converted I ordained priests to serve them — twelve priests. Make a note of their names, my son, and their villages. Some of these villages had no names so I gave them names — after the Apostles, and Barnabas and Stephen, the first martyr."

"You made it easy for me to find them, Master," Linus said, smiling.

"Priests need guidance as well as the laity," Peter said. "I consecrated two Bishops, Irenaeus in Gaul and Clement in Hispania. I set a new policy for them and the others. They will be roving Bishops, and so arrange their schedules that they will visit each church as their bishopric at least once a year."

"You have a talent for system and order, Master," Pudens said.

"Not a talent, my friend. I was pressed by a grave necessity, like a boatsman in a rough sea, so I put the bow of my boat into the wind, hoping to steady her course. You can improve it, Linus, as conditions require."

"I am highly impressed by Irenaeus and Clement," Linus said. "They have given completely of themselves to the service of the priesthood."

"And both of them have abilities that could shape them to be our successors as head of the Church, particularly Clement. When you succeed me it might be well if you brought him to Rome to be your assistant. It would give him an opportunity to be better known."

"You are looking far into the future, Master," Linus said reflectively.

"It may not be as far as you think, my son, but far or near, we must be ever watchful of our responsibilities."

Pulling at his beard, he went on, "A babe is born and in time he grows in strength and durability. Physically, he becomes mature. That person may become a child in his faith in God and never mature, never thrill to the sublimity of faith or the nobleness of Christian works. It is our obligation to help such people grow by giving them holy, dedicated Bishops and priests."

After a brief silence he continued, "But our guidance sometimes fails. I'll give you an example. One of your converts in Hispania, who became wealthy, asked me to consecrate his son Bishop and give him all of Southeastern Hispania for his bishopric. Somehow, I suppressed my indignation but did not give him an answer. Apparently he construed this as a willingness to par-

ley with him. He boasted how beneficial this would be to the
Church and hinted that it would also be beneficial to me, in a
material way. I was so angry I could have throttled him. He was
shocked by my words and my manner of speech, the same words
our Lord once spoke to me. 'Get behind me Satan!' You are a
scandal to me! The holy offices of the Church shall not be dishonored! In deep anger he strode out of the house — and out of
the Church, he and all of his household. I suppose I should have
been patient and gentle . . ."

"No, Master!" cried Linus. "You were justified!"

"The barter of holy things," said Pudens, reflectively.
"More injurious to the Church than a bloody persecution."

"You are right, my friend," Peter said. "There is dignity
and honor in our offices, and in the hands of unscrupulous men
they could become instruments of unjust power and oppression.
This is a warning to us that other men will seek to control or influence the ordination of priests, the consecration of Bishops and
even the choice of the head of the Church. We must be ever
watchful to repel such encroachments."

Under Pudens' direction, the conversation entered a chan-
nel personal to Peter. "Master," he said smiling, "time is beginning to take its toll even of your rugged body. There is much
more gray in your hair and beard, and your step has lost some of
its spring. We presume to suggest that you cast off some of your
burdens."

"So you would gird me and lead me about," said Peter
with simulated grimness.

"No, no, Master. We would steer you into more peaceful
waters, to use one of your nautical terms — lecturing the young
men for the priesthood — we have more than twenty."

"Twenty?" Excellent!"

"Not doctrine, or the old Law, or philosophy — they are
being well trained in those subjects — but the practical side of

the priesthood that cannot be found in any book. Draw upon your experience; warn them of the dangers to the priesthood, and how they can avoid them."

Peter gazed at Pudens. "A good suggestion," he said. "An excellent suggestion."

"And there is another work, Master, most important for the Church and those who will come after us — a record of our Lord's works and teachings as you remember them. One of your old friends recently came to Rome to help you write it — John Mark."

"John Mark," murmured Peter, his face beaming with pleasure. "Dear John Mark. Let me tell you about him, and his father and mother. What dear friends they were of our Lord's."

For the first time since his twelfth year, Peter's life led him into a field of leisure. He lived at the seminary and apportioned his time to lecturing, dictating to John Mark, reading the Jewish Prophets and other sacred Jewish books, the epistles Paul had written to the various churches, working in the seminary gardens and vineyards, and "trying to learn how to contemplate Divine mysteries."

Following Senator Pudens' suggestion he taught the neophytes how to treat cuts and bruises and sprains and fevers and other bodily ills, and how to compound medicine and balms from herbs. "You must be physician to the body as well as to the spirit," he would say. He instructed them how to cook food, and would set them down to a meal of baked fish or roasted lamb or fowl that he had prepared in whole or in part.

When discussing with John Mark, the Gospel he was about to dictate, Peter said, "Jesus was not a recluse immersed in contemplation of Divine mysteries, he was a man of action, of controlled, appropriate action. And that is the view of him I would like to give the Romans. Being a people of action they should be drawn to him. Let me illustrate.

"One Sabbath there was present in the synagogue a man with a withered arm. Knowing his enemies were watching to see if he would cure the man, Jesus bade him come forth so all could see him, and he said to them, 'Is it lawful to do good or evil on the Sabbath?' They would not answer him. He said to the man, 'Stretch forth your hand.' He did so and his hand was cured. Now, Jesus could have cured the man with a thought but he had two purposes in mind: to prove to the people he had the power to cure and that it was lawful to do so on the Sabbath."

"I understand," John said thoughtfully.

Peter's manner of speech was positive and sometimes abrupt, but in dictating to John Mark he spoke slowly, thoughtfully, feeling for the word that would most precisely express his meaning. Only once did he depart from the third to the first person, and then his tone became severe, his words rasped in self condemnation.

"When the Lord told us we would be scandalized in him that night I cried out boastfully that even if all of the others were scandalized I would not be. He gazed at me with eyes that seemed to pierce my soul, yet they were eyes of sadness, not indignation. He said that before the cock had crowed twice I would deny him three times. I said even louder and more vehemently that even if I were to die with him I would never deny him. The words of a braggart, the ranting of a vain, proud man who craved to be hailed as superior to his brother Apostles. John got me entrance into the high priest's courtyard. A maidservant said to me that I was a follower of Jesus. I growled at her that I knew not what she was talking about. Later she said to others standing about that I was one of them. Again I denied it, louder than before. Then one of the men standing by the fire said to me that I was one of them; that my speech disclosed me to be a Galilean. In a rage I cried out that I knew not Jesus. But I did mention his name. I used an Aramaic word of contempt to describe a worthless person. I said . . ."

"Do not tell me what you said," interrupted John Mark.

"The worst crime ever committed," muttered Peter. "Ashamed to have them know I followed him."

"You no longer believed he was the son of God," John said. "All of you had ceased to believe."

"None of us ever believed that — in its proper sense. Jesus often spoke of his Father in heaven, said that he and the Father were one, but he never told us who he was — his true self, I mean. I now realize he desired us to discover it . . . to grow into that truth by ourselves and — and to do it so gradually we would not be astonished by it — its immensity."

"Master, you must have progressed rapidly on that road to truth. When all of your brethren remained silent you cried out, 'You are the Christ, the Son of the living God.' "

"That was a thought in the right direction but I was far from grasping the full truth." Silent for a while, he continued in a tone of awe: "God becoming a man — like all other men — a man so poor he had to work at an humble trade to earn a livelihood — God who created the world having to shape wood into a plow or a bench — that was too much for us. God suffering hunger and thirst and weariness, and pain of body and mind. And finally giving himself — giving himself to the shameful death by crucifixion — yes, it was just too much for us, my son. It was overwhelming — like trying to pour the water of Lake Gennesaret into a wine jug."

"That being true, Master, you exaggerate your offense. You might have been guilty of ingratitude, or discourtesy, even of cowardice, but not of sin. It is no sin to deny knowing a man."

"It was sinful to deny a man like Jesus!" Peter declared. "The most scarlet of sins! A man of perfect holiness and purity, a man of love and compassion, the likes of whom the world has never seen, utterly free from the faintest breath of sin — Godlike in all of his thoughts and actions — specially chosen by God for some great work. This is the man I recognized, even though I was too dull to understand that he was the Son of God."

"You are too emotional to judge your degree of guilt," John Mark said. "I do not think you were ashamed, neither did any of your brother Apostles. When Jesus said he would be rejected by the people and be crucified, you cried out that such a fate would never befall him. Not to contradict him, Master, you loved him so much that the thought of such a death was so horrible you impulsively rejected it."

"I was horrified."

"You objected to Jesus washing your feet. You loved him so much you wished to spare him what you thought would be a humiliation."

"That is true, my son."

"And when he gave himself into the hands of his enemies . . ."

"I was overwhelmed! He could have overcome them with a look but he seemingly abandoned his great mission and gave himself up to death. I was disappointed, frustrated, crushed. Perhaps on my own account, but vastly more on his account. He could have risen so high, accomplished so much good in the world. I suppose I was irritated, as well, as I would have been at King David had I lived in his time, and he had given up Israel's crown for a flock of sheep on a hillside."

"All because you loved him so much," John said.

"Perhaps I spoke out of regard for myself, or in fear."

"One who feared would not have followed him into the courtyard of the high Priest, and only one who loved him much would have so sincerely repented. Would you tell me about that repentance, Master?"

"I will if you promise not to record what I say."

"I promise, reluctantly. I think men would be helped if they could read about it." John Mark listened attentively. For half an hour Peter related his experiences of that night. John Mark shook his head in wonder. "All this," he cried, "because you had denied a holy person whom you believed to be only a man. Grave may have been your fault, stupendous was your repentance. It burned out every trace of guilt and became a holocaust of love. It brought you in remorse to the shadow of his cross. Now I understand why your brother Apostles say you loved Jesus more than they."

"Oh now how could they say that? John showed far more love than I. He remained with Jesus until the end."

"They had in mind what Jesus asked you after his resurrection, if you loved him more than they did. They believed that was his way of saying you did love him more, and that in recognition of your love he declared your primacy over them and bade you feed his lambs and his sheep."

Peter shook his head. "That is mere fancy, my son. The elder and the younger James died for him and probably some of the others. What greater love could one have, to use our Lord's own words."

"They then had come to believe he was the Son of God," John said. "We are speaking of your love for him as a man. When he was seized all save you and John fled in fear. That was a sign of a great love, Master."

"John remained with Jesus until the end," Peter repeated. "He is the one who loved him the most."

"Master, in your generosity you overlook your repentance. It was inspiring. It was the sign of a great love."

"I hope it was, my son."

"And ever since then you have been at peace, contrary to tales that your grief had never ceased and at times was driving you mad."

"How baseless were those tales," Peter said. "One of them

had me in a frenzy of despair whenever I heard a cock crow. As if a crowing cock were necessary to remind me of my sin. Not a day passes that I do not think of it, not in despair — that would be a rejection of God's mercy — but in gratitude for his forgiveness."

"Your faith has given you peace," John Mark said.

"It has," Peter agreed. "Yet how difficult it was for me — faith is a mystery. Rather, its acceptance by man is a mystery. Some accept it in one climactic instant. Faith came to Paul like a flash of lightning. But I — I resisted faith, like a dumb ox shaking off a goad. At times I seemed to have flashes of faith, like the time Jesus asked us, "Who do you say I am? I cried out, 'You are the Christ, the Son of the living God.' I believed that. Yet I know now that I did not understand. Often he told us he would be crucified and would rise on the third day. We seemed to believe but we did not understand. God could not be crucified. Dead men do not rise unless God gives one the power to raise them, as Jesus himself was given. Not until we saw his empty tomb did John and I believe he had risen, but it was a bewildered belief and the others could not believe. And of course, Jesus knew that. When he appeared to us on the night of his resurrection he chided us for our unbelief. My faith — it has grown stronger through the years. The great mystery — God a spirit became united with human nature — he entered into a human body — he remained a Divine person, but with two natures — divine and human nature — and in his human nature he suffered and died for the salvation of men. But how this came to be — why God demanded such a supreme sacrifice — that I do not understand. I have been so steadily engaged in teaching faith in these mysteries I have not had time for contemplation of them. But he will raise up men to make them better known."

Silent for a while, John Mark said, "I have often contemplated these mysteries and I have discussed them with Paul.

He says that because Christ was tempted he sympathizes with us when we are tempted, and helps us if we try to resist temptation."

"What a consoling thought," Peter said. "In my weakness I felt hurt when Jesus reproved me with such severity — at the washing of feet, when he bade me put up my sword, when he called me Satan, and on other occasions. But in time I realized that my sentiments were contrary to his mission and that my failure to understand this required a stern correction. I ceased sorrowing for myself. The truth opened up to me. I try to be patient with one who has difficulty believing God is asking far more from him than he did from us. As to the Gospel, my son, I yield to your judgment when you write of my denial. Say only that I wept."

John Mark began talking of "our beloved Israel," and the loneliness of the Israelite who is obliged to live apart from his native province.

"How truly you speak," said Peter, wistfully. "Galilee — the Lake country. Until I was almost twenty they meant nothing special to me. Then, suddenly, I discovered them.

"We had fished all night with scarcely a catch. My father let the boat drift and I fell asleep. I awoke to see shafts of light slowly mounting behind the Cobalt hills — light of a hundred different shades and hues, soft, glowing, radiant — the advance guard of the sun — gradually illuminating the entire Eastern sky, penetrating the darkness about the western hills, shimmering on the placid bosom of Gennesaret.

"My father dipped his oars, nudging the boat shoreward — through a lily bed. What a delightful odor it gave off. Closer to shore, from a growth of vegetation, other odors came down wind — cinnamon, pomegranate, balsam, pine — seductive, beguiling. How good to live in the Lake country. Widespread were its arms, expansive was its breast. Here men were free, uncrowded, at liberty to wander over its hills. Protective hills! Shielding us in winter from Hermon's icy blasts; soothing us in summer by winds flowing down their canyons. Cool, gentle winds, violent stormy winds, that would churn Gennesaret into a sea of raging billows. In this wise did upper Galilee introduce herself to me — a land of moods and colors and aromatic odors, adaptable to the moods of men — his craving for adventure, his love of fellowship, his desire for solitude, his wonderment that God could be so good to men."

*   *   *

Peter gave more time to lecturing the neophytes and he gave a practical tone to his lectures.

"Teach your people that faith in Christ and belief in all his teachings are not of themselves, sufficient for salvation. They must live those teachings. Remind them that we are so inclined to be self-sufficient, to be independent of all persons, even of God, that total submission to him will require strong self-discipline and humility.

"But after you have taught your people and they ignore you, what will you do? Become discouraged? Frustrated? Say to them in your mind: go to hell? Yes, you will probably do that. But if you are true soldiers of Christ you will fight on and on until you are weary in body and exhausted in mind, even though you are a broken reed shaking in the wind, even though you are a lone voice crying in the wilderness."

Several times a week Crito, a scribe of Linus, would come to the seminary with letters for Peter, and occasionally with a visitor. One afternoon as he walked in the garden he observed Crito and another riding up the drive, but not until they had dismounted and were approaching him did he give them attention. Suddenly he cried out: "Ignatius! Ignatius! My son!"

Hurrying toward each other the young man and the old man fell into an affectionate embrace.

In the privacy of Peter's room, in his direct manner, Ignatius gently cut through the ceremonial courtesy of the older man and said, "Master, I desire to be a priest. I came to Rome to be ordained by you."

"You give me great joy," gasped Peter.

"For three years I have been preparing for ordination. To obtain a clear meaning of the Prophets and other sacred books I learned to read Hebrew. I have pondered the sayings of Jesus which you taught me and as written by Matthew in his Gospel. I believe Jesus is the Son of God, the second Person of the Holy Trinity, that he was conceived by the Holy Spirit and became man of the Virgin Mary so that he might suffer and die to redeem men from the effects of sin."

Peter gazed into the young man's face. "Your profession of faith is most inspiring," he said. "I accept it with joy. Intellectually and spiritually you are ready for the priesthood, but I suggest that you wait a while, until you learn our rituals and know the sacrifices you will probably be obliged to make."

"One sacrifice I have decided to make, Master. I wish to remain a celibate even though that is not required. I wish to give myself wholly to the Church."

"I believed that would be your choice," Peter said.

After Ignatius had been ordained Peter asked him, "Where would you prefer to serve, my son?"

"Wherever you send me, Master. But I do find Rome most interesting."

"The most interesting of all cities, save one," Peter said musingly. "I thought of sending you to Antioch. You know the people there. They might readily respond to your teaching."

"I would gladly serve in Antioch."

"I have another reason. The Church began in the East — in

Palestine, and spread into Asia Minor. Antioch became its heart. So much so that after Christianity came to Rome the churches in Asia became known as the Eastern Church and those in Rome and surrounding countries, the Western Church. I do not like that. It implies disunity. There is but one Church — a worldwide Church. If this idea becomes widespread actual disunity may result."

"There is substantial ground for your concern, Master," Ignatius said.

"Most of the Church elders agree that Rome should be the Seat of Church government, but others, motivated by justifiable pride and sentiment, assert that Antioch should have what they conceive to be an honor. A few of my Jewish friends hope that Jerusalem will be the center of Christianity. They fail to realize that we are not bestowing an honor but establishing a policy that should be most beneficial to the Church for centuries to come."

"Your foresight should be commended, Master."

"Thank you, my son," Peter said smiling appreciatively. "All of us, priests and laity, should do what we can to strengthen the Church, according to our abilities. We have priests who cannot read or write, yet in their humble way they are winning pagans to the true faith. You, my son, are highly gifted, intellectually and spiritually, and you have the ability to communicate your thoughts so you will be understood. The Church will have need of you — to defend her doctrines, to expose heresy, to strengthen her discipline. Should she call upon you to assume the burdens of a bishopric, do not refuse."

"Do you anticipate so much turmoil in the Church, Master?"

The Church will never be wholly at peace," Peter said. "Our Lord told us that he came not to send peace upon earth but a sword, to set a man at variance with his father and a daughter with her mother; that a man's enemies will be those of his own household. But he also gave us words of hope: 'He who loses his life for my sake will find it.' "

"Master, in one of your lectures you warned us of corruption in the Church, corruption in personal conduct as well as in teaching. That disturbed me very much."

"Keep in mind the weakness of our nature," Peter said. "The Apostles closest to our Lord, in varying degrees, were plagued by contention, ambition, envy and the desire to gain some advantage over their brothers. We must expect to find the same weaknesses in other disciples, who were not privileged to associate with him. These corruptions are disturbing but let us fight to expose them and keep intact her pristine purity."

"I come not to send peace upon earth, but a sword." In a reflective tone Ignatius quoted the words of Christ. Then he said, "Now I understand. He made us warriors against all things that would contradict his word."

25

Martyrdom of Brother Andrew

ONCE or twice a week Linus would counsel with Peter at the seminary on the more important matters of Church government. Discussing these meetings with his father, Senator Pudens, he commented on Peter's "Hebrew sagacity." He has had no schooling, scarcely no experience in trade or commerce, yet his intellectual discernments are keen and farsighted; he is sound in his judgments of men and events. He withholds judgment until he knows all of the facts and has weighed them as carefully as a jeweler appraises gems."

"He says he is not sagacious, only wary from many mistakes," the Senator replied.

"I doubt if he was ever the brusque impulsive domineering person he has portrayed for us."

"I believe he was, my son. I have seen evidence of it. He is an example of how restraint and self-discipline can mold an unstable man into a tower of strength."

"He dominates! We must yield to his word."

"Not his word — the Word of his Lord. He declared, Rome is the center of the world. It shall be the heart of his Church."

But on one of his conferences Peter was so inattentive, so engrossed with unrelated matters, that Linus inquired, "Master, is something troubling you?"

Peter gazed at him blankly, then he said, "I dreamed last night — of Andrew — insignificant things, dreams, but this — Andrew seemed to be on Lake Gennesaret — in a light fog. He was calling to me but I could understand only a few words, my name — 'Simon' and something about a storm and to guard against it. He could be dead, but I do not regard this dream as a sign. But it did stir up old memories. Repeat what you are saying, my son. I will be more attentive."

After the conference, as they stood in front of Peter's hut waiting for Linus' horse, they observed a cart approaching. "Crispus," exclaimed Linus, "but I do not recognize his companion."

Upon alighting, the stranger, a lean middle-aged swarthy man, bowed respectfully and said, "Master, I am Silvanus, a disciple of the holy Apostle Andrew. God has called him to his bosom, but I mourn the manner of his death — by crucifixion, on the oblique cross."

Peter stood with bowed head; he wiped his eyes with the back of his hand. Embracing Silvanus, he said, "Come in, my son, and tell us your sad story."

From the cart Silvanus removed a leather-covered jacket which he unfolded, and gave Peter a wooden crucifix. "Your saintly brother bade me bring this to you, Master. The figure of our Lord he carved himself."

Peter gazed at the figure, then holding it for his companions to see, he cried out, "This is reality! How sad and anguished is the face! Observe the blood trickling from his thorn-crowned head, the taut, distorted muscles of his arms and legs, his wide open mouth, his lips parched by the horrible thirst! How bruised his chest from the scourges! Just as John described it to us. What delicate skill guided my brother's untrained hand. I wish the whole world could see! Accept this as a mark of my love, O Lord!" He reverently kissed the feet of the figure.

Linus and Silvanus and Crispus likewise venerated the crucifix.

From Silvanus they learned that for over a year the Christians in Pontus, Galatia, Cappadocia, Asia and Bithynia had suffered imprisonment, confiscation of property and death for their faith. When Andrew protested to the rulers in their defense he was seized and crucified on an X-shaped cross. "Master, I spare you from the painful details of his suffering."

Peter broke a lengthy silence. "Brother, counselor, friend," he murmured. "He loved deeply. My welfare was his chief concern. I mourn his death, yet it was no surprise. Of the Twelve all are believed to be dead save John, Jude and myself, most of them probably martyred. But their blood is not wasted. It will make fertile in faith the stony ground for unbelief."

Speaking of the persecuted Christians, he said, "I should go to them, but my heart holds me here. Little consolation will they receive from a letter but at least they will know we love them. I shall have it for you, my son, when you are prepared to return."

To John Mark he began dictating: "Peter, an Apostle of Jesus Christ, to the sojourners of the dispersion in Pontus, Galatia, Cappadocia, Asia and Bithynia . . ."

He encouraged them to endure persecution and suffering out of love for their Divine Lord, to be faithful to his teachings and charitable to one another. "Charity covers a multitude of sins." He paid tribute to their dignity as Christian persons. "You are a chosen race, a royal priesthood, a holy nation, a purchased people, that you may proclaim the perfections of him who called you out of darkness into his blessed light."

When Silvanus had departed, Peter grieved so much over Andrew's death that he decided to resume his former way of life.

"I should be reconciled," he said to Linus. "I know he is with God, and our association has been severed for many years, yet knowing he lived was a comfort. I could go to him or communicate by letter. But death — how final it is, and so — so irrevocable. It severs the closest of ties and leaves you with a sense of irreparable loss.''

"Our Lord said that he who loses his life for his sake will find life,'' Linus said.

"True. I am grieving for myself, not Andrew. How gentle he was and so good, with an unerring perception of the good in others. The first time he met Jesus he recognized him to be Messiah, he and John. But when he told me he had found Messiah I laughingly scoffed at him and asked how many soldiers did he have. Much of his life he spent trying to refine me, to rid me of my grossness.''

"How blessed you were to have such a brother,'' Linus said.

"How blessed I shall not fully know until I join him. Until then I shall carry on in the way he would advise me. Let us make preparations for my journey into the North Country.''

Unforeseen events obstructed his plans. One afternoon Linus and Joseph came to the seminary, their panting, sweating horses bespeaking their urgency. Peter stood aghast while they reported that Rome had been burning since early the previous evening. The Jewish quarter near the Capena Gate was destroyed and the district about the Circus Maximus was threatened with destruction. Flames were roaring up the Aventine and Caelian Hills. The people were in a panic. All efforts to extinguish the fire had failed.

"What is being done to help our people? All the people?'' Peter inquired.

He was informed that many had fled to the fields beyond the city. Tents and food were being supplied by the government. Country places owned by Senator Pudens and Joseph had been made available and tented camps were in the making.

"We can shelter a large number on the seminary grounds!''

declared Peter. "That was also my thought, Master," Linus said. "I have notified our people to take refuge here."

"Then we must have food, tents."

"My father has been promised help by the Minister of Public Safety. It should begin arriving early in the morning so you need not enter the city, Master."

Joseph had a suggestion: "Master, I remember the sanitary camps you provided during the expulsion of the Jews. A half score of workmen, with tools and equipment, are on the way from my farm to assist you."

"You think of everything," said Peter. "We'll begin at once with what help we have."

Calling together the neophytes, the instructors and the workmen, he told them about the fire and the necessity to prepare for the refugees. "We have about six hours of daylight," he said, "so let us make the most of it. Gather all your garden and vineyard tools. I will direct you where and how to work."

During the night, until mid-morning, more than five hundred refugees had come to the seminary. The women and children were housed in the living quarters. The men were given tools to assist in the work. At dawn, under the guidance of Senator Pudens himself, army wagons arrived with tents and food supplies. These were followed by the wagons and workmen from Joseph's farm.

During that day more than a hundred tents had been erected and assigned to the people, food and water and firewood had been apportioned. To satisfy the demands for water in the torrid heat, two wells were being dug. And during that day, garbed only in a knee-length linen tunic that became plastered to his torso from excessive sweating, Peter was constantly on the move, supervising the erection of tents, the distribution of food and water, the development of the sanitary system, consoling and encouraging the people.

"This is your city," he said to them. "Make rules for its government and choose your rulers to enforce them, for I must be absent much of the time visiting our brethren in other camps. Be watchful of sanitation, lest your health be endangered."

Realizing he had not slept for a night and two days, Peter's friends urged him to rest and take some food. "I am eating," he replied showing them half a loaf of black bread upon which he had been gnawing. "I'll rest after awhile." Finally Senator Pudens intervened. "Sit in the shade of this tree, Master," he said, and Peter sat. A servant brought him a bowl of hot meat stew and a small pot of wine. "How good that smells," he said appreciatively.

Pudens excused himself so Peter might eat in privacy. When he returned an hour later he found him asleep, snoring loudly. He was awakened by the July sun shining in his face.

That morning, accompanied by one of the neophytes, riding horses, he began a visitation of all the camps where "his people" Christians and Jews, were living.

Rome burned for nine days, destroying ten of its fourteen districts. The residential areas of the rich and the powerful on the Palatine, Capitoline and Pincian Hills were spared. So was the Trastevere, wherein festered the Jewish ghetto.

Into the Trastevere, Peter made his way in search of old friends. He found Nicodemus ministering to a congregation twice its normal size, an overflow from the devastated areas. "The Lord has protected us in this area," the aging priest said to Peter.

"He remembers that you were the man who first made him known to the Romans," Peter said.

Peter also found Ebulus, who had trafficked in idols. He had prospered in his weaving. "We have twice the number of looms, Master, and we also make military tents. And the Lord has blessed us in other ways."

"With six children, Nicodemus told me."

"Oh, I am not underestimating that blessing, Master. I meant in a business way. I was tempted to buy some property — would have brought me a good rental, but I held off, and then the fire broke out."

"And the poor have benefited from your good fortune."

"Not very much, Master. And we have been blessed in another way. The most important of all — with the gift of faith. We are Christians now. I finally saw how the teachings of Jesus were a fulfillment of the old Law."

"I wish all of our people could be so blessed," Peter said.

He preached in the churches and visited other friends. Occasionally he would see a house where had lived an old friend, but which was now occompied by a stranger, and he would pass on with a pang of sadness.

One day he paused in front of a tavern above the door of which crouched a shiny brass lion. "Someone told me he owned such a tavern here," he muttered, "but I can't remember — why, it was — it was Askar! He boasted that a Jew could always obtain genuine Kosher food. Askar, you rogue, you man of good heart. I'll probably never see you again." He moved on. A hand on his shoulder stayed him. A man's voice said, "You look weary, Rabbi. Come in and have a glass of wine with me."

"Askar!" he gasped. "Or am I dreaming?"

"You've been dreaming, for thirty years," twitted Askar.

He conducted Peter up a stairway to a room furnished with a table, chairs and a couch. A glass window, something most rare, looked down upon a small garden. "You have elegant taste, my son," he said.

Sitting Peter upon the couch, Askar lifted his feet to a chair. A servant entered with wine and withdrew. Askar placed a cup of wine in Peter's hand. "I hope this will revive you, Rabbi," he said. "You seem quite dull."

"God brought us together again," Peter said, "so I might thank you for your generous gift."

"Chance, Rabbi, mere chance. I was in the North Country two days from Rome where I have some stone and marble quarries. Word came to me of the fire, so I hurried here to protect my property, but I was too late."

"I regret that, my son."

Askar shrugged. "One should not expect the dice always to roll in his favor."

Peter gazed at Askar. "Fifteen years," he murmured, shaking his head, "yet you have scarcely changed."

"I am living a more virtuous life."

"Your generous gift — it brought relief to many who were in need."

"I intended it for you."

"Oh, I didn't stint myself. I never expected to see you again."

"Meeting you was no great surprise. I heard you were back in Rome and I knew you frequently came to the Jewish quarter. It was just a question of time."

"Then you should have come to me," chided Peter.

"And have you try to convert me?"

"Did I ever try to do that?"

"You are older now, and less tolerant, I'm sure. Besides, I come here only a couple of times a year. I have been living on my island, a delightful place. I do wish you would make it your home. After your years of wandering, you're entitled to rest and leisure."

"I'll have plenty of leisure in heaven."

Askar laughed, hilariously. Then, becoming serious, he said, "I fear you may be faced with the most severe trial of your life. The fire has enraged the Roman people. They seek someone to blame, so they looked upward, to the Imperial throne. Two days ago a mob stormed up to the Palatine and beat upon the palace gates. Nero came out expecting to quiet them with promises of games and more food, but they reviled him, cursed him, called him a buffoon, and charged him with murdering his mother. But what frightened Nero was the accusation that he had set fire to Rome, so he could build a new city and name it after himself."

Peter gravely pondered how this might affect his people.

Askar had a definite opinion of its effect. "Nero is a coward, with a coward's low cunning. He will point his syphilitic finger at another — at the Christians or at the Jews, or both the Christians and Jews."

Peter stared at Askar aghast. He recalled how the occasional public quarreling of the Jews over religion had been grossly exaggerated into incidents threatening to the state and resulted in their expulsion. But the burning of the city, with all of its attendant horrors of death, injury and vast destruction of homes and property! If the Jews and Christians should be blamed — Askar supplemented his thought. "Nero has ways to divert from him the anger of the people — wily servants with promises of more games and more food, the employment of men to rebuild the city, the Roman's deep distrust of the Jews and their hatred of the so-called Jewish religious cult which is practiced in different forms by Jews and Christians. Rabbi, you recall the abominable charges made against the Jews in the past. They could be revived. They could be disastrous. Of course, none of this may come to pass, but you should make preparations for protecting your people."

"What shall I do?" cried Peter. "Oh, Lord, direct me what to do."

He consulted with Senator Pudens. Peter was greatly concerned over his people.

"Master, your friend did not exaggerate. Nero probably could turn the people against us and the Jews. But the severity of

punishment — how widespread — possibly only to the Church
leader — you, the priests . . ."

"Oh if he would be satisfied with punishing only me!"
cried Peter.

"I have a few friends — I shall inquire."

Whether through fear or ignorance, Senator Pudens received no information from his friends. They were disinclined to
discuss the matter. When Peter was so informed, he turned to
Linus and said, "We must act now as if we were sure of danger.
To protect the succession of the earthly head of the Church, I
wish you would leave for Gaul or Hispania on the first ship."

"And leave you alone to combat this danger?" protested
Linus.

"If there be danger, my son, I will not be alone. But do not
consider me, only the welfare of the Church. This I desire. This I
command in the name of our Lord Jesus Christ."

"I shall obey you, Master," Linus said humbly.

"If I die, do not return until the danger has passed. Where
you abide will be the seat of Church government."

To protect Senator Pudens, Peter avoided his house and
lived alternately for two or three days with Joseph and with
Nicodemus. Since nothing could be learned from those above he
turned an attentive ear to those below — the people in the street.
Shortly after dawn he would go forth, strolling aimlessly, or
standing near men in conversation or at work removing debris
from the ruins, listening the while for a word that might be a
warning signal. At midday he would sit on the ground and eat a
crust of bread, a bit of fruit, and drink watered wine from a flask.

Days passed. He heard no word. He might never hear such
a word. Peace stealthily linked arms with him. Then suddenly it
was disjoined. A Praetorian guardsman, strutting about the
Forum, bellowed from his alcoholic mouth: "The Christians to
the lions! The Christians burned Rome!" In chorus his three

companions echoed him. "Throw the Christians to the lions! The Christians burned Rome!" Laborers paused in their work and stared at them; merchants and customers exchanged troubled words. Peter heard: "If the guard says it, it must be true. Christians, they feed on human flesh and blood!" He sank weakly upon the base of a statue; sweat broke from his forehead; in anguish he pawed at his beard. "Oh, no, Lord," he moaned. "Save them from the lion's claw."

Strength gradually welled up in him. He rose and cried out in astonishment upon recognizing the statue of Mars, the Roman God of War, from which he had first preached to the Romans. "Twenty years," he murmured. "Thousands now bend their knee at mention of your holy name."

Then, realizing one must work with God as well as pray to him, he said, "Oh, Lord, direct me what to do. Give me the courage to do it and the wisdom to do it well. If I do not respond to your guidance, inspire others to prod me into the right way."

With resolute feet he strode up Pincian Hill to the villa of Senator Pudens, subconsciously wondering why God had saved the homes of the rich and the powerful, while punishing the poor. "But did God actually do that?" he pondered. "How much do the ways of men intermingle with the ways of God and bring about a good end as well as an evil one? Oh, Lord, how inscrutable is your will."

With grave countenance, Senator Pudens overheard Peter relate what he had heard. "I agree with you, my friend. This seems to have been instigated by our enemies to rouse the people against us. If a sufficient number respond—" he shook his head, and said, "I can suggest no appropriate action to combat the conspiracy, but one thing we should not do — make this known prematurely to our people lest they be thrown into a panic with tragic results to themselves."

"You speak wisely, my friend," Peter said. "But the inaction! How difficult for me to be idle while the storm gathers. I wonder if Askar could suggest something."

Askar concurred in the idea of a probable persecution. "I have heard the same thing as you in other sections of the city. It is becoming widespread. Christians will be thrown to the lions. But you need not be inactive, Rabbi. You can save many of your people!"

"How, in God's name?

"Go underground. Lead them into the catacombs."

"The catacombs?" gasped Peter. "The burial vaults?"

"Under Roman law the catacombs are protected from desecration and invasion. Lead your people into the catacombs. Their discomfort will be great but they will be secure."

During his residence in Rome, Peter had learned that the origin of the catacombs could be traced to Jewish captives of Pompey who had been brought to Rome. Their respect for the body of him who had been a person, a believer in the true God, forbade their following the Roman custom of cremation. They interred their dead in tunnels carved out of the soft tuffa soil. The Christians interred their dead in the same manner.

"They could be reasonably comfortable," he said tentatively, "but would the Rabbis permit it?"

"Will a mountain crumble at your command?" snorted Askar.

"You might persuade them, my son."

"How child-like you can be, Rabbi. In their eyes I am a renegade. You must rely upon yourself."

"And God," added Peter.

"Poor God. How you burden him with your troubles."

Peter confided his fears to Nicodemus. "We should do as Askar suggested," he said, "act boldly! I would have you go with me to Rabbi Josephus."

"He is not friendly," said Nicodemus.

"You thought he seemed friendly when we attended his father's funeral."

"I was wrong. I heard him say that of all the Christian leaders you had most injured Judaism."

"He may have spoken in sorrow for the synagogue, not out of enmity for me."

"He is forceful. He could influence the other Rabbis against you . . ."

"I know. But my appeal first to him he might regard as a recognition of his superior influence. And he might also perceive he was being given opportunity to rise above petty disputes and be of service to God and man."

Nicodemus shook his head dubiously. "You must have deep insight into his character," he said, "or perhaps you will resort to subtle flattery.

"A little of both perhaps. Sometimes they blend well."

Rabbi Josephus received Peter with reserved cordiality. In a low formal tone he thanked him for attending his father's funeral. Peter expressed his fears of a Christian persecution. In a tone of sympathetic interest, Rabbi Josephus interrupted him. "I, too, have heard men voice that slander, men of substance and position. It troubled me. It could grow and grow until it becomes a formal accusation."

"That is our fear, Rabbi Josephus," Peter said. "We are seeking means to protect our people . . ."

"And I wondered about that, too." The Rabbi's tone bespoke deep concern. "If such a persecution became widespread, hundreds, even thousands of the innocent might be slain. How could they be saved? And then it came to me, like a flash. Shelter them in our catacombs!"

Peter stared at the Rabbi. "Would you . . . ?" he cried out. Then recovering himself, he said, "Pardon my astonishment, dear Rabbi. I failed to discern your innate goodness. Brother

Nicodemus and I — another — a son of Abraham advised us that the catacombs were protected by law from invasion and to lead our people into them. We feared you might oppose us, but we hoped that by prayers and pleading we might overcome your opposition . . ."

Rising, he crossed the room to where Josephus was sitting and placing a hand on each of his shoulders, cried out, "Again I pray your forgiveness. Why should I be astonished? Do you not preach the love of God, even as I? You are a noble son of Abraham. I feel honored to be in your presence."

Rabbi Josephus rose and embraced Peter.

"We work for the same ends, Rabbi Simon," he said, "the love of God and men. I shall be pleased to work with you. I shall consult with your brother Rabbis and let you know their decision."

The following morning, Rabbi Josephus talked with them in the home of Nicodemus. "All of my brother Rabbis agree that your people should be given shelter in our burial vaults," he said. "Later today Baruch ben-David will come to you. He is skilled in excavations. You will need numerous large rooms, with air vents and security from flooding and provisions for sanitation. He will need many workmen, who must be paid for their labor. We will help you in that, if . . ."

"Thank you, my friend," Peter said. "For the present, at least, we can pay them."

After the Rabbi's departure, Peter hastened to the Royal Lion in search of Askar but was delayed over an hour in seeing him. "A builder wishes to buy all of the stone from my quarry," he explained. "How did you make out with the Rabbis!"

When Peter had told him Askar said, with a tone of raillery, "What sanctimonious flattery. You're a man for all situations. But you have overlooked one thing — food. The government would not feed people they wish to feed to the lions, and besides, it would reveal their hiding places in the catacombs."

"How did I overlook food?" muttered Peter.

"Mountains of food and an orderly system of distribution. You've got your hands full, Rabbi."

At a meeting of the Church leaders and Joseph with Baruch ben-David, plans were made for enlarging the catacombs, the collection of food and furnishings and the solicitation of money to pay the expense. The work began without delay in many areas of the city and at the seminary, wholly unobserved by Roman officials. With so much activity in progress, clearing of burnt buildings and preparing for new construction the nature of their operation was never suspected.

26

Peter Blesses the Prisoners

PETER prayed for time, "For one more day, for one more day." When he had been given nearly a score of days, the Lord let it be known that there would be no more days. Time had run out. Praetorian guards raided the tented camps, seized men and women who would not deny they were Christians and herded them into underground prisons.

Immediately men, women and children began leaving the camps, not in panic or hysteria but orderly, for they had been forewarned of the danger and had been assigned to particular places of refuge. The retreats were dark and damp and over-crowded; the air was musty and sanitation facilities were inade-quate, but they were grateful and offered prayers of thanksgiving for their deliverance from a torturous death.

And time ran out for the cowering, impatient Nero. Heralds rode through the city and the camps announcing that Imperial Caesar had declared the morrow to be a holiday for all of his beloved subjects. They were invited to attend the games in the new circus he had built where the enemies of the empire would contend with the wild beasts of the jungle. Meat and bread and wine would be served free to all who attended the games.

Against the urgent pleas of his friends, Peter was on his way to one of the camps when he heard this announcement. The shock of it overwhelmed him, and to keep from falling he sat upon the ground. "Contend with the beasts of the jungle," he muttered, "Women and children. Oh the wickedness of it!" His imagination conjured scenes of horror. "If God permits this to be, some good will surely come from it. Perhaps a strengthening of faith in men yet unborn."

Regaining his strength, Peter continued to the camp where he mingled with his people and spoke to them words of encouragement. "If any of you should be seized for slaughter in the arena, offer yourselves to Christ with love and resignation. Encourage one another to put on this spiritual robe of offering. Keep in mind that he could save you, even as he once saved me. If he does not, if he permits you to suffer this horrible death, he does so for a purpose. It is within his plan for your salvation and the salvation of ther men. He will be choosing you. The world will not know you. Total obscurity will be your lot. You will be regarded as creatures without attraction, without endowments. But you will not be obscured to Christ. He will know you, he will give you his love a hundredfold."

While grateful for his solicitude, the people feared for his safety and urged him to hide in one of the catacombs.

"And become a mole?" he asked with a gentle smile. "No, my children. Our Lord bade me do this work, but in doing it I shall keep a watchful eye and an attentive ear."

But he did agree not to go forth until after dark, and when he departed for Nicodemus' house he was escorted by three stalwart young men.

Askar was waiting for him when he arrived. "Ah, my son," Peter said sadly, "You knew whereof you spoke."

"Rabbi, do you intend going into the circus?"

"I shall if necessary for my children to see me when I bless them."

"Then you should cut your hair and shave your beard."

"Shave my beard!" cried Peter indignantly.

"How strange that you of all people should be so vain over a bush of hair on your face."

"The beard is our ancient honored custom! It marks me for what I am, a son of Abraham!"

"The Romans identify the leader of the Christians as an old Jew with long white hair and beard. You would surely be recognized. You should at least shorten them and dye them black."

"I'll not have time."

"Come with me to my apartment. My barber is waiting. You shall sleep there."

Peter shook his head, marveling. "You think of everything," he said.

As they breakfasted together, Askar said in a bantering tone, "You look years younger. What a handsome fellow you must have been, with many women in your life, no doubt."

"Six," said Peter tersely. "My mother, my two grandmothers, my sister, my wife and my wife's mother."

For the first time in their numerous discussions Askar was silenced. After a while he said, "Forgive my obnoxious levity in this trying hour." After another silence he spoke again, "If you entered the arena you would cry out in horror and betray yourself. So we must use trickery."

Rising, he removed some garments from a closet. "Try these on, Rabbi," he said. Peter donned a sleeveless knee-length soft leather tunic and bound it about his waist with a leather thong. Into two front pockets Askar placed a palmful of nails, slipped a hammer into a socket on one side and a hand-saw into a slot on the other. "Now you're a carpenter," he said.

Peter stared at him, amazed. "Forgive my seeming doubt," he said, "but I hope you know what you're doing."

Askar put on a tunic similarly equiped and said, "The weather is quite warm, so we'll not need shirts. Yes, I think I

248 UPON THIS ROCK

know what I'm about. You see, I am skilled in deception."

They proceeded to the circus, which was not fully completed, and stopped near a wide entrance, near which stood a pile of timbers and a pile of logs each about two cubits in height.

"The prisoners will approach down this street," Askar said, "and will enter through this gate. The man sawing a log has been employed in building the circus. We shall begin sawing a log or a timber and when we see the prisoners coming you shall stand on one of these piles so you may look into their faces and they will recognize you. There is no reason why the guards should not accept us for what we appear to be. But if some unforeseen incident should threaten you, this fellow and I shall attempt to confuse those involved so you may lose yourself in the crowd."

Peter shook his head, wondering. "What a talent you have for planning," he said. "How my Lord would have enjoyed knowing you."

Now it was Askar who shook his head. "How strange," he muttered, "that an experienced man of the world should be so free from guile. Or are you secretly having sport with me? But no matter. Let me introduce you to my friend Adrian and begin working."

"Just a moment," Peter said, "and you even had those logs and timbers piled here. Yes, my Lord would have enjoyed knowing you."

While he sawed his log, Peter faced in the direction from which the prisoners would come. Finally he saw them, a formless group herded by numerous guards. Then he heard them, chanting in unison in praise of Christ. "Christ has come! Christ reigns! Eternal love and glory to Christ our Lord!" Peter laid down his saw and stood affixed with joy and admiration. At a word from Askar he stood upon one of the timber piles. In the front line he recognized a young priest he had ordained, who was singing aloud. He recognized Peter, for he started when he looked in his direction and reverently bowed his head when Peter's hand moved in an unobtrusive sign of the cross.

Elevated they are in spirit, thought Peter, but how decrepit their poor bodies.

Their bodies were dirty, half naked, encrusted with dungeon blight, cadaverous in their leanness. Some were limping, several were being half carried, their feet stumbling over the cobblestones. An elderly woman was trying to console a weeping teen-aged boy. As they trudged past Peter, he leaned forward and looking into their faces spoke in a low tone, "I glory in your faith. I am humbled by your love."

For some time after the gate had closed on the prisoners, Peter stood, head bowed, in tears. Finally Askar said, "Let us be gone, Rabbi. We have finished our work for the day."

They returned next morning, and for a number of mornings, and on each occasion Peter blessed his condemned people. Askar became concerned for his safety and finally voiced his fears. "Rabbi, if you keep tempting chance it will trip you up. Let us go in hiding for awhile."

Peter reluctantly agreed, but an official proclamation that the games would be temporarily discontinued for another form of public entertainment, eased his conscience.

Brief was his respite. From Askar he learned that the new entertainment would be held in Nero's gardens on Vatican Hill, at night. "I hate telling you this, Rabbi. They will make torches of the Christians. They will be burned to death."

Peter groaned.

"And you will have no opportunity to communicate with them. Fate is being harsh with you, Rabbi."

"Not fate, my son," sighed Peter. "This, too, is within the providence of God."

After the second or third night in Nero's garden the exhibitions were discontinued. They lacked the element, the fictional element, of contest, and for several months, at lengthening intervals, the Christians gave up their lives under the tooth and claw of lions, tigers and leopards. But in fewer numbers, and to diminishing spectators. Public hatred was giving way to pity and revulsion. And there was still another reason, perhaps the most influential reason, which Askar made known. "There are no more victims, Rabbi. The catacombs have saved your people."

"And who first suggested the catacombs as a refuge? A cynical, mysterious, scoffing, unbelieving son of Abraham named Askar. That, too, was within the providence of God."

Askar shrugged. "Rabbi, your troubles have muddled your brain."

Since the first arrests of the Christians, Peter had indeed become "a mole," abiding for a time in each of the catacombs, or in Askar's apartment, and avoiding the homes of Senator Pudens, Joseph and his other prominent friends.

"And we should thank another son of Abraham for saving us, Baruch ben-David," Peter said to Askar. "How simple his plan, yet how effective. And how skillfully he organized the workmen, hundreds of them, so as to get the best results from their labor. Several thousand vaults, I am told, some of them large enough to house half a score of people in reasonable comfort. This, too, my son, was in the providence of God. But while we are thankful for those who have been saved we must not forget those who still languish in prison. I would visit them and bring them the comfort of the blessed bread."

"How childish you can be at times," grumbled Askar. "You'd be like a hare falling into a hunter's trap."

Peter looked startled.

"Don't you realize you head their list of wanted criminals?"

"I suspected that. But I am not important now. I would not risk the life of a young priest who might give many years to the

Church. These innocent people should not be neglected. I should also try to bring about their release from prison."

"How many soldiers have you got, Rabbi?"

"Once I asked that same question," Peter replied with a guilty smile. "My brother Andrew and our friend John met Jesus of Nazareth and with overwhelming enthusiasm, told me they had found the Messiah. In my superior wisdom I inquired, in your words and with the same irony, how many soldiers has he got?"

"You were more practical then than now."

"No, I could not see so well. And I have soldiers — in the form of prayers."

"I have heard you say that one should act as well as pray."

"I am acting, in the only way open to me — making known my thought to one of youthful vigor and daring, who has friends in high places, so he may carry it out. And I shall make it known to Senator Pudens. We should take advantage of this lull in the persecution and arrange for the prisoners to be released, two or three at a time at short intervals over a period of two or three months. Their absence would not be noticed by those in high authority."

"How bold you are!" cried Askar.

"I regret we did not join our talents years ago! We could be masters of Rome!"

Peter smiled at his friend's exuberant exaggeration.

"So bold I cannot ignore you. I have no friends, Rabbi, only former companions in adventure, Lucanus, deputy minister of prisons, is one."

"If he is not your friend you may be in grave danger."

"There will be no danger — to me," Askar said.

A few days later they dined together in Askar's apartment. "This brass disc will get you into the prison, and get you out again," he said. "You will be permitted to talk privately to the prisoners for an hour every day and you may bring with you bread and wine for your religious service."

Peter reached across the table and gripped Askar's arm. "How good of you to think of that," he said. "May God bless you."

"And every time you leave the prison you may take with you one or two prisoners."

"Thank God," cried Peter. "I had hoped for that, but really did not expect it. You're a man of prompt action."

"Prompt action, without reflection is not always wise, Rabbi."

"How long I was in learning that," Peter said reminiscently. "Yet I have been troubled by my hasty suggestion. I got the impression you distrusted Lucanus and might be exposing yourself to some grave danger."

"Oh I trust him," Askar said, with a grim smile. "We dealt with one another under our old code. If he violated that code he knows he would not live long."

"My God!" gasped Peter. "Surely you would not murder him!"

"It would not be murder, Rabbi," Askar said, taking a draught of wine. "It would be an execution, lawful under our code."

"An execution! For violating an agreement?"

"Violation of that agreement would result in your imprisonment and after a while in your death. I gave him gold."

"You bribed him?"

"I paid him for a service, one that would not injure his master in any way. He would not betray me unless — unless he were sure of a richer reward from another. I see no immediate prospect of that. And besides, as I told you, he knows he would not live long. So you need have no fears. There will be no violence."

"Oh my son!" cried Peter, putting hands to his head. "I could not be a party . . ."

"You are not a party. Lucanus and I are the parties. I should not have told you this, but I thought you were wise enough in the ways of the world to understand."

"You terrify me. And you fascinate me, too. You are so resolute, so — so implacable. You hint at a — a predatory time in your life, yet you risk yourself for my people . . ."

"I tell you again, I risk nothing, so . . ."

"You give me gold so they may have comfort. . . ."

"I assure you that was no great sacrifice. Let me pour you some more wine."

"He might accuse you of being in secret alliance with the Christians, hoping for that rich reward."

"Oh, he is capable of that, Rabbi, but one thing deters him — love of life. He knows he would not live a day after his betrayal. He knows he would die dishonored by men in high place whose favor and esteem he covets — Cassius, Commander of the Praetorian guard, Urbanus, an officer of high rank in the Imperial Palace, Rufus, a general in the Imperial army . . ."

"Were these men your former companions in — in . . .?"

"My brother predators," Askar said.

"Yet you have no position of power."

"I craved the power of wealth. I have wealth — silver and salt mines, spice farms, vineyards, wineries, stone and marble quarries. Many herds of sheep, tanneries, a score of ships and other properties."

"You astound me! How can you manage so many affairs?"

"I don't. I manage men. They know I trust them and pay them generously. They know the penalty for betraying my trust."

"Then you do trust Lucanus?"

"I distrust him. But I gave him a way to protect himself,

and insure your safety as well. He removed the superintendent of
the Tullianum Prison and two guards to other posts and put my
men in their places. Should he ever be questioned why the prisoners were freed, he can say he was betrayed."

Peter shook his head. "I would never have thought of that,"
he said.

"You are too trusting. Most men are ravenous wolves. I do
not trust until one proves he is trustworthy. When I was young I
trusted one who stole a year's profit from a silversmith operation. When he refused to make restitution I hung him by the
heels, expecting he would reveal where he had hidden it.
Whether he would not or could not, I never knew. He died."

"Surely the law would have protected you," said Peter.

"The law!" scoffed Askar. "I have seldom found a law,
from Hispania to Syria, that was not the caprice of a tyrant or
administered according to a tyrant's caprice."

"From Hispania to Syria," murmured Peter, "and Palestine. You are the wandering Jew."

"For thirty years I have been a wandering Jew," Askar said,
putting down his wine cup.

"Too restless to take root and found a family."

"As restless as the tide, Rabbi. But I did found a family. It is
scattered from one end of the great sea to the other."

There was a wistfulness in his tone that Peter had never
before heard; an expression on his face he had never before seen.
Regret? Could this proud, independent man of the world experience regret? Or was it the wine that had spoken? Askar continued, in a tone that belied his independence but he spoke a
desire for Peter's respect.

"But none of my family ever suffered for lack of food and
shelter. Most of them have a kind word for me, a few even words
of love."

"You are like the rest of us," Peter said, "a mixture of good and bad, generosity and greed, indifference and compassion. How generous you have been to my people."

Askar drank another draught and settled comfortably in his chair. "In a sense you had some claim upon that money," he said.

Peter waited for an explanation.

"When the Jews were expelled from Rome, many of them blamed you. They were bitter. Two of them put a bag of gold on my table and said 'get rid of this Simon Peter.' We had been companions in similar adventures. They and a few other Jews and some Gentiles, preyed upon people of wealth."

"The Goliath?" inquired Peter.

"I have heard them called that. The Jews in the group were subject to expulsion and would sustain a heavy financial loss. They believed that if you were removed the emperor could be persuaded to rescind his decree. I looked into the bag of gold and told them they must do better. They put another bag on the table, and then another."

Rising, he paced about the room and then stood, facing Peter. "I inquired about you. I was told you had tried to restore peace to the Jews, and that you had pleaded with Claudius on behalf of the sick and the aged. And I was reliably informed that nothing could induce Claudius to revoke his decree. My employers angrily asked why I had failed in my agreement and demanded the return of the gold. I reminded them of the covenant, 'get rid of Simon Peter,' and that this gave me discretion as to how and when I should get rid of you."

Peter nodded approvingly. "You should have been a lawyer," he said.

"I had heard so much of Simon Peter, good and bad, I thought a good look at him might help me decide how I should get rid of him. I went to the Port Ostia where you were assisting in the embarkation. I was disappointed. I expected to see a militant leader strutting about giving orders and demanding instant obedience. Instead, I beheld a placid old man with the face of a child and the pleading voice of a woman, encouraging his people to remain firm in their faith and loyal to 'their Jewish heritage and the religion of the greatest of all Jews, Jesus of Nazareth, the Christ and Redeemer.' Your patience irritated me. Were you a weakling or a tower of secret strength? I concluded you were not an instigator of dissension or ill will. You actually love men — all men."

"I would like to think you are right," Peter said.

"And then, in my heart, I betrayed my employers. Fearing they might hire others to get rid of you on board ship, or after your arrival in Judea, I decided to stand between you and them until you could lose yourself, and I took passage on that voyage, and followed you to Jerusalem."

"Now I understand certain things that puzzled me," Peter said. "Several tims James' servants said they had seen a man standing near their house, as if he were waiting for someone. It was you, or one of your men keeping watch and you followed me about Jerusalem. That is how we met several times."

"You were probably in no danger, Rabbi, but I did not rest easy until after you left the ship for Antioch."

"And you said our meetings were mere chance," Peter said.

Askar smiled and continued. "I was sure I would never see you again; that the East would smother you in its aromatic bosom. I had a tinge of regret — you were such an interesting companion, with the wildest of dreams — a Jew fisherman bent upon reversing the morals of the world — but since that was what you willed — and I experienced a sense of loyalty to my employers. You had been gotten rid of and I could conscientiously keep the money." He chuckled. "Don't think Rabbi, that I would ever have returned it. Time and chance often bring about a desired end."

"All in the providence of God," Peter insisted. "Nothing happens by chance."

"Whatever it was, Rabbi, it smoothed my way. One of my employers was taken to the bosom of Abraham; another acquired much wealth in Alexandria; the so-called Goliath gradually fell apart. And I must confess my business enterprises crowded you out of my mind. I believed you had found your way into the bosom of Abraham. How astonished I was to see you in the Forum one day preaching Jesus Christ to a group of Romans. It was almost like seeing Moses coming down from Mount Sinai! But I passed on. You didn't seem to be in need of any assistance."

"Ah," said Peter, "you put your finger on the heart of the matter — my need in time of great peril." After a reflective pause, he continued:

"I was in Herod's prison, doomed to death by Herod's sword. An angel of the Lord walked me to freedom. In Rome I was again threatened with death and God again sent one to aid me, not an angel, a Jew, a ruthless, cynical, profane, rebellious son of Abraham who had turned from the God of his fathers for the gods of the world — power, wealth and the pleasure of the flesh. But God could see in the heart of this man what even he himself did not know he possessed, a sense of indignation at injustice, compassion for those who suffered. He did not work a miracle as did the angel, but in his own way he delivered me from the threatening danger. Inscrutable are the ways of the Lord."

"You exaggerate, Rabbi," Askar said, "but I appreciate it. Now let us go to bed. The hour is late."

But Peter would not be stayed.

"How I mourn for this son of Abraham," he said wistfully. "He accomplished what he set out to do, but at what a price — thirty years of wandering, sacrificing what is the Jews' dearest possession —a home, a wife and children, rejecting that which alone can give one happiness in this life — a hope of a life with God after death. Oh, Lord, give light to this man. Restore to him the faith of his youth."

Askar slowly paced the room. Peter rested his head in the palms of his hands. He, too, had been a wanderer. Now he wandered in thought, back to Gennesaret and the Galilean Hills, to the jovial scenes of his youth and young manhood, the sad memories of deceased relatives and friends. He began humming one of the Psalms, taught him by his father. In a louder voice he sang the ancient lament of his people. "By the waters of Babylon we sat and wept, O Sion, whenever we thought of you."

"My father often sang that dirge," Askar said. "I wonder why the Jews enjoy being mournful."

"They mourned in repentance for turning from God," Peter said. "Such mourning brings happiness, not sadness."

27

A Visit to Tullianum Prison

THE MAMERTIME or Tullianum Prison was near the Forum, at the foot of Capitoline Hill. Originally, it had been a deep well. Later, the shaft was enlarged, windlasses were installed to lower and raise people and materials, tunnels were run from it in various directions, at several levels, off which prison cells and rooms had been carved out, similar to those the Christians had hewn for refuge in the catacombs. Over the opening, an apartment of several rooms had been built in which prisoners were received from above and below ground. Standing apart in a fenced-off area stood the house of the warden, a barracks for the guards, a stable for horses and storage places for materials and supplies. Still farther apart, a low stone structure partially hidden by shrubbery could be seen. Here the bodies of dead prisoners were cremated.

Askar conducted Peter to the prison and introduced him to Appia, the substitute warden, and to Javenal and Tirus, the substitute guards. Under arrangement made by them, Peter met with the Christians at the close of day in a large candle-lighted room on the first level. He did not preach to them. He lauded them for their courage and fortitude. "I am unworthy to be in your midst. Your faith in Christ is so strong, your love for him so deep that you suffer for him with sublime joy and offer yourselves to a cruel death rather than deny him. You are willing to

259

do for him what he did for you. In this wise you bring yourselves into closest bond with him."

He moved among them speaking intimately with one, and then with another. He prayed with them — prayed to prepare them spiritually for the reception of the blessed bread. When he had officiated at this rite he gave each a portion of the bread and wine, saying, "Receive you the body and blood of Jesus Christ." They ate and drank of them with an adoration so pure and entire that he was moved to cry out: "Oh, Lord, give me the grace of a faith and love like unto theirs."

The substitute guards entered. One of them herded the prisoners, except four, back to their cells. These four, the eldest of the women, and Peter, were led up a ramp to the ground level. Here the women were directed into a carriage. "You are free," Peter said to them. "You will be taken to one of the catacombs where you will be cared for." He was joined by Askar and another man who conducted him to Askar's apartment. Peter spoke once. "It has been a blessed day, my son, thanks to God — and you."

Before beginning the religious service the following night Peter told his people that "through the intercession of a compassionate man," the four women had been released from captivity and were receiving aid and comfort. "During our service let us keep this man in our prayers so that he may progress in God's grace."

At the conclusion of the service two women and two sickly elderly men were released from captivity and conveyed to shelter.

"All is going well," said one of the guards. "Only old Galen seems to be aware that something unusual is happening."

Galen, a disabled veteran foot soldier, snarled at Peter: "Freeing the burners of Rome! Someone will pay for this with his head!"

"Perhaps those in authority believe they are innocent," Peter suggested.

Galen's retort was shut off by a fit of coughing and a wheezing struggle for breath. Looking at him more closely, Peter observed jaundiced eyes and the liverish color of his face. "You seem ill," he said. "Have you been treated by a physician?"

Galen's puzzled stare gave Peter his answer.

"I know a little about treating sickness," he said. "I'd be pleased to bring you something that has helped me, and others."

Galen looked at him suspiciously.

"Your bowels are clogged. You struggle for breath. You do not sleep well . . ."

"Are you a physician?"

"No, but most Jews learn something about treating sick. I'll not poison you, my friend."

"I have no money," grunted Galen.

"I want no money, no favors."

Galen shook his head. "I never heard of anything like this. But bring your stuff. It can't make me feel worse than I do now."

At the end of five weeks all of the prisoners had been freed. Galen had faithfully taken Peter's remedies. "I feel better," he said, "but my shortness of breath . . ."

"May not be fully cured. But it will improve if you continue taking the medicine. I will keep you supplied."

Some weeks later Galen came to Peter at Askar's apartment. "I heard something," he said in an agitated tone. "The regular superintendent of the prison — he came back. I overheard him say there would be no more punishment of the Christians, at least for a time."

"You bring me good tidings, Galen," Peter said.

"But the rest is not so good. He said you and the other Christian leaders would be arrested."

"I am not surprised," Peter answered Galen. "You should protect yourself —shave your beard and cut your hair and dress like the Romans."

Peter affectionately fingered his beard. "I suppose the sacrifice is worthy of the risk," he said sadly. "I am grateful for your warning. Let me give you — no, I have no medicines — but come with me."

He conducted him to the house of Nicodemus and introduced him to Deborrah: "My good friend, who has been ill."

After describing Galen's symptoms and his treatment, he said, "Look at him, mother. Tell me if I acted wisely."

Deborrah rolled back his eyelids and peered into his eyes, looked at his tongue and teeth and poked a sturdy finger into his midsection. "You treated him well, Master," she said, "but I will give him something besides. Come back in a week," she said to Galen.

Galen opened his mouth but no words came out. A woman physician! A Jewish woman physician! He was bereft of speech.

When Peter told Askar of Galen's suggestions, Askar said, "It was good advice. And you should live in the catacombs, going from one to another. When you do go about, have a sack of tools on your back. And direct all of your priests to do the same.

The rebuilding of Rome created such a demand for skilled craftsmen and sturdy laborers that the Christians began leaving the catacombs to take employment, timidly at first, and then in great numbers. When there were no more arrests Askar explained to Peter the government's policy.

"Even the Romans sickened at Nero's brutality, and he cunningly conformed himself to their mood. He promises to build for them the most beautiful and comfortable city in the world and to pay the builders higher wages than they had ever received.

"Your friend Senator Pudens and the other prominent Romans who became Christians are in no danger. Nero plans to turn the people against the Jews. The old bigotry is again raising its head. The people make no distinction between Christian and Mosaic Jew. Their religions are one cult to them — a strong contradiction of their own religion. But you and your priests have been so prominent that you overshadow the Rabbis as leaders. It is generally believed that if you and the other Christian Jewish leaders are put out of the way the cult will die. We must contrive ways to throw them off your trail. It might be well if you went into hiding for a while. My island would be a safe place."

Peter turned a grateful countenance toward his friend. "I am sure it would," he said, "but should a shepherd seek safety when his sheep are threatened . . . After his resurrection our Lord appeared to us in Galilee, and he said to me 'feed my sheep, feed my lambs, feed my sheep.' "

"And here you belong, Rabbi. I should have known better than to suggest such a thing."

So Peter continued shepherding his sheep, not carrying a shepherd's crook, nor playing a shepherd's pipe, but with a leather bag of tools slung from his shoulder. He did not think it necessary to seek employment to maintain his disguise, but as he was passing a building in the course of construction a heavy hand fell on his arm and a gruff voice said, "If it's work you're looking for you can find it here."

"You would give me work?" asked Peter registering pleasurable surprise. "Many say I am too old."

"Can you lay stones?"

"Not as skillfully, I fear, as you would require."

"You're not too old to carry stones to the mason's. What is your name?"

"Petra (Stone)," replied Peter smiling.

"You should do well with stones, since that is your name. Come. I'll show you where to begin."

He worked as one who was grateful for work, as one who enjoyed work, and unobtrusively established a friendly relationship with his fellow workers. But not with all. A small youthful group seemed to resent him. He did not smile at their obscenities or participate in their criticism of other workmen, nor accept their invitations to drink with them. Neither did he attempt to correct them. Finally one of them said, with a suspicious frown, "Who are you? You talk like a Roman and wear Roman clothing, but you look like a Jew."

"My mother's grandfather was a Jew," he replied amiably. "It is said that I inherited some of his features."

To avoid the eyes of spies, Peter lived in Askar's apartment and did not mingle with his people except in an emergency. His wages he gave into a fund for their support. After a while he sought an opportunity to cease working without casting suspicion upon himself and finally it came — one that deeply saddened him — Nicodemus became gravely ill. He besought his employer. "You have paid me well and treated me fairly. I would continue with you, but a dear friend, an aged man, lies ill, in need of much care. I would help him. I ask to be released from your employment."

"That you do not need. You may go when you please." Regarding Peter with curiosity, he went on. "Some of the workmen think you are a Jew. Your courtesy marks you for a Jew of high rank. But Jew or not, if you ever wish employment, come to me."

Nicodemus was only an obscure humble priest, but in Peter's mind he was a superior person, the equal of an Apostle. He should be ministered to in a manner befitting his lofty stature. Fearing that delirium might permanently incapacitate him from participating in the rites, he hurried to Nicodemus' house.

"My friend," he said, "together we shall eat the holy bread."

"How I would love that, Master," Nicodemus said. "How I would love that."

Sitting up in bed, he joined with Peter in the prayers and in the ritual of consecration. Before partaking in the consecrated bread and wine he said solemnly, "My Lord Jesus Christ, firmly and entirely I believe that the bread and wine we consecrated is now your sacred body and blood which you gave to the world for the salvation of souls."

"I bow in awe at your faith," Peter said. "Of the faithful who had not seen him, our Lord said, 'Blessed are they who have not seen, and yet believe.' "

Many devoted friends offered to attend Nicodemus, but Deborrah chose only those whose service would not impose a sacrifice. Peter included himself in this group. "I have no family to support and no employment to protect. I will stay with him every other night."

When a Jewish man attended a sick man he did not feed him and give him medicine and leave the unpleasant services to a servant. He bathed him, helped in calls of nature and cleansed him from the excess of such calls. He rubbed his body with oil and unguents to prevent the formation of bed sores. In these ministrations Peter had become highly efficient and he instructed some of his associates who lacked experience.

These ministrations brought physical comfort to Nicodemus, but they were not expected to cure him. And they did not. At the end of a fortnight he died with the words of the priesthood on his lips, "You are a priest forever."

As Peter had washed Nicodemus' body in life, so he cleansed it in death, bathing it and swathing it in linen and ground aromatic spices. He helped bear it to a stone table in one of the catacombs, and all that night in an unbroken line, the faithful slowly filed past as a mark of their love and respect. At dawn, upon a stone altar at ground level, before a large congregation, he celebrated the rite of the holy bread "for the soul of our beloved Nicodemus," and spoke in brief but solemn tribute.

"Our brother Nicodemus was our Lord's Apostle even as were we, the Twelve. Even as is Paul. He was the first to carry our Lord's teaching to Rome — to an humble son of Abraham who worked in his weaving shop, and then to others until more than five hundred men and women believed in Christ when I came to Rome. This he accomplished without the aid of a priest, without the grace-giving ceremonies. So strong was his faith in Christ, so deep was his love for him, so completely did his works harmonize with the Divine word that men regarded him as a saint and readily accepted his teaching. Let all of you try to believe as he believed, to love as he loved, to sacrifice as he sacrificed."

For several months no Christian had been arrested, but remembering Askar's warning, Peter expected the persecutions to be resumed. Askar had said, "Under Nero, Rome will not tolerate what is regarded as a 'barbarous Jewish religious cult.' It will attempt to destroy your Church by making war on your priests." His prediction proved to be true. Within a fortnight eight priests were imprisoned.

Peter cried out in grief. In desperation he besought his Lord. "The anti-Christ besieges your city! He imprisons your shepherds! Your sheep will be scattered! Direct me how to repel him!"

In an underground room he stood before a large gathering of men. "The war on Christ has been resumed!" he declared. "The teachers of Christ's word, the ministers of his rites, are being imprisoned!"

His body was tense, his countenance grave, his voice vibrated. "What are you going to do? Surrender to the enemy or fight him?"

They stared at him, dumbfounded. He continued.

"A near score of priests died in the arena; neophytes preparing for the priesthood I sent into the back country to save their lives. Our training of other neophytes was disrupted. You can fight the anti-Christ, not with spears and swords, but by teaching Christ's word, by administering his rites. You can fight him by becoming priests!"

After a brief silence, he went on, in a quieter, a more persuasive tone.

"You think you are unworthy, or have not sufficient learning, or that you have no vocation. For many of you that is not true. You know your religion well, and much of the old Law. Inability to read and write is no obstacle. Most of us, the Twelve could scarcely read or write. All you need is the will. If you have the will and the determination to serve Christ faithfully, then you are worthy. You know what a priest's life should be. It will not seriously interfere with your family life or your means of livelihood. With these responsibilities you can be only a part-time priest, but as these responsibilities are discharged, your service to the priesthood may be increased. Ask our Lord to guide you in your choice."

He spoke in like manner to other gatherings, with gratifying results. Over a hundred men offered to receive instructions. Peter concentrated upon what he said was his most important work, "training men to be like Christ." Since most of them were employed by day, he arranged to meet them after the evening meal, in three separate classes according to their learning. That this would require him to lecture almost three hours every night caused him no concern. But some of his friends were concerned. Senator Pudens came to his quarters in one of the catacombs and offered to share the burden. Peter graciously declined. "No, no, my friend. I shall not expose you to such risk. You are too important to the Church."

Joseph, the former priest, expressed his concern. "You should have some assistance, Rabbi."

"Assistance would be welcome, my son, but where shall I find it?"

"You might give me a trial," Joseph said, timidly.

"Try you!" cried Peter. "Do you mean? — Let us go up and walk while you tell me."

Pacing slowly under a half moon, Joseph said, "Rabbi, this is not a sudden notion. It goes back to the time when I rejoined the synagogue. My wife asked me to explain the difference between Judaism and Christianity. To give a true explanation I studied them carefully. Later I explained them to my older son, and daughter, Mariam. She thought she might like to be a Christian, I suggested that she study them and decide for herself."

"Prudent counsel," Peter said.

"My belief in Judaism remained strong, yet I marveled at your faith in Christianity. It absorbed you. It seemed to be merged with your being, like your blood with your body. I studied it more carefully, reading the Prophets, weighing your teachings. Slowly it came to me that God's law given us through Moses did not conflict with the teachings of Jesus. The contradiction lay in its innumerable interpretations, by the many Jewish sects that had accumulated during the centuries, which were in themselves conflicting. There was no spiritual authority to resolve them. The members of the Sanhedrin were in conflict and the high priests had repudiated many Mosaic teachings."

"And yet God did not abandon our people," Peter said. "He chose a Jewish maiden to be the mother of our Redeemer."

After a silence of some duration Joseph continued. "Many sons of Abraham suffered martyrdom for their Christian faith. That stirred me to the depth of my soul! Not for refusing to deny their faith — many other men have done that — they refused to deny a man! They died out of love for him! Out of gratitude for his sacrifice for them! Rabbi, that broke my resistance, my proud stubborn resistance. Faith overwhelmed me! I would be a priest again. I beg of you give me back my priestly powers."

With deep emotion Peter embraced Joseph. "My son! My son!" he cried huskily. "This has been a blessed day."

"After twenty-five years," Joseph said reproachfully. "For the fires of youth I offer you the lethargy of incipient old age."

"Faith and love will rekindle that fire," Peter said joyfully.

In the beginning Peter limited Jospeh's activities to teaching at night so he could continue his way of life by day. After six months he began detaching himself from his business so he could assist other priests.

"Let us do this unobtrusively, so it will not be noticed," Peter said, "so we may avoid the wrath of our enemies."

But they did not wholly escape that wrath. Within the six months' period four other priests had been imprisoned. Joseph suggested that he visit them. "I can get into the prison without danger," he said. "No one suspects I am a Christian. My wife is in full accord with me."

"I thought you might have that in mind," Peter said, "and I felt sure your good wife would agree, but I cannot permit it. The Church would be hurt if she lost you now. But I have another plan I might try."

The key of his other plan was Askar who had recently returned to Rome after several months' absence. "I would not ask for their release," he said. "I know that would be futile, but only to obtain a few privileges — receiving bread and wine so they might celebrate the Holy Rite, walking serveral times a day in the fresh air . . ."

"Oh, Rabbi! How childish you can be! The Romans are not interested in the comfort of their prisoners!"

"I should know that," Peter muttered. "But if they are ex-

270 UPON THIS ROCK

ecuted — could we have their bodies for Christian burial?"

"I can be quite persuasive about that," Askar said gently.

But his persuasiveness was ineffective. "He laughed at me," he said. "Bade me wait until they were executed. And I have other sad tidings for you, Rabbi. Your friend Paul is again returning to Rome a prisoner. But this time he will be tried and executed."

"What a loss that will be to the Church," mourned Peter.

"Nero is determined to destroy Christianity so he concentrates on executing her priests. The police are confident they will finally track you down."

Peter said, "But you — I've been fearful — you might be suspected of helping us."

"I guarded against that, Rabbi. I let it be known that I extracted a sizable bag of gold from you to obtain the release of the prisoners and I offered to divide it half and half. Knowing how much I craved wealth, they believed me, but I did not tell you for fear of outraging your scruples."

"Now they refuse to accept your gold," Peter said. "Only God can save my sons."

Askar flicked his red beard, now thinly streaked with gray. His deepset amber eyes fixed upon Peter's somber face.

"If he does not save them you will console yourself by saying it was not his will. I intend no disrespect, Rabbi, but I am impatient with such abject resignation. These men would serve him, teach his doctrine, carry on his work. Why will he not save them? By a miracle if necessary?"

Peter spoke in a quiet reflective tone: "Many times I have asked myself that. Why does God permit certain happenings? Why did he not save the Apostle James instead of me? He was a far more capable man than I. I cannot know God's mind, so I resign myself. Not idly, not indifferently but trustingly. Trustingly, yet always groping for the truth. God gave us free will — the power to decide, to make a choice, and so much does he respect that gift that only rarely will he interfere with our exercise of those powers, even to avert a grave injustice or to prevent suffering or sorrow. He did not prevent me from denying him, or Judas from betraying him, but he did intervene miraculously to save me from Herod's sword and to make an Apostle out of Paul. So my son, I resign myself, trustingly."

28

Paul's Execution

PAUL was brought to Rome in chains and confined in the Tullianum Prison. Peter spoke to Askar concerning him.

"He has been confined for two weeks, yet he has been allowed only one visitor, Senator Pudens, for only a brief half hour . . ."

"That is more than I expected, Rabbi."

"Isn't there some way you could obtain permission for me to visit him?"

"Nothing could be easier. How the Romans would rejoice at having you in their trap!"

"I mean so they would not know . . ."

"Do not underestimate your enemy, Rabbi."

Peter raised both arms in an emphatic gesture. "Paul is the most important man in the Church!" he declared. "He is entitled to our utmost respect and veneration! I cannot ignore him."

"Why, he would urge you to remain in hiding — for the good of the Church, and your own good, as well."

"Of course he would! But that does not satisfy me. I suppose I should pray more."

"That might help, Rabbi," Askar said with a shrug.

Peter did pray, and he put his mind to work. One evening he called at the house where lived Deborrah, the widow of Nicodemus, who still compounded medicines and ministered to

272

the sick. Deborrah knew his purpose for calling and said, "This is his night to come, Master."

Within half an hour the person for whom he waited arrived. "Ah, Galen," he greeted him. "You are looking well."

"Deborrah is keeping me alive," Galen replied.

When Galen had received two small jars of medicine from Deborrah, Peter said, "Let us talk, my friend," and conducted him into a room where they could be alone.

"You have an important prisoner, Paul of Tarsus," he began.

"Yes, your friend you told me about."

"I would like to visit him, bring him some bread and wine."

Galen's face clouded. "The Senator — Pudens — he brought him some bread and wine. But other visitors — only men high in authority can permit that. And they do not favor visitations."

"I know. I was hoping a way might be found."

Removing a small leather pouch from his pocket he emptied its contents on the table and picked up a small brass disk with a number stamped thereon. "This got me into the prison before," he said. "I thought it might . . ."

"Why, I thought you had turned that in!"

"So I thought it might get me in now."

Galen stared at Peter. "I see no reason why it should not."

"But I will not subject you to punishment."

"I am head day guard now; the other one died recently. If you should show this to the guard at the outer gate and ask for me, I will take you to the prisoner."

"I repeat, Galen. I will not expose you to any risk."

"I do not see any risk. If they should question me I will tell them the number on the disk and state that since it had been used before, it was natural to think it could be used again."

"You comfort me, my friend."

Pointing to an object in the contents of the pouch, Galen inquired: "Is that some kind of a jewel?"

Peter smiled, sadly, Galen thought. "No, it's a stone native to Galilee. It is highly polished and skillfully cut into an ornament."

"What beautiful coloring."

"A present from my dear wife Anna on our wedding day."

Galen remained silent, leaving Peter alone with this treasured memory.

After a while Peter picked up a short silver chain. "What's left of a wrist ornament," he said. "A gift from my mother when I was fifteen. While in a storm on the lake one night it got foul of an oar handle and broke into several pieces. This is all I was able to save."

"This is a strange looking money," Galen said, examining one of the coins.

"Old Galilean money, before the Roman conquest. My father was a flaming patriot and made a hobby of collecting Galilean coins and pottery and other things. These came to me at his death."

Galen gazed at Peter. "You're a mystery to me," he said in a musing tone. "A Galilean fisherman, as far from Rome in some ways as the moon from the earth, yet now you are Rome's most hated rival. It growls in anger that you have escaped from its claws."

Peter smiled. "That time may come. When it does, I would like you to have these trinkets." He replaced them in the pouch. "May I enter the prison in the morning?"

"Be there a half hour after sunrise," Galen said.

The next evening Peter called on Askar at his apartment. "I visited Paul this morning," he quietly announced, and proceeded to tell his astonished friend how the visit had been arranged.

"How tricky you are," sniffed Askar. "I suppose you are quite proud of yourself."

"Let us say I am pleased," replied Peter amiably. "Paul reproved me for taking what he called 'a most daring risk,' but how grateful he was! Galen brought two of the prisoner priests and we celebrated the Holy Rite together. He did not bring more for fear of attracting attention, but each morning two of them will celebrate with Paul. A shrewd courageous man is Galen."

"You've probably cast a spell over him. His shrewdness may cost him his head."

"To protect him I shall not return to the prison for a week when Paul will need more balm."

"More balm?" cried Askar, striving to curb his impatience.

"He has a persistent skin rash, very itchy, smarting, most uncomfortable. Deborrah's ointment helped him more than anything he has ever used. I taught the young priests how to apply it and rub his back."

Askar shook his head in frustration. Peter continued to laud the man from Tarsus.

"But Paul gave me far more than I gave him — confidence that the Church will grow, courage to foster its growth. Paul, the man whom God most honored. He invited us to follow him but left the decision to us. But Paul — he wanted him so much he got rough with him, threw him from his horse, demanded to know why he was persecuting him. This assures me that Christ's Church will endure forever. When her enemies are assailing her from within and without, when they rebelliously proclaim, 'A way with your doctrine of only one wife, and chastity and self sacrifice,' he will raise up men, and women, too, who will steer her through the storm into calm waters and equip her with new strong sails and sturdy rudders and stout oars."

"How eloquent you can be when speaking of Jesus and his

Church," Askar said, a note of admiration in his voice. "You remind me of a line from Scripture my father often quoted: 'The zeal of your house is eating you up.' Do not let your zeal destroy you. Do not return to the prison. I am sure Paul prefers that you do not."

Peter slowly nodded. "You are right," he said. "He urged me — he said, 'Simon, I am grateful for your coming, but do not return. The Church needs you,' so I shall yield to him — and to you."

Askar sighed, in simulated relief.

In the seclusion of the catacombs Peter instructed the neophytes for the priesthood. In the gloom of his prison cell Paul prayed and offered his glorious tempestuous life to God. In the luxury of his palace, while Nero sojourned in Greece, the deputy governor of Rome, Sabinus, pondered when he should order Paul to trial. Finally, he fixed the day. In the new "Forum of Justice" near the prison, a blinking, watery-eyed skeleton of a man stood before a magistrate and boldly proclaimed his belief in "the divinity of Jesus Christ, the second Person of the most holy Trinity." The magistrate sentenced him to death by beheading on the following day.

At dawn of that day Peter presented his brass disk to the outer guard of the prison and asked for Galen. As Galen conducted him within, he cried out, "Rabbi, this is folly! You may be recognized!"

"Oh, my friend, is it folly to do what love and respect command?"

When Peter and Paul had been alone for almost an hour Galen appeared. "It is time," he said respectfully. Peter linked arms with Paul, and they walked up the ramp to ground level where Senator Pudens, Joseph and a half score of friends were waiting. Here he was directed to a cart which would convey him to the place of execution. His friends walked toward their conveyances, but when Peter attempted to join Senator Pudens, a guard he had not seen before stayed him and said, "Come with me."

He conducted Peter to a cell on the second level. About midday Galen came with a small jar of soup. "It's thin, there's no meat in it," he said.

"At least it is hot, thanks to you, I'm sure. And there are pieces of turnip and cabbage in it. Will you sit with me a while?"

"Only a short while, Rabbi — against the rules to be friendly with prisoners. You should not have come here. Surely you knew they would recognize you and keep you a prisoner."

"I thought they might do that, but my life — it is not so important now — other matters take precedence — visiting Paul was foremost."

"I think I understand, Rabbi. Would you tell me something about your Jesus? I saw Paul go to his death singing in praise of Jesus, and also many who died in the arena. What was there about Jesus that so completely captured their thoughts and their will?"

For a quarter of an hour Peter told him about Jesus.

At sundown Galen returned with more soup and a hard lump of black bread and a straw pallet. "They say this tuffa rock is soft, Rabbi, but it's not soft when you try to sleep on it."

"Don't worry, my friend. I've often slept on the ground. What are your rules about sanitation?"

"Prisoners clean their own cells and empty their chambers in the latrine at the end of the corridor."

"How often may we bathe?"

"Bathe? You'll hardly get enough water to drink. Roman prisons are not cradles of comfort, Rabbi."

"I'll try to find comfort of mind," Peter said with a smile of resignation.

He also found comfort in the brief visits of Senator Pudens,

Joseph and other friends. But he discouraged visitations. "I would not expose our beloved people to imprisonment. Urge them to protect themselves, and tell them I will be grateful if they remember me in their prayers."

Nevertheless, he had a visitor, a daily visitor, Galen, the senior day guard. He brought candles to the prisoner so he could read the scrolls of Holy Hebrew books and the letters of Paul, and he smuggled in enough water for an occasional bathing. Gripping Galen's arm, Peter said, "Holy writ tells us that if we cast bread on the water of charity it will be returned to us a hundredfold. You have proven its truth. I cast upon your waters a few crumbs — for your illness — and you send me a boatload of blessings. And with such good will — Oh Galen, I am ashamed to say it but I would ask for something more."

Galen side-glanced Peter with a broken-toothed smile. "Would you like some perfume in your bath water, Rabbi?"

"Some perfume to offer my Lord." After a brief silence Peter continued, "Senator Pudens brought me wine and bread so that I could celebrate every day our sacred rite known as the Holy Bread. We are grateful, my Lord and I, but we are a bit lonesome. If we could have some company — two or three of the priests who are prisoners, or better yet, all of them for, say an hour at dawn — providing that would not endanger you in any way, my friend."

Galen seemed dubious. "I don't know, Rabbi. Most irregular — yet — it couldn't cause any disorder. Why is this — this bread breaking so important?"

For half an hour Peter explained the mystery.

Galen shook his head. "As you said, Rabbi it is a mystery — yet it is so simple — eating a bit of bread and drinking a sip of wine. I doubt if the warden would object. We guards have some choice in the treatment of prisoners. I'll bring two of your priests, Rabbi, and if there is no objection, I'll bring two or three of your priests the next morning and every morning."

"You are a gift from God. I would ask you for still another favor. A stone . . ."

"A stone?" querried Galen.

"To use in place of an altar for celebrating the Holy Rites — a flat smooth stone about a cubit in length, half as wide, and a finger length in depth."

"I think I can find such a stone, Rabbi."

"You are a man of good heart, Galen. I am sure my Lord is pleased with you."

At Peter's invitation, Galen occasionally witnessed these religious rites. Attentive, respectful, yet mystified, as he confided to Peter, "Bread and wine — changed into the body and blood of your Master. How can you believe that, Rabbi?"

Peter explained why be believed it.

"Those priests — they were so — so reverent — so filled up with something — not of this world. Love. That's what it was, Rabbi, love. Like I have never seen."

"You are right, my friend. This is a sacrifice of love — faith and love."

While Peter walked in the narrow corridor facing his cell, a privilege given the prisoners for half an hour twice daily, Galen appeared and conducted him up the ramp to ground level. "Oh, glorious sun!" he cried looking skyward through watery eyes. "How good it is to see you again!"

"Since you enjoy sunlight, Rabbi, let us walk in it for a while."

"Ah, Askar!" said Peter turning about to face the speaker. "Something tells me I should thank you for this favor."

Askar drew him out of hearing of the guards. "Yesterday I returned to Rome and learned you had put your head in the lion's mouth. But don't be disturbed. I'm not going to scold you."

"That is a comfort," Peter said, with a smile.

"You must realize what is facing you — a trial, conviction, and execution."

"That wouldn't surprise me."

"You'll not be tried until Nero returns to Rome from Greece. I told Lucinus that if he wished to keep you alive until then he should give you several hours a day in the fresh air. He agreed to that."

"That is good, my son. I am grateful to you. I'm sure I'll be able to pray with more fervor."

"It's too late for prayers, Rabbi. You must act boldly."

Peter peered inquiringly into Askar's face.

"If we act boldly we can get you out of here."

Peter gasped.

"This rebuilt prison is an invitation to escape. That stone wall on the south of the enclosure is about six cubits in height. One could easily pass through those iron spikes sticking out of the top. There is a narrow court between one section of the wall and the rear of the south wing of the guards' barracks. If you walked in that court at dusk I believe we could devise a way to get you over the wall."

"Such boldness!" cried Peter. "You take my breath away!"

"I am trying to keep breath in you. Standing on a horse, I could fasten the hooks of a rope ladder to the top of the wall. You could climb the ladder and slide down a rope to the ground. I would unhook both ladder and rope and hide them. We would travel all night and about noon next day board one of my ships in an isolated cove on the Adriatic Sea."

Peter put hands to his head. "Madness! Madness!" he muttered. "Coming from any other man — but you — it is fantastic — bold beyond imagination — yet I am confident you could carry it out."

"I could if given a week's preparation. On my island, a day

off the Dalmatian coast, you would be safe and close enough to Rome to govern your Church. Or, if you desire, you can lose your identity in the fisheries there until this storm blows out."

Peter paused and gazed into Askar's face. "What genius you have for planning," he said. "No wonder you have succeeded so well."

"No flattery, Rabbi," twitted Askar, good humoredly. "By your standards I am a failure."

"Only in the ends you sought, my son; not in your use of the means available to you."

"What a subtle distinction," laughed Askar. "By that reasoning, Satan was a success."

"Ugh!" growled Peter, frowning. "You, a son of Abraham! How could you say such a monstrous thing?"

"I beg your pardon, Rabbi. I should have known how real the devil is to you."

Recovering from his indignation, Peter said, "I am grateful for your concern, but even with the most careful preparation you might have to use violence."

"No more than a knock on the head or a gentle throttling . . ."

"A gentle throttling!" gasped Peter.

"Just enough to squelch a howl. But even that is remote. Escape from Rome prisons — well it just doesn't happen, Rabbi. I could almost assure you there would be no obstacle."

"But Galen, he would surely lose his head."

"He is on day guard. You would not escape until after the night guard came on duty."

"Some of them would surely suffer — perhaps be executed. Oh, I could not be a party to that!"

"You would not be a party!" Askar spoke sharply. "Your imagination is curdling your thinking. You had no such thought for the guards when you were delivered from Herod's prison."

282 UPON THIS ROCK

Peter slowed his pace and gazed skyward. "I did give them some thought," he said reflectively. "I asked God to be merciful to them. If I were ten years younger — even five years — but I am close to the end, my work has been curtailed. My value to the Church is outweighed by the value of life to those humble obscure men."

"You don't know that, Rabbi. You speak out of humility, a spirit of excessive self-abnegation."

"I think I speak out of experience. I have come to believe that sometimes we can more perfectly serve God in death, especially when we are old."

Askar shook his head. "I do not understand such a philosophy. It irritates me."

"Nor do I understand it. James, the prudent one of the Twelve, the sound thinker, God did not save. He saved me: the blusterer, the unstable one, the slave of his emotions. An incomprehensible mystery."

After a brief silence he resumed. "So, my son, with gratitude for your concern, with regret for disappointing you, I must decline your generous offer of assistance."

What an exciting adventure!" cried Askar with a sigh of regret. "It could have been the master stroke of Roman history."

"Indeed it could, my son! Oh, if I were only ten years younger."

29

Peter's Imprisonment and Trial

WHEN Galen brought Peter his breakfast of soup, he seemed sad and depressed. "I hate telling you this, Rabbi," he said, "but all privileges have been taken from you. No more water for bathing, no more wine. Your only bread will be in the soup. No more visitors or walking in the sunlight. But you can have your candles. They probably think you will not need them, for you are to be brought to trial this morning.

"My captors would prevent me from celebrating the Holy Bread," Peter said. "I am pleased they recognize its significance. But they shall not entirely have their way."

From his neck he removed a flat silver flask, suspended by a cord, and exposed its contents — several wafers that looked like bread.

"Little things often become very important in life," Peter said, reflectively. "My son, Joseph, once befriended a young Roman who is now a secretary in one of the Government offices. He learned that I would be deprived of my privileges and informed Joseph. Yesterday Joseph brought me this bread, and this morning when I celebrated the Holy Rite I consecrated all of it. I shall take a portion each morning but should any remain at my death I wish you would burn them."

"Burn them?" cried Galen.

"To save them from desecration. Be sure to do that, my friend. Put one in a candle flame until it is consumed."

"I will do that," Galen said, gravely. "I must go now. In about an hour I'll return to take you to your trial."

On Galen's arm Peter tottered into the courtroom, officially designated the Hall of Justice, and gazed wonderingly at the crowd of spectators. Years ago, stalwart and confident, he had stood in a Jewish Hall of Justice before the High Priest Annas, and had spoken with such authority and eloquence that he and his companions were let off with a scourging and a warning to speak no more about the man Jesus.

He was not stalwart now. Months of solitary confinement in a dungeon cell had shrunken him to a gaunt skeleton bound by a jaundiced sheet of wrinkled skin, sagged his shoulders, bleared his eyes, crusted him with grime and infested his shaggy hair and beard with crawling things.

But his mind bore no affliction. He listened attentively while the Imperial Prosecutor acquainted the two magistrates with the charge upon which he would be tried.

"Simon Peter is the leader of a Jewish religious cult that feasts upon human flesh and blood. He instigated the people to revolt against Imperial Caesar in an attempt to gain control of the government. This cult desecrates the religion of the Roman people, defames their gods and charged his Imperial Majesty with having fired the city."

The Prosecutor then offered in evidence the official proclamation of the Governor of Syria reciting disorders among the Jews under Pontius Pilate which had been incited by the seditious activities of Jesus of Nazareth who had set himself up as King, and who had been executed by Pilate, the Roman Governor of Judea, for his crime.

He read another proclamation, by Pilate's successor as Procurator of Judea, which declared that after the execution of

Jesus his followers under the leadership of Simon Peter continued to preach his doctrine, and bestir the people to rebellion and disorder. For this crime he and some of his associates had been arrested and tried before the High Priest Annas, who extended clemency to them upon their solemn promise to cease their agitation. But they continued to defy lawful authority, and one of them, James, was executed by King Herod. The prisoner Simon had also been arrested but men who had been seduced by him bribed his jailers, and they permitted him to escape. Fleeing Judea, he journeyed to Antioch in Syria and thence to Rome where he continued to stir up public disorder. Finally he and all other Jews were banished by the Emperor Claudius. Although he never became a Roman citizen he returned to Rome and continued his teachings that Jesus rose from the dead, that he was the Son of God and rules the world. Thousands of people have been deluded by him, and hundreds have been lured to a martyr's death. "What I have said is contained in official documents. Formal proof of them would be repetitious. Many more people will suffer if this man is not brought to justice."

Peter did not wait to be told that he might speak in his defense. He promptly rose, bowed respectfully to the magistrates, then to the Prosecutor and began speaking in a low but firm clear voice.

"I would acquaint the honorable magistrates with other historical facts that require no proof. My Lord Jesus did not teach sedition or rebellion against lawful authority. He bade us 'Render to Caesar the things that are Caesar's and to God the things that are God's.' These words are recorded in the Gospel of Matthew, one of his disciples. He taught us that we should love other men as much as we love ourselves, not love Jews only, but Romans and Greeks, and men of all races and all colors. He showed us what he meant by love. By a touch of his hand or the speaking of a word he cured lepers, the sick and the lame. He even raised the dead to life. When a large crowd of people had no food he fed them with five loaves and two fishes until all had satisfied their hunger. The only compensation he asked was that they be strong in their faith and sin no more. When he fed the multitude the people were so grateful they cried out to make him King, but he fled from them. Many times he told us his kingdom was not of this world. The Imperial Prosecutor said that my Lord Jesus was condemned for sedition and inciting public disorder. He has been misinformed. The records of the Sanhedrin, the Jewish high court, reveal that Jesus was condemned for blasphemy for saying he was the Son of God. The Roman governor recognized that Jesus was the center of a dispute between Jews over a question of religion. I was in the crowd that day. I heard Pilate say he found no fault in Jesus. He examined him privately and again announced that Jesus was without fault, called for water, washed his hands, and spoke words that men will repeat to the end of time: 'I am innocent of the blood of this just man.' "

After a brief silence he resumed, his voice resounding vigorously. "Honorable magistrates, I give you the words of another witness, the Roman centurion who carried out the sentence of execution. When Jesus prayed for his executioners, 'Oh Father forgive them, they know not what they do,' the centurion cried out spontaneously, 'truly this man is the Son of God.' "

Again he paused, head bowed, as if to dwell upon that scene. The spectators, restless in the beginning, sat silent, motionless. Slowly raising his head, he said, "Honorable magistrates, thus does truth sometimes crash into our minds — a flash of lightning. But as a rule it comes to us gradually, as if it knew we could not accept it all at one time. So did truth come to the Prophets of my people, some twelve in number, during a period of over five hundred years. These truths they wrote into a record. While you are considering the historical records mentioned by the Prosecutor, I invite you to consider the writings of these men. You will find foretold every event in the life of my Lord Jesus Christ from the time of his miraculous conception to the day of his ascension to his Father, written by different men at different times. I shall not weary you with numerous references to their writings, but I would ask permission to quote a few words from Isaiah written over six hundred years ago. 'Therefore the Lord shall give you a sign. A virgin shall conceive and bear a son and his name shall be called Emmanuel. For a child is born to us and a son is given to us and the government is upon his shoulder, and his name shall be called wonderful, counselor, God the mighty, the Father of the world to come, the Prince of Peace.' "

"The Prince of Peace," he repeated slowly, his arms uplifted, his face aglow. "Honorable magistrates, had you known him, that is what you would have said of him, the Prince of Peace. I confess that for thirty-five years I have been teaching his doctrine of peace and love."

Lowering his arms, he said, "With your gracious permission I would conclude with a brief comment."

In a wistful musing tone, as if he were addressing his Lord in person, he said, "Jesus of Nazareth. The most mysterious paradox in the history of men. You are God the Son, the second Person of the most holy Trinity. For the salvation of man, you became a man so You might die in expiation of his sin. Begotten by the Holy Spirit you were born of Mary, a Jewish virgin, in Bethlehem and grew to manhood in the village of Nazareth in Galilee. You earned your living by working as a carpenter, and at the age of thirty you began preaching your doctrine of salvation. You wrote none of your thoughts, you held no place in government, you owned no property; you had not friends of wealth or influence, you never traveled beyond the limits of Palestine, you exerted no force; men were free to accept or reject your doctrine. After preaching three years you were condemned for blasphemy, crucified between two thieves, buried in a borrowed tomb, and deserted by the men you had chosen to carry on your work. By the standards of the world you were a failure. But you conquered death. You raised yourself from the tomb. Today thousands believe in you, in many countries, hundreds have suffered death for their faith. No, honorable magistrates, my Lord is not dead. All the armies that will ever march, and all the navies that will ever sail, and all of the philosophers who have written or will ever write, and all of the kings who will ever rule, will not so vitally influence the lives and thoughts of men as you, the gentle teacher from Nazareth. Worthy magistrates, pray that your hearts be opened to his ourpouring of faith and grace, but if they will not, if my death be your judgment, then I shall pray for you as he prayed for his executioners: 'Father forgive them.' "

Bowing to the magistrates he sat wearily upon a bench.

One of the magistrates announced that judgment would be reserved and Peter was conducted to his cell by a guard he had not seen before. He hoped to see Galen, but for fear of embarrassing his friend did not inquire about him.

Several days passed. He wondered why judgment had not been given. On the fourth day he had a visitor, Joseph, who looked so sad that he said: "Do not be distressed, my son. We must be reconciled to my death."

"True, Master, but you are faced with an even greater sorrow — your friend Askar . . ."

"Askar!" gasped Peter.

He witnessed your trial, Master. Before he could leave he was arrested for giving aid to the enemies of the Empire, the Christians, and for being a Christian. One of his associates betrayed him."

Putting the palm of a hand against the wall of his cell, Peter sank into a sitting position. "Askar," he murmured. "My son Askar."

"His betrayer said he gave the Christians food, clothing and money, knowing that they were secret enemies of the Empire and had put the torch to Rome.

"Askar had able counsel. Four Jewish Rabbis testified that he had given them money, food and other things for the Jews and for any other persons who might be in need, and that he did not specifically mention the Christians. All of them repeated his exact words which seemed to impress the magistrates, 'You will be doing a valuable service to the Empire, heavily burdened as it is with so many people to care for.' The Rabbis said that they distributed this food impartially to Jews, Christians and Romans, and that many people would have suffered but for Askar's abundant contributions." .

"God bless them!" cried Peter. "But why did the magistrate . . . ?"

"Let me tell it as it occurred, Master. Aware that this charge had failed the prosecutor turned to the other — that Askar was a Christian — and again sought evidence from his betrayer. He testified that Askar was friendly with many Christians, naming you and Nicodemus especially, and that he had given them money to help them in their work of spreading Christianity; that he had heard him speak in praise of the Christians for their belief in Christ and of their bravery in suffering for their faith.

"Under questioning by Askar's counsel, he admitted that he had heard other people, including Roman policemen, speak in praise of the Christians; that he'd never known Askar to attend a Christian worship, or express an opinion favoring Christian doctrine. He was evasive and self-contradictory, but finally admitted that Askar was indifferent to all religions. The Rabbis testified that Askar was a Jew in religion, but that he never attended a synagogue, and two of them said they had heard him say that Christianity was only the dream of a gentle man from Nazareth."

Peter sadly shook his head.

290 UPON THIS ROCK

"Sensing that this charge was likewise failing, the prosecutor became desperate and inquired of Askar, 'Do you deny that you are a Christian?' How relieved we were. A vigorous denial would destroy the charge. But he did not deny. He parried. 'Define what you mean by Christian,' he said.

"The prosecutor seemed disconcerted. 'One who has been baptized in the Christian rite,' he said. 'I have never been baptized,' Askar retorted. Even more disturbed the prosecutor said, 'one who regularly attends a Christian worship.' Askar replied, 'Never have I attended a Christian worship.' "

After a brief silence Joseph continued:

"We — the Rabbis and I — we exulted. The prosecutor turned from him in humiliation, his shoulders sagging in defeat. Suddenly he again faced Askar, and with an accusing finger pointed at him, cried out: 'A Christian believes that Jesus of Nazareth is the Son of God! Do you not so believe?' "

Peter gripped Joseph's arm. "I know what he said!" he cried huskily. "He said he did believe!"

"As cooly as a philosopher explaining a thesis, he said, 'In my youth I firmly believed in Yahweh, the Jews' name for God. Gradually I lost my faith, but not entirely. Belief in God is too deeply rooted in the Jewish heart to be wholly obliterated. Some years ago I came to know Simon Peter, the leader of the Christians. I thought he was a fraud seeking to advance himself by preaching Christianity. But I was wrong. Wealth and fame and praise have no attraction for him. He depends upon the alms of his people for his living. His faith that Jesus Christ is the Son of God absorbs him. His every word, thought, and deed is dedicated to worship of Jesus, and to making others worshipers of him. Yet he never suggested that I be a Christian. Occasionally I would inquire how he could believe such a doctrine. He would explain, but never in an accusatory tone for my lack of faith. Often I heard him say that the Jewish Prophets had foretold all the events in the life of Jesus. But I could not believe they were inspired by God, as Simon Peter believed. Mere chance, I decided.

" 'But it was not chance that made me a spectator at his trial. It was respect for him, my desire to mourn his prosecution for his religious beliefs.

" 'But I did not mourn! I rejoiced! Oh, the sublime faith of that grand old Jew! With an array of indisputable facts, and a spearhead of irrefutable logic, he made known the doctrine of Jesus, and there swept through me like a great wind the overpowering majesty of Divine truth. I believed without reservation that Jesus is the Son of God, the promised Messiah, and became man to die for the salvation of men!' "

Peter wept. In a voice choked with emotion, he cried out. "Oh Askar, my son Askar! What joy there is in heaven!"

Peter rose, assisted by Joseph and together they moved slowly about the cell. "When is it to be?" Peter inquired placidly.

"In the morning, Master. The cross for you, the sword for Askar."

"The sword for Askar," murmured Peter. "How incongruous. A hundred times you have cheated the sword. Ruthlessly you have forced from life her choice nectars. The headman will be vexed, for you will not bend your proud head. If could talk with you, even for only . . ."

"That has been arranged, Master," Joseph said. "At dawn he will be brought here so you may talk privately."

Peter smiled. "Ah, Joseph, how I benefit by your gift of tactful persuasion. That hour Askar and I shall cherish through all eternity."

Slowly disengaging from their long embrace, Askar said to Peter: "I believe all that the Prophets wrote about the coming of the Messiah. I believe that God inspired them to write. I also believe that Jesus of Nazareth was that Messiah and that he was crucified to death and rose from the tomb. I believe you saw his empty tomb. I believe he appeared to you through the walls of your room and joined you at the table. All of this I believed when I heard you speak in the Hall of Justice." After a pause, Askar continued: "I could not deny that I believe. As much as I love life, I could not deny that I believed . . ."

Peter rejoiced. He was pleased, not only with Askar's words but at the tone of his voice, and his manner of speech. It was calm, clear and reverent. The proud, disdainful Askar had given place to Askar the humble. His mannerisms were somewhat reverent. His pride revealed a holy ardor.

"How Jesus rejoices in your faith," said Peter.

"I doubt if he is rejoicing, Rabbi. I feel no pulsation of nobleness. I was angry at my betrayer and I could have slain him. But, I could not stultify myself and say I did not believe. The Prosecutor left me no other choice."

"The Lord understands," Peter said. "You need have no reluctance to being baptized. Galen wishes to be baptized, why not join him?"

"I seek all the blessings I am entitled to, Rabbi."

"Practical wisdom," said Peter. "Galen, bring us some water."

Galen departed and soon returned crestfallen. "The water barrel is empty," he said.

"Be not disturbed," Peter said, "Let me have your helmet."

Holding the helmet against the rock wall of the cell, he said: "My Lord, if it is your will give us water."

Immediately, water spurted from that mark on the rock wall until the helmet was about half filled.

Pouring some of the water upon the bared heads of the two men, Peter baptized them "In the name of the Father, the Son and the Holy Spirit."

After a brief silence Peter said, "Now you are entitled to receive other blessings . . . those which come from eating the flesh of Jesus and drinking his holy blood." In considerable detail he told them how that came to be, and said: "Believing that bread and wine can be changed to be the body and blood of Christ will put you to a stern test of faith."

"Christ said that," declared Askar. "It is true," replied Peter.

Galen also professed his faith.

From his locket, Peter removed two fragments of bread which had been previously consecrated, and gave them to eat. From the wine flask which Joseph had provided, Peter likewise bade them to drink of Christ's blood. Then he said, "Worship your beloved Lord in silence."

To Galen, Peter gave his locket and the small flask of consecrated wine. "Every morning before breakfast take a small portion of these sacred elements," he directed. "They should last you for a considerable time. . . . Now, let us be going lest you be censured for delay."

Drawing a grimy hand over his eyes, Galen the worshiper became Galen the guard, and he led the way out of prison.

30

Crucifixion on Vatican Hill

AT A NOD from Galen, Peter and Askar drew apart and arm in arm began pacing slowly in the court. "All this seems most unreal, Rabbi," Askar said. "I was given money to get rid of you but you got rid of me. You thrust me into the arms of Jesus Christ."

"No, my son. Impelled by an irresistible surge of faith you thrust yourself into his arms."

"Faith," murmured Askar. "How mysterious. More dominating than knowledge."

"Knowledge we acquire," Peter said. "Faith is a gift from God. He offers it in abundance. Blessed is he who becomes saturated with faith — in his blood and in his bones and in his spirit."

"And how exhilarating! The satisfaction of knowledge is lusterless compared with the joy of faith in Divine Truth."

"You are saturated," Peter said smiling.

"Not since my youth have I thought about God. He became a myth, created by our priests and Rabbis to suppress the people and enrich themselves. Then less than a week ago I began thinking of him constantly — because of you. How did that come about?"

"You set out to get rid of me, but you saved my life. Whenever I seemed to be in grave danger you unexpectedly appeared to help me and my people. How did that come about?"

"If I said by chance, you would say it was the mysterious providence of God."

"Mysterious, but not mystifying, as you imply," Peter said. "God respects our free will, but he does not abandon us. He uses natural events to give us a choice of decision to do his will. I think you and I have done that."

"I wonder if that is true of me," Askar said. "Had I remained silent at my trial I could have served him for the remainder of my natural life."

"And both of you would have been saddened by your failure to confess him before men. This is the better way, my son. You are about to enter upon a service far superior to that which you could have given him here."

"You are the great comforter, Rabbi."

In front of the stable two men were harnessing a horse to a wagon.

"I wish we had more time," Askar said. "This experience bestirs old memories. My father — how vigorous was his faith in Yahweh. How he loved our ancient hymns and chants — by the waters of Babylon . . . Rabbi, let us sing that lamentation."

Peter's baritone voice blended with Askar's basso as they sang, "By the waters of Babylon we sat and wept, O Zion, whenever we thought of you."

"And there was a psalm," Askar said, "the Lord sits forever — I have forgotten most of it."

Peter led in singing the psalm: "The Lord sits forever on his throne of judgment. He will judge the world with justice. He will be a refuge for the oppressed."

Two guards emerged from the barracks and stood, looking toward them. "There is one psalm he liked most," Askar went on, "the Good Shepherd. We might have time . . ."

"We shall take time!" Peter declared, and they sang: "The

Lord is my shepherd, I shall not want. He invites me to lie down in green pastures. He leads me beside the still waters and gives refreshment to my soul . . ."

"The most beautiful writing in our literature!" said Peter. Embracing Askar and kissing him on the cheek, he cried out, "My son, my son, you have given me great joy."

Askar circled an arm about Peter's shoulder, saying, "Rabbi, I have enjoyed life with a gusty relish. I exulted in wresting from life its most alluring pleasures. But because of you — I give it up without regret — perhaps even with just a flutter of exulatation."

Taking Peter in his arms, he continued: "Many times you have called me son. I would be honored to call you Father, for father you have been to me — patient, kindly, understanding, teaching me by example, not by exhortation, always respecting my right to choose. You have guided me into eternal salvation. My father, I give you the kiss of a loving son."

After a long embrace he disengaged himself and nodded to the two guards who stood waiting a few paces distant. As he walked away with them, Peter gazed after him until he turned and waved his hand in farewell. As the door of the low stone building shut him from view, Peter's right hand moved in a solemn sign of the cross.

The approach of the wagon bestirred him. One of the guards said, "It is time." He entered, and seated himself beside Galen. Noticing the timbers that were to be his cross, he said, "I am more favored than was my Lord. He carried his cross."

"The place is too far," muttered Galen.

Rome teemed with activity, heavy traffic slowed the wagon, but Peter was unaware. The deck of a ship at sea loomed in his mind: the jeering voice of a man taunted his ear: "Rabbi, are you scheming to corrupt the ship's crew?"

He smiled, a sad smile, yet savoring a gentle triumph. "Ah

Askar! You proud disdainful son of Abraham! You heaped ashes on the fire of faith but not even you could smother that last dull ember. Had I known you years ago — what a priest you would have made — but who am I to challenge the providence of God?"

The rumble of wheels upon a bridge withdrew Peter from the ship. They were crossing the Tiber. Ahead loomed a large hill — Vatican Hill, upon which he once had hoped to build a monumental temple to God, presently giving occupancy to Nero's racing stables. The roar of chariot wheels speeding over a race course and the strident shouts of charioteers contrasted harshly with its pastoral serenity.

Peter stepped from the wagon into a circle of friends, including Senator Pudens, Joseph, Ebulus and Linus whom he embraced with joy. "Forgive me, Master, for disobeying you and returning to Rome," pleaded Linus. "I am in need of your counsel. I crave your blessing. Impart to me some of your strength and fortitude and wisdom."

Drawing Linus apart, Peter gripped his shoulders and spoke with quiet intensity. "Urge your priests to remain close to their people. Teaching the Divine Word must be joined with its practical application — helping the sick and the aged and the orphan and the destitute, instructing the ignorant, improving the conditions of the slave and the serf, and crying out against the injustices of our time. All this did Christ, the first priest. Teach them to be like Christ."

While others were beseeching his last blessing, a guard touched his arm and pointed to a timber lying on the ground. Removing his robe and tunic he gave them to Galen, saying, "Give them to the prisoner who needs them most." Then he lay on the ground, his open hands upon the plank. Like our Lord he was crucified. Unlike our Lord Peter was crucified with his head downward.

Death often has its moments of pity — even death by crucifixion. It brews a potion against the sufferings of the flesh, even though it accentuates the torments of the mind — the potion of delirium. Midway in the second hour Peter cried out in vexation, "This log of a boat! Where were your eyes when you bought it — those thieving salterers! Wink your eye and they will rob you of half your catch — rash, impetuous. Always you fling that at me, when I am only firm and decisive." "How he lashed me! Get behind me, Satan, you are a scandal to me!"

Gradually, the delirium passed. In painful gasps he entreated his friends gathered about the cross: "Have charity — one for another — for the stranger — and for him — who would do you ill. Charity covers — a multitude — of sins — a mul—ti—tude . . ."

He groaned. Delirium again plagued him. "The son of man — has no place — to lay — his head."

"May a legion of angels come and bear him victoriously into heaven!" cried the young priest Clement.

If the angels were waiting to escort Peter's soul into heaven the group about the cross was unaware of them. And the only note of victory they heard came from the charioteers speeding about the track.

At the moment of his death, Peter's Lord had triumphed over the Cross and in a loud voice had cried out, "Father, into your hands I commend my spirit!" But there was no triumph in Peter's death. His gaunt body seemed to shrink into the wood, his stentorian voice had dwindled to a tremulous whine; his flesh writhed, delirious mutterings fell from his lips. Then, suddenly, he did cry out, but not in triumph. Again he stood in Herod's courtyard. Again he heard a cock crow. And as on that night there erupted from his soul the same anguished shriek of guilt and anger: "You jeering cock! You croaker out of hell!"